Nevermore

A Novel

By Glen Adams

This is a work of pure fiction. All the characters, places, organizations, and events portrayed in this work are purely products of the author's creative energy and are used in a fictitious manner.

ISBN: 978-1-7369268-2-6
First Edition 1c

www.glenadams.com

Dedication

I dedicate this book to you! Thank you.

Acknowledgements

I would like to acknowledge those who
made this book a reality;

My writing posse who inspires me.

For graphic artist Arena Ada Villanueva
who transformed my rough sketch
into the cover art used for Nevermore.

To Jess who worked on the amazing
author photos used in the promotional
materials for this book.

You, the reader. Thank you.

Prologue

Since the beginning of civilization, humans have been led by a heart made up of two distinct parts. One half was imbued with the ability to know right from wrong, the definition written directly into its DNA. While the other half, corrupted by outside forces, works to influence human behavior towards self-serving interests.

But the heart was never designed to serve two very different masters. Millenia ago, the battle fell so far out of balance that evil, having gained such an upper-hand, took on physical form. Foul creatures, remnants of the darkest human souls, coalesced into entities referred to as the Sael Lords, drawing on our pain and suffering to fuel their war on humanity.

In the distant past, on the verge of losing their battle with evil, those few remaining righteous individuals fought back and restored the balance. Assuming that if someone should need again the key to overcoming the darkness in the future, humanity recorded the instruction in a prophecy which has been handed down through the generations. Because the Sael Lords could also wield the weapon against the forces of light, the prophecy was described in the most ambiguous of terms. Only those rightful individuals, possessing the necessary wisdom and knowledge, it was assumed, could decode the clues, and faithfully execute the plan.

Ch1 – Auvergne Region, France 1204 A.D.

Oriel Toussaint stared ahead at the unassuming lump in the landscape, knowing it was their final destination. What it lacked in majesty, it made up for in its importance. A spot atop that small hill was critical to their planned objective.

As one of the few female fighters remaining, and the only one on horseback near the front of the line, she had a decent view of the path ahead. It was clear and unobstructed, free of any apparent dangers, but with the forest encroaching from their left, an entire army could lay in wait for them and they wouldn't know it.

Her horse didn't need any guidance, the animal obediently following those in front, so Oriel shifted her attention to the dark woods for any signs of movement. She could sense that the others around her were thinking the same thing, their heads turned in that direction.

"Almost there," the man riding next to her said in a way of encouragement.

Oriel knew that their leader, Felix Hatt, meant well, but he had been saying the same thing for days as they battled their way across the grasslands. Despite wanting to toss out something sarcastic, she kept quiet, knowing the man had good intentions. In either case, they were nearing the end of their journey and the fulfillment of the prophecy which had guided them all to this spot.

Knowing that their enemy could be waiting ahead for them while others were pursuing their forces from behind, the small army tried to pick up its pace.

The daylight was slipping away as darkness crept into every corner, shadows lengthening. The rhythmic sounds of hooves on beaten soil and armor banging against shields had lulled the fighters into a trance-like state, which made the shouts and noise of fighting at their rear easy enough to detect.

Felix and Oriel could see that the dark army, which had been pursuing them for days, had caught up and had begun their assault. With the distraction underway, the other half of the evil forces charged out from the forest and into the line of fighters on the road. As though sensing an opportunity, the first wave of attackers had targeted the horses, requiring the warriors to travel on foot as they fought off the enemy. Their army's advance had slowed, but was still inching its way forward.

While Felix, Oriel, and those fighters closest to them charged single-mindedly towards their objective, the others ringed the group, trying to hold back the forces meant to stop their progress.

The hordes, directed by the evil Lords, pushed in from all sides as the band of warriors continued to fight their way up the tiny, unremarkable hillside. Nearing the top, which no one would ever consider a summit, stood a ruin of stones, barely something one would recognize as handmade. The knights pushed ever higher, driving the magician onward towards the finish line.

"We can't keep them off you for much longer!" one commander yelled over his shoulder, sword lifted high, seeking a target.

Felix heard the warning, but couldn't reply, his chest heaving for air. He had gathered the meager forces and had managed the cross-continent race to stay ahead of their enemy. But even tossing aside stealth in favor of speed, the army of darkness, driven more by madness than focused direction, had still run them down. The bloodlust that motivated the army of evil creatures was reaching its crescendo, the base of the hill now entirely encircled. No escape afforded them.

"If we succeed, there won't be an army left," the old magician mumbled, smiling, encouraging the boy, the Chosen One, ahead of him with a gentle hand on his back towards the broken stone structure that lay only a dozen yards ahead.

To each side, dark creatures fought the lines of knights, who were struggling to hold the line, necessary to keep their forces from being cut off from the ultimate objective.

"Why aren't you fighting?" Oriel screamed over the roar of battle at the young boy, standing there as though he were taking a stroll, suddenly inconvenienced.

The Chosen One looked up the hill at their destination before turning back to face her, a look of displeasure at his being questioned, the answer obvious. "Because that's not why I'm here," he declared, dismissing her by turning away.

She screamed again, this time in frustration directed within instead of at the enemy, which continued to press their advantage. Most of the dark creatures were taller than Oriel's five-foot frame, but what qualified as marginally higher ground here, only put her even with most of the dark forms who were clawing their way through the last ring of defenders.

The young woman's arm grew weary, so she switched the magical blade to her left hand. Although it was just as effective at keeping the enemy at bay, it was far less efficient. She backpedaled, trying to hold her position.

15

Sensing a weakness in their opponent, Oriel's determination faltering and body growing tired, the individual dark forms, hacking and slashing and biting at the army of light with talons and teeth of smoke, consolidated together, growing darker and taller, more solid. Instead of ghostly arms passing through the fighter's defenses, causing internal damage if hit, the enlarged beast standing in front of her swung long limbs at the remaining knights, bodies driven to the ground where evil scavengers fed on their prone, injured forms. The writhing black fog hanging close to the ground smothered those who were still fighting to stay alive. Anyone who couldn't gain their feet quickly risked having the evil tendrils worming their way inside their armor, lively flesh their preferred meal.

Screams merged into a chorus of bone-chilling horror. The sound was like music to the ears of the beast staring down at the Oriel, its deep sockets for eyes now visible as it searched the area for any remaining threats. A crude horizontal slash, looking as though in had been torn open by a dull knife, widened, and a sickening sound emerged, the reverberation shaking Oriel's body and the ground upon which she stood.

The rest of the dark army, gaining strength and ground around the dwindling human forces, joined in on the battle cry, the volume so loud that the army of light cowered under the audible assault. Although Oriel heard no message discernible in the unholy bellow, her heart recognized it loud and clear.

You are useless.

You can't win.

You will die here.

She hurt, was tired, and in pain, but the worst feeling of all was an unshakable sense of hopelessness and defeat.

The Dark Lords collectively roared again in some kind of coordinated attack, wave after wave slamming into her and the other defenders. The dark minions, now energized, clawed their way over the piles of the dead to overwhelm the living. The sole aim of the evil forces was the magician with the crown, who was weaving his way towards the summit of the low hill, still making progress, a half-dozen dedicated knights clearing a path for the man and the boy with him, the Chosen One from the prophecy whom the knights had sworn to protect. But the human resistance, under brutal physical and psychological attack, faltered, weapons and resolve dropping before the enemy.

The Sael Lord in front of Oriel turned the deep pits of its eyes away from her, as though dismissing the young woman as any kind of ongoing threat, and trained them on the magician, who was nearing the collapsed tower. It was there that the dark enemy would win the battle and this Lord's corrupted soul wanted to be there for the end.

Oriel turned to look in that direction, watching the wall of darkness rising to either side, as it tried to swallow the last of the humans and to end the existential threat to their dark existence.

Swiping at the remaining knights with the back of its beastly limbs, only Oriel stood in its way. As though sensing the end of the fight was near, and not wanting to be left out of the last moments and the carnal feasting on flesh to follow, the dark beast, dragging its evil followers with it, turned towards the final melee.

While armor crumpled under the footsteps of Sael Lord, now risen to nearly ten meters in height, its denser physical form also made it more susceptible to weapons, now barely transparent in the faltering light.

The beast roared again, any thoughts of Oriel now pushed away by the bloodlust feeding its anger.

Ch2 – Auvergne Region, France 1204 A.D.

"Hurry," the magician urged, feeling the breeze of unholy talons slicing the around him, dark eyes and bright teeth pushing in from either side of the narrowing path ahead. The smell of blood and the screams of friends and allies wafted through the air, as even the long grass seemed to reach up and grab hold of them as they climbed the ever-steepening hillside.

"Faster!" he huffed out, no longer able to catch his breath. Only a few minutes more, he thought, and then the prophecy would bring this entire chapter, this nightmare, to a bitter and costly end. A glimmer of hope grew inside him, as it looked like they were actually going to make it.

Felix had almost given in to his dark thoughts that their crusade, a decade in the making, would be over before it had even begun. Then a series of fortunate events and the blessing of the fates had brought everything into proper alignment. He could even envision what had to be done, as though someone had carefully sketched it out on the wall in front of him. And with the help of a few trusted advisors, Oriel included, he had located the young man who the prophecy had foretold. Taking the boy, an infant really, from his family had not been difficult. A few bits of gold had relieved them of another mouth they couldn't feed, and the wealth would buy his parents a bit of breathing room. By now, almost a decade later, it was likely that they had all but forgotten about their son.

Somewhere off to his left, a heavy object attached to a long chain swung into view, and the magician's tall frame ducked, as much from instinct as conscious thought. And although his ill-fitting helmet, loaned to him only a short while ago, had absorbed most of the energy before flying away, he still felt his neck and spine compress from the solid blow.

He had feared that the grasp of hands that followed was that of the enemy looking to claw him away from the completion of the quest, but a reassuring voice whispered in his ear.

"You're going to be fine." The voice said, sounding calm despite the chaos of the moment. It was the captain of the guard who was assigned for their personal protection, though the magician had hoped that the fighting force of men and women wouldn't be necessary. The reassurance made his heart leap as the same set of hands practically carried him forward, the weakness in his body from the blow subsiding. "At least for the next few moments," the captain added, following it all up with a hearty laugh that seemed terribly out of place here.

The roar of the beasts surrounding them melted into a hideous symphony that assaulted the last vestiges of their fighting group. As they neared the opening in the small stone tower at the top, sheared off a few feet above the ground by some unimaginable force, the army of evil seemed to lose their bloodlust, replaced instead by something akin to doubt. The volume dropped as the sounds of battle once again displaced the uncontained fury of their opponent.

19

As the humans pushed into the entrance of the broken tower, a half-dozen members of the evil army materialized out of the deepening shadows. It seemed logical that this would be the magician's ultimate destination, but he had hoped the trail of false clues they had left behind the previous days might have confounded their enemy. He clearly hadn't given them enough credit, a shortcoming that may ultimately cost the army of light their hard-fought victory.

A few of the knights, having seen the ambush in time, reared back and parried the assault, drawing the knot of fighters to a temporary draw.

Felix hadn't expected their enemy to be so strategic in their planning, given their animalistic nature, but even the higher forms of monsters had a cunning about them when you watched the horde collectively work out a problem. Here, they were wary to step out from the keep, assuming incorrectly that the small group and tiny protecting force must have been employing some kind of ruse to draw them further into the open.

"Desperate times," Felix muttered, removing the leather satchel he wore around his neck and held it out before him.

While the light show momentarily transfixed, the monsters on the hill, those within the stone structure positioned on the very portal itself, didn't stand a chance. The presence of the golden crown, shining through every tiny opening in the bag, had activated the ancient magic which had been cast here long ago. The flagstones that lay inside the broken tower, which had been nudged out of place by centuries of ground movement, sprang instantly to life. The swirling maelstrom of light, like a furious hive of angry lightning bugs, lasted only a moment, an electrical charge spilling out into the evening air.

Then it ended just as quickly, the light dimming to where it was barely discernable even inside the enclosure, unable to compete even against the darkening shadows.

Having been full of evil darkness, and within the keep itself, when the portal activated, the vile creatures were annihilated. Only a few wisps of smoke on the gentle breeze remained, and then they, too, were gone.

Raising a torch inside to get a better view, the fighters could see it was now empty. Any threat now lay solely outside and around the hill.

"Think we can get them to assemble inside the tower a few dozen at a time?" the captain quipped with a grin, slapping Felix good-naturedly on the arm.

The magician ignored him and kneeled, setting the sack beside him. The young lad, with the bright blue eyes and golden hair, who Felix had been raising for nearly five years, stepped forward, seemingly unphased by the chaos of their arrival. He watched it all with a calm and clarity that bordered on boredom.

Disconcerting, Felix thought to himself. He could not grasp how the boy could be so unaffected by the terror and bloodshed. The magician tried to smile, a bit of hubris reaching his eyes, assuming that the years of preparation he had passed on to the boy, a young man really, had prepared him for his journey ahead and that leaving this place meant leaving all this carnage behind. He might have felt the same way if he were making this journey, but he knew, like those awful creatures who had just been obliterated, that he too wasn't worthy to pass through this magical portal undamaged.

His eyes swung from the darkening shadows to the sun edging ever closer to the horizon, before settling on the boy who looked at him, chin up, knowing that his destiny had arrived.

Ch3 – Auvergne Region, France 1204 A.D.

Seeing the tidal wave of darkness, comprising arms and legs and jaws full of potential death, collapsing onto her friends and threatening to end their righteous crusade, caused a resurgence in Oriel's resolve that she had not been expecting. The dark beast's dismissal of her had done even more to energize the young woman. A fire growing in her soul silenced the doubts and pushed away the doubt which had immobilized her.

No longer frozen in fear, but energized by a vindictive need for retribution, she chose the closest target and lifted her sword, its edge crackling in anticipation. As the Sael Lord moved to step past her, focused solely now on the melee happening around the crumpled tower, it failed to sense the threat before it was too late.

With a two-handed grip on the magical sword, she swung the blade with deadly intent, full force behind the arc that sent it biting into the dark beast's thick leg. While it didn't cut all the way through, it buried deep into the phantom flesh before stalling. A roar of pain, shared by the entire dark army, drew a collective cry, tinged with disbelief and fury.

The beast collapsed forward under its own weight, crashing to the earth, the ground shaking from the impact. Sensing a potential victory of her own and a distraction for the enemy, she leaped upon the beast's back and drove her magical sword into the back of the Dark Lord's deformed skull. Oriel ripped it back out, but before she could drive it in a second time, a wave of darkness, using her own moment of distraction against her, slammed into the young woman, driving her away into the long grass, her consciousness flickering in and out of focus before it gave way to its own darkness, this one peaceful.

Ch4 – Auvergne Region, France 1204 A.D.

A far different roar rose up from the bottom of the hillside. Instead of it encouraging the dark army to finish the fight, it seemed instead to confuse and confound the enemy, their fight temporarily suspended.

Felix too was confused, eyes searching in that direction. He saw that a Sael Lord was down, a familiar flash of sword catching his attention. He smiled and silently wished his friend the best of luck, but turned away to not waste the precious seconds that his protégé had just bought them.

"I *am* the Chosen One," the boy repeated, looking around at the small group that encircled him. There was pride in the way he carried himself, a smugness that those around him had always detested. The magician had done what he could to bring up the boy with a sense of humility, but it was an impossible task when the child learned it was he alone who held the keys to the kingdom and its survival.

"I guess you're ready," said the only father-figure the young man had ever really known, as he held out the crown to his young charge. The boy, a smirk upon his lips and an air of expectancy on his face, stepped closer, but didn't move to take the crown from the Felix. He just tipped his head forward in one last act of power.

The old man, no longer trying to hide his irritation at the attitude, reached out quickly and without ceremony, placed the crown upon the boy's head.

"Go!" the magician said, fearful that they might lose their slim lead.

The fighting resumed, the evil ones gaining momentum. As though sensing that its permanent defeat was near at hand, the darkness had called in reinforcements. All the evil that lurked in the area had manifested itself into a dark creature of immense size. It surged forward, crushing and shredding the forest as it crawled free and began its ascent. The dark storm rolled up the hill from all directions, scouring the land as it climbed towards the remnants of battle.

Rallied by the reinforcements and encouraged by the prospects of satiating their bloodlust, the enemy renewed their attack on the dwindling forces remaining in defense of the hilltop.

"Go now!" the magician screamed over the roar of their foe. Any hope of surviving another sixty seconds seemed unlikely.

Driven by the Sael Lord's insanity, the beasts rushed towards the faltering defenses and threw themselves mercilessly at the remaining fighters. Hoping to gain only thirty more seconds, the humans switched tactics, brandished shields rather than swords, to hold back the surge in the shrinking battle area.

The blackness howled in madness, gaining volume and encouragement as the remaining knights were hammered to the ground, one by one, and were ripped away. The defensive ring shrank in order to fill the growing gaps. Screams mixed with the chorus of chaos.

Felix snatched up a sword lying at his feet, the unfamiliar grip feeling alien in his hands. Having nothing else to contribute, he hoped to help stem the tide of the enemy's advance, only a few more critical seconds needed. If he had to give up his life to ensure the prophecy's fulfillment, the permanent banishment of evil from this world, he was determined to make the sacrifice.

Captain Abad Alvarez, no longer willing to risk this entire endeavor and the lives of his fighting force on the pompous vanity of the youth, snatched up the boy and literally threw him into the broken remnants of the tower and onto the portal. Despite the less than graceful landing, the young man stayed on his feet, straightening the crooked crown on his head. The Chosen One turned, shooting the soldier a disgusting look as he smoothed out his clothes and tried to reestablish his composure. Raising his hands high, his eyes looking out across the encroaching darkness, he exclaimed once again, unnecessarily, "I *am* the Chosen One!"

A bright flash blinded those in the immediate area, the evil cringing and recoiling at the sight. The blast of pure energy stopped even the advance of the monstrous wave of darkness which had closed within feet of the melee.

As the intensity dimmed, the magician's eyes recovered in time to see the delicate golden crown, hanging in the air of its own accord, tumble, clanging a few times off the stones, before bouncing to the edge of the broken tower where it hung up in the long grass near the entrance. The light breeze blew away the static charge of ozone, only the acrid smell of burning flesh remaining.

The collective, demented laughter of the enemy echoed over the hillside. Any existential threat to the darkness, now eliminated. As quickly as the dark forces had overrun the defender's precarious position, they dissipated from view. The only evidence that it had ever been there was the wake of death and destruction strewn across the landscape.

"Apparently, the pompous little turd wasn't the Chosen One after all, eh?" the captain noted dryly, slapping the haggard magician on the shoulder.

Ch5 – Auvergne Region, France 1204 A.D.

The first thing that registered in the Oriel's mind was pain. Not enough to cause her to flail about, but just enough to sharpen her mind and cut away the fogginess that clung to the inside of her skull. Pin-pricks of light danced in the periphery of her vision, the only evidence that she was still alive. It took a few moments, but she pieced together what had happened. The surrounding silence told her that either she had been left for dead or that the battle had ended, the enemy vanquished. Could it have worked? She wondered.

Looking up the hill towards the broken tower, she could see the remaining fighters milling about, taking stock of the situation. Along that same direction, only feet from her face, stood the largest black bird she had ever seen. Its color was so deep, in fact, that in the parting light of evening, it would have been invisible had she not viewed it against the slightly lighter color of the faltering sky. It was studying her, as though curious.

"Maybe I did die?" she whispered to herself, hoping that hearing her words would provide evidence to the contrary. "Are you here to carry me home?" she asked the bird, thinking it might belong to the mythical clan of soul carriers charged with dealing with the dead, either carrying the souls of the righteous to an eternal existence or carrying away the flesh of the wicked, one bite at a time.

Wondering if the bird was only an illusion, she extended her hand, beckoning. As though knowing what she wanted, it rocked back and forth, stepping awkwardly closer, closing the distance between them. It placed its head in her hand, rubbing it against Oriel's fingertips, until she took over and stroked it gently.

"Oriel, you're alive!" the magician called out in obvious relief, chasing away the crow, which fled in noisy agitation.

"I'm not entirely sure I agree with you, Felix," she said, trying to make an assessment of any injuries from her prone position.

"Looks like you still have all of your limbs. That's something."

"You always are the eternal optimist," she replied, accepting his help to roll over and get to her knees, shedding bits of armor. "Did it work? Did we win?" she asked, noting no signs of the enemy.

"To your point," he said sadly, "I think I was too optimistic."

Ch6 – London, England – Last Year

Explosions shake the ground nearby, bits of mud and grass racing skywards. Pounding rain crashes down, concussions from the blasts launching the liquid in all directions. Two men, burdened with an empty stretcher, stumble and fall across the battlefield, taking more and more precious time to get to their feet and scramble forward. One soldier they find is sheered in half, while another is missing limbs. They see a third nearby waving at them, mud covering his uniform. After racing across open ground, shells falling around them, waves of compressed air slamming them to the side, they reach the downed soldier only to find that he's been caught by friendly fire, his Nazi brethren fighting to hold the Normandy shore against the surging ally army.

One man drops his end of the stretcher and pulls his firearm from the stiff holster on his belt. Resigned to a certain fate, the man closes his eyes right before the rounds penetrate his flesh, his blood splattering across the medic's filthy uniforms.

The gentleman witnessing the phantom vision reels in shock, almost able to smell the gunpowder and taste the mud as though he was physically there. He stumbles, his hand losing its grip on the black metal handrail which borders the tiny patch of perfectly manicured lawn. He reaches out blindly, as though his vision is blurred by the smoke of battle, ears ringing, and feels his hand gain purchase on the next section of fencing. His eyes can see again, not the world around him, but another time and place.

Two men sprint down the irregular trench, legs churning through the knee-deep, freezing water, mud threatening to pull the boots from their weary legs. Fighter planes buzz low overhead, fighting for dominance of the air, bombs raining down on both lines. A mix of soldiers from the UK, Canada, and the US scramble up narrow ladders and crest the lip of the trench before machine gun fire sends them tumbling backwards, bodies slamming into the churning water of surf. The two men carrying the stretcher already have a wounded man strapped to it. His injuries are not deadly, though he may lose a leg they suspected. He is screaming in agony, his cries mixing with the chorus of all the others yelling and pleading for their help. But the stretcher continues on, turning down a side channel heading back to the coast where medical staff can lend additional help.

The man clinging to the antique fence stumbles again, coughing in fits, the phantom air burning his lungs, eyes watering so badly he can't see the modern sidewalk under his feet. He nearly trips over tree roots, only his iron grip on the railing keeping him upright. He moves further down the line, feeling his way, breath ragged as sheer exhaustion comes close to shutting down his consciousness. "More", he demands incoherently, experiencing the terror and pain felt by those who had come before, while morning commuters around him, side-eyeing the wild man with apprehension, continue on, assuming someone else will help him.

31

Missing most of his lower body, the bloodied man strapped to the bent stretcher is already dead, he just doesn't know it yet. His screaming has thankfully stopped. The two men bearing the stretcher thank God for that as machine gun rounds pepper the surrounding ground. Ten feet, five feet, and then they duck behind the cover of a landing craft, relatively safe from the assault by the German fortifications. There's a lean-to of sorts, partially assembled in haste inside the abandoned boat, and the two men, both bearing gunshot and shrapnel wounds themselves, aim for it. When they get inside, they drop the metal stretcher onto the ground and fall away, exhausted, relishing the few moments they have as a blood-soaked doctor races forward and kneels beside his latest patient.

As though sensing relief might be at hand, the bright sunshine blotted out by the camo covering, his injured man's eyes flutter open, mouth moving. "Please save me," the man pleads, words barely discernable above the sounds of war. A shell whistles by, everyone dropping for cover as it lands on the beach next to the makeshift field hospital. The steel walls of the landing craft absorb most of the explosive energy, and a shotgun-like blast of stony debris launched against its steel hull. Outside, screams reach their ears, even though they're still ringing from the concussion of the explosion.

"I have to get back to her," the dying soldier begs again, mouthing the words now, no air left in his lungs to generate sound.

The doctor, making a quick and final decision, pulls the man off the stretcher and down to the hard steel floor of the landing craft. He signals to the two soldiers that they can head back out, and they reluctantly scramble to their feet.

"Please," the man begs one last time, tears in his eyes, realization hitting home. But the doctor has already turned away, moving on. The man watching the vision kneels down next to the dying man, tears of his own streaming down his face. Lying there bleeding out, the dying man's gaze seems to fall on the invisible visitor who's sharing the corporal's last seconds.

Using his fleeting strength, hope still shining in his eyes, he reaches upward towards the man. The visitor takes the offered hand into his own. Though he doesn't feel the physical touch, he can feel the coldness in his grip, even if it's only in his mind.

The soldiers with the stretcher raced back outside, moving away with the object to which he is both mentally and physically tied. He wants to follow, but he can't leave, not now. He stares down at the dying soldier and cries out to the man, "I'm sorry. I'm so sorry." No one here in the small landing craft will hear it, and neither will the soldier, already gone, lifeless gaze forever staring, hope extinguished.

The man, back in his own reality, loses his grip on the short fence and flails about desperately, trying to find it again, his own useless eyes overflowing with tears. "I'm so sorry," he cries out again before falling to the sidewalk. Pedestrians try their best to sidestep and ignore the crazy man who's interrupting their morning routine, their conversations, and their phone calls.

When he opens his eyes again, swiping away the tears with his hands, he can see the buildings reaching skyward, a single leafy tree directly above him. He can sense the foot traffic on the London sidewalk flowing around his prone form, but gives it no mind. He's so used to episodes like this that the stares and whispered comments no longer register. Thankfully, it's rare that anyone even acknowledges his presence, but today, however, is one of those occasions.

A shape stands over him, his mind assuming it's a police officer or medical professional. Occasionally, it's a priest or somebody that helpfully recommends a local hospital, treatment center, or shelter.

This morning it's a young woman. Scratch that, he thinks, once his eyes focus. It's a young girl, maybe 12 or 13 years old, studying him with curiosity. This is new, he notes. It's usually apprehension, or concern, or something akin to angry righteousness, like he was intentionally creating a scene, but not her. There's a gentleness in her gaze, but it contains none of the usual pity he's used to seeing.

The man looks around, assuming the young girl's parents, or nanny, given that he was in a wealthy neighborhood, had to be hovering nearby, but no one seems to rush over to pull her away from the crazy guy laying on the sidewalk. The girl extends her hand as though offering him help with getting up, but she couldn't have weighed more than a hundred pounds, half his weight, and he isn't looking for trouble from the law by taking it.

He waves her gently away and rolls to his knees, getting up and dusting himself off, taking stock of how he must look.

"Thanks anyway," he says, noticing his voice is hoarse, wondering how much noise he must have been making. He combs back his hair with his fingers, inspecting his hands and clothes for signs of scuffs or tears. Far better than he's fared in the past, he notes, noticing the young girl is still beside him, eyes watching. Her curious stare seemed to drill into him, a smirk on her lips as she takes in the sight. Normally, he doesn't care what others think, but that she's noticed him and wasn't going away has put him off balance.

"I'm Lily, Jacob's daughter," she says, as though it should ring a bell, but it doesn't.

She offers her hand again, and this time, he takes it, surprising himself. He looks around, assuming it's some kind of trap, but no one comes running to tackle him. Or Taser him. God, he hates when that happens. Non-lethal doesn't mean gentle, and people were way too quick to use it, in his opinion.

"Neal."

She nods, as though she already knew this, and then motioned towards a row of businesses.

"May I buy you a cup of coffee, Neal?"

He nods, wondering why he feels no apprehension in accepting such an unwise invitation.

Ch7 – London, England

A coveted two-topper in the front window opened up just as they approached and they took it. Lily, daughter of Jacob, had gone with a chai tea latte with a spot of soy milk. Although her words sounded British, he detected no hint of an accent in her speech. He could only assume she lived in the area and was on her way to school, but wore none of the requisite private school uniforms, nor was she sporting the usual backpack.

"Why do you do that to yourself?" she asked, focusing her gaze on him.

Neal heard the simple question, but it carried knowledge in the way she said it, implying that she knew at least part of his story. Only a select few knew what made him tick and he wouldn't have put it past any of them to be setting him up here in order to gain his cooperation.

But as he stared at the young girl sipping at her tea, he wasn't picking up any of the usual vibes that his cynical nature often bounced around his brain. Instead, he felt a certain peace, a revelation that surprised him as he sipped his own drink, wondering where to begin his tale.

"It's a long story," he said, averting his eyes, clearly not comfortable talking about the subject or about himself.

"I have nowhere to be," Lily answered simply.

So, he laid out his background in succinct, chronological order, hitting all the hidden key points in his life. Faltering a bit at first, trying to tease out what was and what was not important, he soon found his groove, confessing all kinds of sins from his past. With each new revelation, he felt a weight being lifted off of him. And after nearly an hour, having asked no questions or given off any vibes of judgement, Lily asked for refills and some scones from a server that wandered into their orbit. Once reloaded, she turned her focus back to Neal.

"Let's talk about your gift," she said, redirecting the conversation.

"You mean my curse?" He replied, surprised to find it so easy to acknowledge what he worked so hard to keep concealed.

"It all depends on how you use it, Neal," she said, smiling.

He certainly didn't feel that way, but there was no use in ruining a perfectly pleasant conversation by debating something that had tortured him since his youth, his gift only having grown stronger and more disruptive with each passing year.

"You're able to see an object's history, if I'm not mistaken," she stated, not asked.

He nodded, almost imperceptibly, confirming her suspicions.

"But you have to be in physical possession of it."

He nodded again, feeling better that he could talk about it, even if the young woman seated across from him was only a child. Maybe he felt she didn't have an ulterior motive, only a simple curiosity. And who would believe her? He could just deny the accusations. This was London after all, not Salem, circa 1875. The question, though, was how she knew what she knew. And did he know her father, Jacob? The name still didn't ring any bells, but he hadn't found an opportunity to inquire.

"Yes, I have to physically touch it."

"And the fence outside?" She asked, though he got the impression she already knew the answer.

"On my first visit to London, I was tired from walking around the city and sat down to take a break, leaning against one of the short stretches of fencing near where you found me this morning. I noticed the strange design and instead of pulling out my phone to Google it, I took a shortcut and had a look for myself, reaching up and grabbing hold of the section behind me."

"Got more than you were expecting?" She asked, a conspiratorial gleam in her eyes, eyebrows arched.

"Way more," he said, shaking his head at the memory. "The next thing I know, I'm seeing horrible visions from the second World War. Wounded ally soldiers being carted around the battlefields. It was some pretty gruesome stuff. I've seen some things in my life, but nothing prepared me for that. The intensity and pure rawness of the experiences cut deep. Not just a vision, I could literally feel it, hear the horrors, smell the gore and even taste the mud on my lips," he said, the words spilling out quickly.

"You weren't expecting it," she reminded him gently.

He shook his head, laughing a bit, eyes darting around the immediate area to see if anyone was listening in. Neal could feel his face getting flush at the thought. "If you stop to look at the fence sections, you'll notice they're of a peculiar design, no rhyme or reason for them to be formed the way that they are. I doubt most of the folks walking these streets have any idea what they are or what they've been through. The pedestrians just go on about their lives, clueless about the horrors that happened here relatively recently."

Neal shifted in his seat, and cleared his throat, realizing that his façade was slipping and the bitter and angry man inside him was coming out.

Lily reached out her hand and placed it on his.

It was calming, reassuring. Not weird, like his logical brain might conclude.

"Go on," she encouraged.

He didn't want to, but he did anyway. "It only took a quick search online to find what I wanted. All those fence sections were stretchers from World War II, used to cart the wounded and dead from the battlefields. After the war, they were just surplus scrap, no longer needed, thank God. And after the people here had sacrificed so much for the war effort, they weren't about to just toss them all away. The repurposing folks today would celebrate, if they only knew the story," he laughed, hearing the bitterness in it. "So, they were purchased, painted and installed as fencing around some of the small properties here in town."

"Thank you, Neal, for caring so much," Lily said, withdrawing her hand.

He nodded again and smiled at the compliment, not sure on how to respond to such a gracious comment.

Their table fell into silence for a few minutes, but it wasn't the awkward kind that Neal hated. It just felt like a lull, with more to follow.

"I need to get going now," Lily said, and asked Neal to get in touch with her. "And these are for you," she added, passing him the bag of scones. "Thank you for talking with me."

"Thank you for listening."

She exited first and turned right, merging smoothly into the pedestrian flow, her short frame disappearing from view. A moment later, he stepped out of the shop and turned left, intending to walk upstream in the foot traffic, but was intercepted by a familiar face.

"Hey, it's you," the man said, playing it off as an accidental encounter, when clearly, it wasn't.

Neal dodged one way, then the other, trying to dance around the man, but others on the sidewalk had the pair hemmed in.

"I told you I'm not interested!" Neal said, shouldering past the intruder and walking briskly away.

"But Oak Island is practically on your way home!" The man called out to him.

Neal did his best to disappear by leaping into the morning traffic, crossing the street, and darting around the nearest corner.

Ch8 – California, United States - Tomorrow Afternoon

As Oriel emerged from the bright California afternoon and into the windowless establishment, it took her eyes a moment to adjust to the relative darkness. A few folks looked her way, but quickly lost interest. The bartender eyed her with suspicion though, having recently been burned by an underaged police decoy.

Confident that she could once again move safely about the space, she navigated a path through the few tables in front of her and saddled up next to the lone patron at the bar. Seated, she noted, was not entirely accurate. While the man occupied a chair, he was face down, unmoving, arms used as a pillow. A tall shot glass, filled with an amber fluid, sat undrunk in front of him.

Oriel poked at the man's shoulder, but got no reaction. A large mop of greasy locks cascaded down over his face, so she couldn't verify if he was the person she was seeking.

Another poke, still no reaction.

"Is he dead?" She asked the bartender, only half joking.

"You a cop?" He inquired, wondering if the city had changed things up and were trying to catch him for over serving a patron.

She shook her head. "No."

"He's probably alright," the man answered, turning away.

The woman prodded harder and longer until she roused the old man, who seemed unconcerned about his current situation. It wasn't her kind of place, but if the folks watching them now were allies of his, she could see that he might feel comfortable here.

His face rose far enough for her to confirm her suspicions; it was the man she was seeking. When his eyes opened, seemingly oblivious to her presence, they focused on the glass in front of him and a shaky hand reached out and drew it to his lips; the alcohol disappearing with practiced ease.

"Can I buy you some lunch?" She asked. If she had startled him, he didn't show it. Or his senses were just too dull to react to her sudden appearance.

"Oriel?" he croaked out, saying her name as though he had worked hard to dredge it up from memory. His eyes found hers via the mirrored wall behind the bar, their gazes meeting in the reflection.

"Can we eat something?" She repeated, her stomach growling at having skipped dinner the night before and missing breakfast on her morning flight.

The man turned, taking in her appearance directly as though needing the confirmation. "You are here."

"Can we grab a booth?" She asked, thumbing behind her, hoping to gain some space from prying ears. The bartender, who continued to study Oriel, wasn't the only one watching her exchange with Felix.

"You're just full of questions, aren't you, Oriel?" He said, repeating her name as though tasting it for the first time. He had thought of her occasionally, but it had been such a long time since he spoke her name aloud. Sliding out of his seat with surprising agility, she followed him to the farthest booth, the one she would have chosen.

He slid into the seat with ease and looked comfortable on the bright red fax leather bench seat.

"How is it you still look so young?" He asked, smiling.

"How is it you've gotten so old?" She countered, concerned at his appearance.

The man laughed, looking less tired. "It's not the years, honey. It's the mileage." he quoted, his smile faltering when he noticed the server eyeing him dubiously. Trying to deflect her suspicions, he quickly added, "She's, my granddaughter."

The server's eyes shifted to Oriel and then back to the old man, her poker face not revealing how successful his ploy had been. Regular or not, the server clearly had limits to patron behavior.

"What are you drinking?" She asked, giving in for now, but she made a mental note to approach the young woman to confirm the story if an opportunity presented itself. She withdrew with their order, leaving the pair alone for the first time.

"Not really the mileage, is it, Felix?" Oriel asked, motioning towards the bar.

"It's just an expression," he defended, rolling his eyes and throwing up his hands, exasperated.

This was definitely him, Oriel thought to herself, the man barely able to speak without waving his arms about. Some things never change. It was her time to crack a smile.

"Why here?" She opened, genuinely interested in his circumstances. Felix Hatt had never been a man who was comfortable in rich surroundings, favoring instead similar 'hole in the wall' type places, as the expression went, but this place seemed to lack the action he had usually sought.

"Why not here?" He challenged.

She heard no heat in his words, as though defending the small establishment against her criticism, but he posed it more as an intellectual inquiry, another trait he was famous for.

A cloud of steam, tinged with grease, blossomed up from the far end of the room, drawing her attention. It seemed the bartender also doubled as the cook, a small grill and fryer tucked behind the bar so he didn't have to leave his workspace. Made sense, Oriel thought, since the building itself wasn't that large from the outside and it was unlikely that any magic was at work here in such a public place to mask its true size. If it were, it might explain why Felix seemed to feel at home here.

"But it's Hollywood," she challenged, noticing the server headed their way with plates of cheeseburgers and fries that were laid on the table in front of them.

"Still good?" the server inquired, focused solely on Oriel.

Oriel wasn't sure if the woman was asking if she was OK on her drink, or whether she was still OK sitting here with a far older man who was acting out of character. She nodded.

Satisfied for now, the server drifted away to her only other table.

"Hollywood is a perfect place for people like us to live. A knight on a horse could turn up on the roadway outside and just as quickly vanish again, and people here would barely question it. It's crazy the kinds of things I've witnessed. Most people think it's eccentricities or movie special effect being tested out."

Oriel had already dug into her hamburger, never one to stand on protocol when there was food in front of her. There had been far too many missed meals in her life and when you know hunger that intimately, it wasn't something you got over easily, no matter how much time has passed. Delicious, she thought, juice trying to escape down her chin from the greasy sandwich. Steak-style potato planks were perfect too.

"And you have this place," she added around the big bite of beef in her mouth.

He pointed at her in agreement with the long fry in his hand. "Hang around a while and you'll see the charm."

"Seriously though, Felix. Have you been seeing anything strange?

"Besides, what's considered normal for this town?"

She nodded, not fully grasping what he was implying, but assumed it had to be something special if he had bothered to call it out.

Felix ate in silence as he pondered the question, creating a mental checklist in his head. "I had my doubts at first, maybe a year ago. The quirky stuff around here helped to mask the magic, so I expanded my range a bit, searching for confirmation."

"Did you find anything?"

"Nothing I could pin down conclusively. It was subtle. Kind of thing you catch out the corner of your eye but it disappears when you look directly at it. I was out of practice, you understand," he stressed, gaze distant. "I found nothing definitive, no smoking gun if you will, but enough to make me suspicious. It was maddening."

"Do you think they've returned?" She asked, watching him for a reaction. Oriel didn't have to specify who she was referring to. If she had spent the energy in tracking him down after so many years, it wasn't just to catch up on old times.

"How did you find me?" He dodged, steeling her with a stare that proved he hadn't lost all of his intensity.

"The world might be bigger now than what we originally thought, but it's not that large," she replied. He had his secrets, and she had hers. Right now, she wasn't feeling that forthcoming. Oriel had narrowed down her search area to California, but Felix had hidden his tracks well. It took skills to mask one's magic, and it didn't come without considerable effort. That's how she knew he hadn't lost his edge, despite his humbling appearance. She had had to call in a few favors to locate him, though. More than she would admit, but once she triggered the search and made the investment, there was no turning back.

"You've seen some signs too?" He asked, unnecessarily, as she wouldn't have exposed herself by coming here if there had been any doubt in her mind. She had never been one to get excited without cause and he doubted that time had changed that. That she was playing her cards so close to her vest showed that her cautious nature was alive and active. Probably for valid reasons, he thought, given the number of enemies they had gained over the centuries.

She finished the last of her fries and pushed the plate away, buying time.

"A few. Like you, they seemed to evaporate if you looked too closely. But what I saw seemed indisputable. I don't have your 'experience' in such things, though," she said.

He laughed at the emphasis she had placed on his 'experience', normally a jab taken at people older than themselves, but he knew better.

"You're nearly as old as I am," he reminded her, unnecessarily. They both knew that looks could deceive in a world woven through with magic.

They stared at each other, smiling, ruminating on the breadth of history and secrets they shared.

"Touché," she said, flagging down their server and switching to something stronger to drink. The server, urged on by the reluctant bartender, sent her back to the table to check her ID, taking no chances.

"You get that a lot, I bet," Felix said, holding out his hand.

Seeing no reason to deny his curiosity, she handed her passport over, watching him as he flipped through the pages, noting the travel stamps and bio.

"Only twenty-one?"

She stared at him, smirking. "I can look older by the way I carry myself, dress, wear my hair, and by putting on makeup, but the charade is tiring. I went with an age that was old enough for complete freedom, yet young enough to be plausible."

He handed the passport back, and they sat in silence for a moment, resting, before Oriel broached the unanswered question again. "Do you think they're really returning? I mean, after what we did?"

"After we failed?" He said, looking at her with a deprecating demeanor. "After I put all the evidence together, raised and instructed the child, and convinced the local aristocrats to give me a small army and the resources so I could march them across the continent, most to their deaths, and then not deliver on the objective?"

She had played this conversation over and over in her mind on the way here, and it had gone a dozen different ways. So, it didn't come as a great surprise when Felix took the pitiful route, shouldering most of the failure. While he had convinced many that their quest was true and important, it was not without evidence that the dark Lords and their minions were planning something. Both he and Oriel, and their small coalition, had seen the signs for themselves, long before they had arrived to ask for their help.

"But it turned out to be true," she countered, reaching out and taking his weathered hands in her own. "The Sael Lords and their dark followers were assembling for something big."

It had been so long since he had enjoyed something so unassuming and pure as the holding of hands that he grew still, eyes cast downwards. Felix tried to stretch out this humble event, but his mind was racing through the past, eyes glazing over. When he spoke, his voice sounded distant.

"It was nothing we did, Oriel, you know that. The prophecy wasn't fulfilled. And although the Evil Ones had vanished, and our support with it despite our objections, they never truly left. No matter how much we wanted them gone, they weren't going away. Maybe it was our singular desire for wanting them gone, which corrupted the prophecy. How's that for some messed up logic?"

When he returned from wherever in the past he had gone, and their eyes met, she could see the pain and hurt in his eyes and he could see the pity in hers. Felix looked away, unable to hold her stare.

"You think that us wanting them destroyed meant that we couldn't destroy them?"

He laughed now as though it just was a silly theory, but he wasn't going to admit how strongly he held that belief. It was karma incarnate, he thought, the most likely of explanations. But no, that was an idea he was unwilling to share so openly. "Of course not," he lied. "The prophecy was wrong, my interpretation of it was faulty, or I chose poorly," Felix concluded, memories of the young man he had led to his untimely death playing over in his mind.

"Do you think they led us astray?" Oriel asked, throwing him a bone meant to assuage his bruised ego.

If Felix supported her comment and the Council of Advisors had been wrong, it would allow Felix to save face personally, but it meant bad news for the Council, who relied on its reputation for infallibility for its authority. Worse still, if the Council had become corrupted and had intentionally deceived their coalition. While the Council's influence had waned over the centuries, he shivered at the prospects that the one remaining stabilizing force in the magical realm might falter, or worse, be turned against them.

"Not intentionally," he said, not wanting to project any doubt in the Council, in Oriel's mind, or to convince himself that things had gone so wrong. Maybe the Dark Lords, sensing some kind of opening, were looking to exploit it. "It's been a very long time since those prophecies were recorded, the original sources unknown and language exceedingly difficult to decipher. There were gaps in our own history when there was no one who had the knowledge to advise the Council. You know, they shut down the great libraries and sealed them until they could find suitable replacements following the Great Corruption. It was a time filled with ignorance, people living with their heads in the sand, not wanting to know or admit the truth."

Oriel had heard much of this before, but never any of the details behind it. It was when chaos ruled the world and the mighty temples went back into hiding, locations scrubbed from memory. 'The Gap' as it was known, were dark days when few were safe from the evil forces that dared to walk openly in the light, unchallenged. It took centuries for order to be reestablished. For the world to push back against the tumultuous times and regain some control, preventing all of civilization from burning to ash.

"In some small way, though, we must have helped," she said, more to bolster her own faltering morale than to help Felix's damaged ego.

"Maybe we played a small part," he was willing to admit, a sad smile on his lips.

Ch9 – Hollywood, California, US – Day after tomorrow

Felix and Oriel left the bar on foot, following a circuitous route through several neighborhoods. Taking a shortcut through a weed infested, fenced-in lot that Felix insisted he owned, they approached an abandoned warehouse from the rear.

"Making it look abandoned is the best way to keep people out," he said, swinging a loose piece of sheet metal aside so she could enter.

Oriel wasn't expecting much, so she wasn't disappointed.

Continuing through the space, she followed Felix towards what looked to be an office structure inside the larger building. Unlocking it with a key, he ushered her inside. This time, though, was different. Instead of an abandoned office with desks and dry erase boards lit by harsh fluorescent lighting, the room featured an elaborate, heavy wooden dining table and chic leather furniture. Throw rugs and polished wooden floors had replaced yellowed linoleum. Decorative wall sconces and subdued lights created a peaceful and inviting environment.

"Surprised you, didn't I?"

"Yes, it's very tasteful," she replied. Trappings of society had never really held much sway for the magician. 'You are born into a spot in society, wealthy or poor, powerful or helpless. But knowledge used for good is available to anyone who wants it,' she remembered Felix extolling. It hadn't always been that way, Oriel knew. Keeping knowledge from people, or feeding them false narratives, had always existed as a method of control. The only thing that changed over the centuries was the speed at which information, or disinformation, could be disseminated and acted upon.

He seemed pleased by her assessment.

And he should, Oriel noted.

While Felix disappeared into the back of the space, she milled about, taking in all the details. Tasteful art, much of the works being original, mingled on the walls with framed movie posters. A lot of signed Hollywood paraphernalia, props and such, were inscribed with personal messages written out to Felix, she noted, assuming it involved work he had done on various film projects. There was even an academy award with his name on the metal plate for a movie she would have to look up later. Wondering if it was real, she hefted it in her hands, as though the physical weight might make it more authentic.

"It's real," Felix said, returning.

Startled, both at his sudden appearance and his having guessed her true motivation for picking it up, nearly dropped the golden statue.

"I had no doubts," she lied, with a grin, returning it to its specially made stand.

"Welcome back," a young man said, sweeping into the room. "Oh, I'm sorry. I didn't mean to intrude."

"No need, Nathaniel. Please come in and meet an old friend of mine, Oriel," he said, staying the man from leaving. "Oriel, this is Nathaniel; he keeps things in order for me."

"It's nice to meet you," she offered.

51

"Oriole, like the bird? That's cool. Likewise," he responded, looking clearly uncomfortable. "Can I get you anything, sir?" He asked, hoping to flee from the stranger's sight.

"No, thank you," Felix answered, when Oriel shook her head.

The young man withdrew, disappearing deeper into the peculiar home.

"Still collecting strays?" She asked, once the man had gone.

Felix smiled, studying her. "Yes, but you certainly were no stray."

Ch10 – Hollywood, California, US – Day after tomorrow

Oriel awoke, taking a moment to figure out where she had spent the last night. It wasn't an odd sensation any longer; her pulse no longer racing after so many years of being on the move, one night here, a week there.

"Hollywood," she mumbled, studying the memorabilia that decorated the guest room in which she lay. Getting up and cleaning up, she got dressed and stepped out, exploring a bit more of her mentor's home, as she went in search of Felix.

She passed a room, which anyone else would have considered a study, but what some in the military would have called an operations center. She could see that it had all the usual trappings: a desk, tasteful armchairs, and a beautiful desk lamp, but each wall had a different series of maps tacked to it, sticky notes stuck everywhere. Although she didn't bother to step inside, feeling some kind of moral apprehension, she could tell that a lot of what she had uncovered about the growing threat posed by the dark armies was mirrored in what Felix was already monitoring. It gave her a sense of satisfaction to know that she had been on the right track.

She edged further down the hallway, examining all the prints and wall art as she went. Most of it was movie industry related, but the rest was an eclectic mix of subjects and formats, apparently chosen based on what Felix enjoyed or was gifted, rather than trying for a consistent theme. The collection truly reflected the man, she thought, smiling.

Although the house within a warehouse was a bit of a maze, she suspected she was moving in the right direction, the smells of breakfast getting stronger with each step.

Around the next corner, she emerged into the kitchen, the young man Nathaniel standing at the very professional and expensive looking gas stove, working several pots and pans.

He leaped when he noticed Oriel standing there.

"Whoa! You're like a breakfast ninja," he said, trying and failing to appear relaxed and indifferent. "Good morning," he added, turning back to the frying pan, as Oriel circled the room full of modern appliances.

"Good morning to you too," she said, studying the contents of the well-appointed room. "Is all this for you?"

Although it looked like he was focused on his work, he was watching her out of the corner of his eye.

"No, it's not mine. It was all already here when I started working for him."

Felix had found a hobby, it seemed, one she wouldn't have guessed.

"Please," he continued, laying a plate on the table and pulling out a chair for her. "I hope the meal is acceptable. If not, I can make you almost anything else."

"This looks wonderful, thank you."

He smiled shyly and nodded, still struggling to make eye contact.

"Coffee? Expresso? Cappuccino? Tea?"

"Expresso sounds great."

He went to work on a complex countertop contraption with practiced familiarity, and returned a moment later with her selection, before returning to cleaning up the kitchen. She looked around for Felix, but detected no signs of the man.

"Is Felix joining us?"

"No, he finished hours ago and left to make preparations. He said you two were taking a trip today and had to get some things in order. I usually take care of those for him, but he didn't ask me to help this time."

Oriel detected a hint of frustration at that last comment as she studied Nathaniel.

She would put the young man in an awkward spot, Oriel knew, but she couldn't help herself. "Are you joining me?"

"Oh, no, but thank you, I've already finished eating," he answered quickly, an acceptable answer, true or not, that got him out of having to take part in an awkward social situation.

She nodded and dug into the meal, noting the perfectly prepared frittata. "This is great, Nathaniel. Well done."

He beamed with pride at the compliment. "The market around the corner has the freshest ingredients."

"Is there goat's cheese in this?"

Nathaniel paused in alarm until Oriel added she loved goat cheese.

Relieved, he spoke at length about his local sources. "It also has gruyere and fontina."

"It's delicious," she said, and meant it. Further attempts at small talk were rewarded with furtive and evasive answers, so she let slide.

When she finished with breakfast, he swapped out her dishes for a sealed envelope, returning to the sink to complete his duties.

Not sure what to do, Oriel opened it and found a single sheet inside, featuring Felix's horrible handwriting, and studied the simple instructions.

"Thank you, Nathaniel. It was very nice to meet you."

"Nice to meet you too," he said, not turning from the sink.

She retrieved her bag and reversed course through the warehouse and abandoned lot. Orienting herself, she took off on foot, navigating the streets like a savvy native, critical eye studying her surroundings without giving off a touristy vibe. A few blocks down, Oriel spotted Felix standing in the shadows of an industrial park. As she continued forward, he spotted her and waved.

Oriel was watching for any signs of a warning, having flashbacks to a time centuries ago, when an unknown enemy had dangled Felix in front of her as bait, trying to lure her into their trap. This time, though, he looked relaxed and not resigned to a certain fate. Still, her eyes searched the area for any signs of trouble, but found none.

"Ready to go?" he asked, seeing that she wasn't carrying anything more than a backpack.

"I told you, I travel light," she replied, noting that he was strangely attired for the sunny and warm morning.

"Are you carrying more than three ounces of liquids, anything flammable, weapons including knives, nail clippers with attached file, loose nail file, box cutters, or any other long knives such as daggers or swords?"

Oriel smirked at the familiar but odd inquiry. "No."

"Are you carrying any electronics not powered down, any cellphones not already set to in-flight mode, or loose lithium batteries that might pose a fire hazard?"

"No."

"Any food or animal products like fresh produce or uncooked meat?"

"No," she said, rolling her eyes, wondering where this was going.

"Anything else to declare or carrying over ten-thousand Euros?"

"Why would I be carrying that much cash?" Oriel replied, looking around to see if anyone was within earshot.

"I guess we're ready to fly," he said, reaching out and placing a gentle hand on her shoulder.

Ch11 – Paris, France – Twenty-two minutes later

"You could have warned me!" Oriel screamed over the thunder that echoed down the street. She was more pissed that he didn't tell her than surprised by the unexpected change of location.

Eager to get free of the swirling rain, she pressed tighter into the doorway, but the stone lintel above her provided little in the way of shelter.

Felix stepped closer to her and knocked harder on the thick wooden door.

"And how the hell did we get to Paris?" She asked him as she retrieved and slipped into her own windbreaker. Oriel had a pretty good idea about how it happened, having heard rumors of such magic, but was unaware that he possessed such skills.

While Felix upped his efforts at rousing someone inside, she slid out her cell phone and checked the screen, confirming that they were indeed in the French capital.

"And what happened to the last twenty-five minutes?" she asked, protecting her phone from the mist, but turning it so he had a view of the glowing screen.

"Twenty-two minutes," he corrected her without consulting the tiny screen.

Felix quit pounding, and Oriel turned when they heard activity coming from inside.

As soon as the door opened wide enough to push through, Oriel darted inside, nearly knocking an old man down whose eyes went wide in surprise at the unexpected intrusion. She stayed close though, allowing the water to run off her and onto the well-worn flagstones near the entrance. The air from inside was the only warm welcome they received.

"How did you do that?" The man stammered. "How did she do that?" He demanded, turning to Felix, who remained outside in the rain.

"Wouldn't you like to know?" Oriel asked, playing along with the old man's confusion despite not knowing herself what he was referring to. The answer, she thought, was perfectly obvious, which made the question only that much more obtuse.

"How did she do that?" The man asked again to Felix, the magician looking equally baffled.

"Let me in and we can discuss it," he conceded, shivering on the front step.

If the weather had been the least bit hospitable, Oriel suspected that both of them would have been left outside on the sidewalk. But the man conceded and waved Felix inside, slamming and bolting the door again behind him.

Proper introductions had not yet made, but she had learned his name was Rosario, no surname offered. After leaving them seated near a burning fire, he disappeared deeper inside the sizeable structure.

She shrugged out of her coat, saying, "Getting here was a new trick for you."

Felix mumbled something under his breath as he stepped around the room, examining various knick-knacks and framed items on the walls, noting some recent additions.

"And why did it take twenty-two minutes to get here?"

He turned, looking at her as though noticing her for the first time. "We just traveled over 9,000 kilometers and you're criticizing me because it took a little over twenty minutes to get here?"

"Of course not," she replied, impressed, if confused, by the feat. "I'm just wondering what happened from the time we left to when we arrived."

He huffed in mild irritation, remembering just how inquisitive his former protégé could be. "I don't actually know."

"You don't know?"

"No, I don't. I just start in one place and finish in another," he defended before switching tactics. "Are you missing anything? Worried someone went through your stuff or searched your pockets?"

"I don't think so. Why?"

"Then what's the problem?"

"It's the time," her curiosity winning out on worry. "Is it always twenty-two minutes?"

"Yes, always."

"So, if you were to travel from your bedroom to the kitchen, it would take twenty-two minutes?"

"Why would I expend all that the energy to go from my bedroom to the kitchen?" He asked, no longer trying to hide his exasperation.

"I dunno. To get a snack maybe?"

"Why would I spend twenty-two minutes of my life just to get a snack, when I could literally just spend seconds walking to the kitchen?"

"So, it is twenty-two minutes to travel between two points. No matter the distance between them?"

"Yes," he confirmed, suddenly tired and taking a seat directly on the hearth next to the fire.

"So, you go from here to the moon then in twenty-two minutes?"

He was growing tired and concerned that his old acquaintance had been gone far too long. Where had he gotten off to?

"Yes, it would take that same length of time to travel from here to the moon theoretically," he began, holding up a finger to hold her next follow-up question before continuing, "but I can only travel between two points where I've physically been before, the old-fashioned way. And no, I have not been to the moon."

Progress, Oriel thought to herself.

"If you have been here before and knew it was raining, why didn't you just beam us directly inside?"

"Would you appreciate someone beaming their way directly into your home?" He said, adopting her Star Trek reference.

Oriel nodded, accepting his argument. "Point taken."

"Besides," Felix said, eyeing her curiously, "I couldn't have done it, even if I wanted to. A series of powerful spells of exclusion seals this structure in order to keep uninvited guests out."

Oriel looked confused. "But I walked right in."

"Yes, you did. How did you overcome the magic?" He asked her, looking around to see if Rosario had returned.

Oriel shook her head, belaying her ignorance. "Nothing that I did. Door opened, and I stepped inside to get out of the rain."

Felix eyed her, but saw no obvious signs of deception. No reason for Oriel to lie about it, anyway. "So, you were just blowing smoke earlier with Rosario, pretending that you had a way around the protection spells?"

She smiled, remaining silent, clearly enjoying the moment, aware now why the pair had been so baffled earlier.

"Well, I'm hoping Rosario is going to cooperate with us and that involves a visit to an especially important room in this building. If he does, I need you to pretend that you can't walk into the room without his granting you an invitation to enter. Like there's a barrier in the way and it's stopping you from entering, got it?"

"Like in *Buffy the Vampire Slayer*?"

Felix's eyes narrowed, drilling into her. "What?"

"Vampires can't enter a home unless they're invited inside," Oriel clarified, as though the answer should have been obvious.

"I don't even know how to answer that," he conceded, noticing movement in the doorway.

"Vampires, Felix? Please tell me you're not here about them again?" Rosario pleaded, a steaming tray in his hands and an alarming look on his face.

"Good heavens no," Felix replied calmly with a disarming laugh as he got to his feet and relieved his friend of the tray. He set it on a low table between their seats and passed out a steaming mug of tea to Oriel, along with a selection of cookies on a plate. "Although you are probably wondering why we've come."

Taking several treats, Oriel offered thanks, shifting her attention from the fascinating structure and artifacts to their host. Much more was lurking here, just below the surface, she suspected.

Rosario settled in, waiting for his unexpected guests to explain.

Over the next few minutes, Felix filled their host in on what he had been up to since their last meeting, glossing over anything irrelevant and centering the narrative around his most recent actions, suspicions, and conclusions.

"What do you think?" Rosario asked, turning his gaze to Oriel, who had been expecting the question. She cleared her throat and started in.

"I'm afraid I can't vouch for anything Felix said prior to yesterday, but I can, however, attest to his conclusions. I independently identified many of the same signs which had caught Felix's attention, and reached the same conclusions; the reason I sought him out." Short, sincere, factual, straight to the point, no embellishments.

The man nodded, holding questions he might have had, and sipped at his tea with a grimace, the steeped brew having grown tepid.

"I suppose you'll be wanting to visit to the observatory?" He asked, turning to Felix, the answer on his guest's face as clear as if he answered with words.

"If it wouldn't be too much trouble."

Rosario rose, looking older than when he had entered the room. "Come on then," he said with resignation, setting down his teacup and walking towards the next room.

They made to follow, but Oriel held him back for a few seconds, relaying a curious observation. "You didn't drink his tea or eat any of his cookies," she admonished. "Manners often opened door better than brute force, I've learned."

"I wanted to see how you reacted first."

"You thought I wouldn't like it?" she asked, confused.

"No, I wondered if it had been poisoned. Rosario and I didn't leave on the best of terms last time, and he has an unhealthy obsession with dangerous plants and animals."

Felix was the worst of poker players, Oriel recalled, but as they both moved to catch up to their host, he gave off no signs of deception or humor.

Ch12 – Paris, France – Ten minutes later

"I swear I just saw him come through this doorway," Oriel stated, her eyes finding no places to hide nor any other exits save for a window in the far wall that looked too small for even she to pass through it.

Felix stood in the hallway, eyes closed, and waited, listening.

"Aren't you going to look for him?"

"No. If he's hiding, we won't find him. And if we keep moving, he might very well never find us. It's best to just stay where we last saw him and wait."

Patience, Oriel thought to herself, was not one of her strong suits. She considered backtracking, but even the path she was sure they had taken to reach this point no longer looked familiar.

They heard a sound behind them and turned in time to see Rosario pushing open a door and stepping inside a room.

"Was that door there a moment ago?" she asked, moving quickly in that direction. Although Felix didn't remind her, she made to enter the room but stopped short, as though some invisible barrier prevented her from doing so. She held her forehead with one hand, as though having struck it on something unseen, while she reached up and felt for an explanation with the other. Seeing a very pleased, if somewhat intrigued, Rosario beaming with pride.

Turning away, their host moved deeper into the room. "You may enter," he called out over his shoulder as he lit a series of long tapers in candleholders on the table in the center.

"What was that?" Felix whispered, sliding up next to her.

"I thought that's what you wanted me to do?"

"The entire 'mime in a box' act, though, was over the top, don't you think? You nearly gave it away," he hissed.

"I'm from Paris, so it was what came to mind," she replied, but it held no hint of an apologetic tone. The smart-ass smirk on Oriel's lips told a different story.

"That's not how it works," Felix countered, but fell silent when Rosario finished his task and turned back to them expectantly.

"What is it you seek?" He asked, hands raised in dramatic fashion to stress all of what the immense room had to offer.

Felix looked around at the shelves of books, scrolls, and loose vellum that was squirreled away in every available nook and was literally licking his lips in anticipation.

"Let's start with, *The History of the Lonely Isles*, volumes 1 and 2, Frode's *Folklore of Scandinavia*, and the scrolls of Demetrius, ideally in translated form. My ancient Greek is a bit rusty."

Oriel saw a look of disdain come over Rosario. "I won't have translations in my house!" He exclaimed, pointing a bony finger at Felix. "Only originals, and I will translate them for you if necessary."

"Demetrius? As in the founder of the Library of Alexandria?" Oriel asked in amazement, the obscure reference dredging up ancient memories.

"Brava, my dear, very good," their host beamed, a wide smile on his face as he scurried away to retrieve the requested items.

"One time, I brought him an ancient treatise by Omar Khayyam on cubic equations. When he unrolled the scroll and saw it was only a thirteenth-century copy from Spain, I thought for sure he was going to wad it up and throw it in the fire," Felix laughed, with a deep, booming, intensity she had never heard before. "The man only revels in originals and first editions."

"Rosario has great tastes," Oriel said in way of defense of the man who wasn't here to defend himself. Distancing herself from Felix, she got to her feet and strolled a few feet away to examine a painting she hadn't noticed until now, but was instantly recognizable.

"This is extraordinary!" she declared, edging close enough that her nose could smell the hint of pigments.

She heard Rosario returning, followed by a rebuke from Felix. "You said you were going to return it!"

Oriel turned, seeing Felix pointed in her direction. Although she did not know what he was referring to, Rosario recognized the reference and had turned a deep shade of red, looking chagrinned by the accusatory comment.

Their host laughed uncomfortably, setting down the documents, hoping they would pose a proper distraction. "I could have sworn I had," he defended weakly. He looked like a child caught with both hands in the proverbial cookie jar.

"What's happening?" She asked, not afraid to admit that she was lost.

"The painting," Felix said, getting to his feet and pointing. "You said you were going to return it," he repeated.

"But you needed it for your research," Rosario stammered in his defense.

"It took me only a few minutes to conclude it didn't have the information hidden in it like I thought. You could have put it back that night!"

The foggy picture came into focus as Oriel's mind cleared. "Wait, you're saying this isn't a copy of the Mona Lisa? This is *the* Mona Lisa? From the Louvre, just across town? How did it get there?"

"I *borrowed* it," Rosario defended.

"If you take something that doesn't belong to you and don't return it, that means you *stole* it!" Felix clarified.

"Did you take it recently?" Oriel asked, trying to give their host a way out.

"1911. He *stole* it over a century ago."

Rosario shrugged. "I guess we'll have to agree to disagree."

"Wait, what's hanging at the Louvre, then?"

"I put a copy in its place to keep security appeased. And I planned on swapping it out again after he," Rosario said, pointing at Felix, who had returned to his seat and began flipping through the various books and scrolls, "was done with his examination."

"What happened?"

"My copy was stolen that night."

"Why didn't you just return the original?" Felix asked, feigning disinterest, while apparently still listening in on the exchange.

"What was I supposed to do? Just walk up to the museum and hand it back?"

With no response from Felix, the debate had ended.

"Do they know it's a fake?" Oriel asked.

"Oh yes, my dear. It was talked about, at great length, following the recovery of the painting. All behind closed doors, of course."

"Your painting?"

"Yes, they recovered the copy two years later. Upon further examination, they determined it was a fake. Secret talks with the insurance company resulted in a cash offer in return for the museum's silence. Everyone just wanted the entire episode to go away. They hung up my duplicate and since then, no one's been the wiser. Increased security and the glass barrier keep anyone from getting a close look. Examination by experts not in the loop is strictly forbidden."

"That's because you suggested the buy-out *and* hanging up the fake," Felix added.

"I was on the museum's board of directors," Rosario explained. "Had to give it up after fifty years because it was getting hard to explain my lack of significant aging. People were starting to do the math in their heads."

He looked sad at the explanation and Oriel could relate, as could Felix. In the modern age, it was getting even more difficult to create new and secure identities, unless you were willing to live like a monk, much like what she saw here in Rosario's Paris hideout. Wanting to change the subject for their host as much as for herself, she finally had time to ask a question that had been nagging her for years.

"If this is a library, why do you call it an observatory?" Oriel asked, pleased to see the man's disposition brighten. The sordid affair with the priceless painting now set aside for the moment.

Rosario pointed up towards the ceiling, Oriel's eyes following. With a flick of a switch, the high ceiling of the room slid away, revealing a dark sky pierced by a thousand points of shimmering light.

"The rain has stopped?"

"Outside this building? No. Up there?" He pointed skyward. "It never rains. Come, let me show you."

Ch13 – Paris, France – Several hours later

"How is it going?" Oriel inquired. When she and Rosario had descended from on high, the ceiling above remaining wide open, a blanket of stars stretched out above them.

"Very slow."

"Any way I can help?"

"How good is your ability to read cuneiform?"

She shook her head. "A few rulers, a couple of place names. Not much else."

"Me too," he said, surprising her with the admission.

Facing the prospect of a long night, Rosario declared he was going to make more tea.

"Thank you," Oriel said with a smile, their host returning the gesture as he passed.

"You'll have to drink it fast," Felix warned her.

"So, the poison will work faster?"

He laughed, but it was more from worry and lack of sleep than humor. "I don't think we're going to find what I need, even here."

"Not in this collection?"

"Then the information you seek simply doesn't exist," Felix said in an excellent imitation of Rosario. "Some of it, yes, but it's more of a refresher than any new knowledge. Though I found one interesting anecdote referenced in the back of this version of *The History of the Lonely Isles*," he said, opening the tome to the page in question, and pushing it towards her.

Oriel took the book into her hands and stared at the page. The words were a blur, but the simple sketch of a young woman was intimately familiar, though from an ancient time she wished she could forget. How had the writer obtained it, she wondered, closing the tome, and passing it back?

"Anything else you need to see?" Rosario asked as he returned.

"No, I'm not finding what I need and I've concluded that what we need isn't here, even in your world-class collection," Felix said, trying to ease what could easily be taken as a slight. Rosario really had a top-notch library.

"Then the information you seek simply doesn't exist," Rosario defended, pouring the tea.

Felix and Oriel smiled, sharing a quick glance, grateful that their host didn't have his eyes on them.

"It probably doesn't," Felix admitted, another rare confession.

It was so out of place, in fact, that their host stopped mid pour, and waited for the inevitable continuation of the thought.

"But I think we both know someone who can help us."

There it was, Rosario thought, setting the teapot down with such vigor that Oriel thought it would shatter across the hardened wood surface.

"No, no, no, absolutely not," he said, staring daggers at Felix, who looked as though he had expected such an outburst, but allowed it to happen, anyway. With raised hands in mock defense, he tried to soothe their animated host.

"I wouldn't ask if it wasn't vitally important," he explained. "But what I'm looking for aren't facts and dates," Felix said, waving his hands at the irreplaceable collection surrounding them. "What I need is more like rumor and innuendo. More instinctive and oral tradition than written history and lineages."

"I can't do it again," Rosario pleaded, trying to convey his case.

"I know, old friend. I'm just asking for an invitation."

With a slight shake of his head, Rosario finished pouring the tea and passed each of them a cup, trying to stall, mulling over the options in his mind. He turned to his guest and made to speak, pausing Felix's objection with a hand.

"Do you really think this is happening? That the Sael Lords are making to return?"

Felix had all but decided months ago, but gave the inquiry it's deserved due.

"Yes," he responded. Less was often more when dealing with emotional subjects.

Rosario screwed up his face, nodding. Oriel could see the tumultuous fight going on in the man, though she was unfamiliar with any of the details. It was almost painful to watch, until there seemed to be a decision reached, a nervous glint to his eyes, but a more peaceful look overall.

"I will have to go with you," he declared, surprising even himself. "There's simply no other way."

"That's unnecessary. I know how the location affects you and I can't ask you to go with us. Just send word ahead so they'll be prepared for our arrival," Felix said, indicating that he and Oriel would go on without the librarian.

"You? I'd send in there alone, but your young friend here? I couldn't do that to her," he said. The thought of defending the young woman, while old-fashioned and discouraged in certain times and places, seemed to pump up their host.

Oriel, though, didn't object. "Thank you."

"Don't thank him yet," Felix warned. You don't know where we're going.

Rosario laughed, the sound so seemingly out of place. "It will probably be fine this time," he said, warming ever so slightly to the idea.

"And we can't wait days, we need to go now, tonight," Felix added, as though reading the man's mind. Any longer, and the magician knew his associate could change his mind.

"Tonight? But it will take me days to find someone I can trust to come here and guard this place!"

"Unnecessary, just lock up, and dump out some cat food," Felix instructed, looking around for the furry pets he knew must close at hand. "And set the spells. It will be here safe and sound upon your return."

"I can't do that; you saw how she walked right in!" Rosario said in a panic, motioning towards Oriel. "Something must be wrong with the spells."

"There's nothing wrong here, Rosario. You just have no idea how rare her gift truly is," he defended, even having no clue how Oriel had accomplished it. "And she didn't make it in here, did she? Your mighty spells kept even 'Oriel the Clever' from penetrating the inner sanctum!"

"I'm not sure," he said, eyes turning to study the young woman.

"No one will even suspect you're gone. Just bolt the doors against mortal intrusion and pack a bag."

Oriel nodded at Rosario, not knowing if the encouragement was wise.

Their host finally nodded, perhaps resigned to his fate, and without another word, walked from the room, shoulders slumped.

"That went better than I thought it would," Felix confided, still eyeing the tea warily.

Ch14 – Paris, France – Thirty minutes later

When the trio reappeared, Oriel felt more prepared. She was suitably dressed in long pants and a windbreaker, though the bite of the cold reached easily through the high-tech fabric. She also clicked on her Apple Watch, stopping the timer.

"Approximately twenty-two minutes," she mumbled, loud enough that Felix had to have heard it. "Do you have any idea why it takes that long?" She said, turning to Rosario.

"Cover that up," Felix hissed, panic in his voice, eyes white and wild under the full moon.

Rosario seemed more enthralled by the colorful device on her wrist than panicked by its glaring brilliance in the near total darkness.

"Pi times seven," he answered matter-of-factly.

"Really?"

"Quiet," Felix hissed again, making more noise than the two of them combined.

Seeing and sensing no threat, she treated Felix's statements more like a suggestion. "I thought you said you couldn't beam us to the moon?" She commented, her eyes taking in the most alien landscape she had ever witnessed.

"I fear they might have found us," Felix said in a whisper, his eyes searching the shadows of the abandoned city around them.

"I fear you're right," a voice spoke up from behind them.

Oriel jumped at the presence of the forms that had materialized out of the nowhere.

Only Rosario had expected their sudden appearance, a wide smile greeting the new arrivals. He stepped forward and hugged the man, a long embrace based on shared familiarity.

"It's been far too long, my friend. Welcome."

"It has," Rosario whispered, the explanation on why, passing between them, unspoken.

"And you've brought guests?"

Gathering himself, he first introduced Felix, who had crept closer, inspecting the locals. Rosario went on for a few moments, trying to convey a bit of history about the magician.

"Welcome Felix," the man said in way of greeting, hand upon his heart.

"And this is Oriel," Rosario said, but faltered, not really knowing anything about the stranger who had only just appeared on his doorstep.

"Welcome to you as well, Oriel. I was wondering if the signs were true and that the Angel of Auschwitz would come to our beautiful city."

Oriel felt her face flush at the use of the moniker, glad that it was all but dark out. She hadn't heard it in decades and had all but forgotten the name. If Felix hadn't known that portion of her history, he hid the revelation well. Although it had gone unnoticed by the others, it was Rosario who had reacted to it the strongest, eyes wide and mouth

74

agape. He made to say something, but the whisper was unintelligible and lost on the breeze.

As though sensing his guest's discomfort, their host returned to making introductions. "I am Nikolai, and these two are my children, Anton, and Elana. Welcome to our home," he said with a flourish, arms sweeping out towards the ancient, mountain-top town. "Let us set ourselves by the fire and get you warm," Nikolai said, noting his guests weren't dressed for the conditions. Anton and Elana relieved them of their gear and raced ahead, bounding across the interlocked structures like sure-footed goats.

While it took all of her focus to follow their host through the winding dark maze of rooms and corridors, Oriel couldn't help but sneak an occasional view of the otherworldly realm whenever they emerged from a stone building or a window appeared. She had never truly seen anything like it.

"Where are we, exactly?" Oriel asked, assuming it was no longer forbidden to converse at a normal volume.

"We are in the town of my birth," Nikolai said proudly. "A place that modern maps refer to as Gamsutl, located loosely in the Russian republic of Dagestan."

Oriel nodded to herself, not knowing the exact coordinates, but confident that she could easily find the region on a map. "It's amazing."

"Thank you," he said, pausing on what had probably been a patio in the past. He looked out at the landscape, appreciating it as though seeing it through fresh eyes.

To Oriel, the mountain perch reminded her a bit of the painted white edifices atop the mountainous rings of Santorini, though the air was dry and there was no water in sight.

The four of them continued on in the darkness, when a yellowish light appeared ahead, lazy tendrils of smoke rising into the chilly night air.

"You've answered the *where* question," Felix said, finally speaking, but his eyes were on the small fire ahead, his face wearing worry. "But you never mentioned *when* are we?"

Oriel examined her surroundings and their host with a new inquisitiveness. He was dressed in loose robes that would have fit in here over the past several centuries, she suspected, but he wore a more modern ski jacket over the top.

"We are in your time," Nikolai clarified, pausing in the darkness to gather their small group.

"Aren't you worried about the fire?" Felix asked nervously, wondering if wandering eyes might spot it.

"I am not," their host declared defiantly.

Felix looked to his friend for support, but Rosario seemed unconcerned about their safety, given Nikolai's confidence.

To Oriel's critical eye, they had the entire city to themselves, signs of collapse and abandonment apparent once you knew what to look for. It wouldn't be impossible for someone to be lurking in the thousands of shadows, but if the locals were unconcerned, she had no reason to be on her guard.

"Shall we go? I don't want to keep the others are waiting."

"Others?" Felix and Rosario asked in unison.

"Yes, a man and a young woman. They arrived this morning by more traditional means. We have so few people who come here and they're not researchers in the academic sense, so I assumed your two visits were connected."

Felix and Rosario were sure they weren't.

"You didn't let anyone know of your plans, did you?" Rosario asked Felix.

"I didn't think we would have to come here. Oriel didn't know of this place, and you certainly weren't expecting to be here," Felix reasoned. The pair stared down the steps as though they could infer what might lie ahead, but made no move to see for themselves.

"Let's greet them, shall we?" Oriel offered, surprising everyone as she led the way.

Ch15 – Gamsutl, Dagestan

After navigating the narrows of the deserted town by only the light of the moon, the brightness of the glowing fire felt intense. Shielding her eyes, Oriel could see that the scene was as advertised. A pair of strangers sat on the opposite side of the small patio area, while Nikolai's two children milled about, preparing a meal off to one side.

"Greetings. I'm Oriel," she said, stepping forward and offering her hand, first to the young woman and then to the gentleman, both of whom stood to greet her.

"I'm Lily, and this is Neal."

"Pleasure to meet you both. These are my friends Felix and Rosario," she said, pointing out the pair when they emerged into view. "And you know Nikolai, I assume?"

"We do. We met him when we arrived earlier today. A wonderful host," Lily said.

They sat down, enjoying the warmth of the flames against the growing cold of the night. Only after the children had distributed hot drinks and plates of cooked meat and vegetables to everyone did Nikolai settle his tall frame down into what Oriel assumed was his usual seat.

Unsure of the customs here, she played the waiting game, watching their host. Without fanfare or any kind of visible invocation, Nikolai dug into his meal. She and the others followed suit. She might not have known the source, but she knew it was goat meat, having eaten it for most of her life.

As she ate, Oriel examined each unfamiliar face. Although she was enamored by the world around her tonight, and the new people she had met, it was the mysterious young woman seated opposite her that continued to draw most of her attention. Despite Lily appearing to be nothing more than a typical teenager, the way she carried herself and how she spoke for both herself and the man she was with projected a kind of maturity that hid secrets. And while Oriel had a knack for spotting magic in the world, Lily, like their host Nikolai, was a blank slate. Neal also had a gift, Oriel was sure, but he carried it more like a curse, wearing the pain on his face as though it was physical.

"Rosario tells me you have questions, Felix. Would you like to start?" Nikolai asked, having finished his food.

Felix paused and smiled nervously, as though caught passing notes in class. His gaze fell first to their host and then shifted to the unexpected pair of attendees who were watching him intently. He chuckled, not wanting to alienate them, nor did he want to reveal his questions in front of them, their motivation for being here unknown.

"Go ahead Felix," Lily encouraged, "we're all friends here."

Oriel didn't know if that was true, but Felix launched into his inquiries as though taking her at her word. Even Oriel felt strangely compelled to ask questions, though she currently had none.

Felix continued to outline his various theories, declaring his hypothesis, and that the signs were foretelling the coming darkness after centuries of lying dormant.

As her old friend spoke, Oriel watched the others for any reaction. While Nikolai nodded sagely and Lily listened carefully, Neal was all but lost, his ignorance apparent. He made a good show of it, though, trying to remain engaged.

What are you doing here, Neal? Oriel thought to herself.

It went on for nearly an hour with Felix tossing out a question, Rosario translating where necessary, and then either Nikolai or Lily providing supporting answers. The width and breadth of their shared knowledge was intimidating. While she, Felix, and Rosario had a pretty good grasp on the arcane history of the world and its inhabitants, it was clear from their shell-shocked looks they felt like Neal, who looked totally lost.

Whenever Neal looked her way, she shrugged and smiled back at him, conveying the idea that she too didn't understand a lot of it.

He nodded, appreciating the effort.

When the Battle of Auvergne and the doomed mission to defeat darkness came up in the discussion, Nikolai relayed the story as though he didn't know that some of the participants were seated around his fire tonight. If Lily suspected that Felix, and by association herself, had had a hand in the battle, she hid it well. Although Oriel couldn't look at Felix without fear of potentially tipping her hand, she could feel herself relaxing, as though they had passed a test, when their host moved on to other subjects.

On some unseen signal, Anton appeared, a small burlap sack in his hand tied closed with a short piece of cord. Nikolai took it and opened it, revealing an object which looked like a dark piece of wood, heavy in the man's calloused hands.

"Don't know if it's authentic, but I came into its possession a few days ago, trail growing more and more cold the further I questioned my associates."

Though blackened, the twig-like stick didn't look burned from what Oriel could see in the firelight.

"I can reveal the runes," Nikolai said, running his hands over the dense material, insignificant details springing to life, glowing like blown-upon imbedded embers. "But I've never seen writing like it."

Nikolai passed it to his right, Oriel taking the object and holding it as though it might be hot. It was neither hot nor made of wood, as she suspected. The cold metal, bronze she assumed, seemed to pull the heat from her fingertips, the surface punctuated occasionally by glowing spots which looked random until you put an eye up close to the branch-like object. Like their host, Oriel had seen nothing like it, sure that she would have remembered something so exotic. She passed it on to Felix, who only gave it a cursory examination before handing onward to Rosario, eyeing his friend with rapt attention, hope written on his face.

Rosario examined each glyph individually, but sagged in his seat when he had no answers to give. "I have heard a description of such a language, ancient and rare, but I've never actually seen examples of it."

"Perhaps something in the Observatory could help us?" Felix offered, a gentle pleading in his voice, but his friend just shook his head.

"I'm sorry, Felix, but I know every book, every scroll, and every loose sheet. There *might* be a reference to this writing," he said, holding up the artifact, its script already losing its glow, "but I'm sure we will find nothing there to help us decipher it, if that's your desire."

Rosario passed it on to Lily, who took it and rolled it in her delicate hands.

Oriel perked up, wondering if it had been because of her fatigue or a trick of the light, but she could swear that the font had grown in intensity under the young woman's touch.

Oriel looked around the fire for support, but found everyone else lost in their own thoughts.

As though trying to quell Oriel's suspicions, the script seemed to go out completely, disappearing from view.

Lily did not indicate that the object registered with anything in her memory. Turning to Felix, she asked, "You're trying to use this to find the tree, I assume?"

Felix eyed her for a moment before confirming with a nod. "That is my intent, yes."

Lily held the object out to Neal, who stared at it as though hesitant to touch the artifact. Their eyes met, an unspoken message passing between the odd pair.

Oriel watched Neal take the item, but didn't seem to examine directly. She watched the man look around at the group, his eyes landing on hers for the briefest of moments, a look that Oriel couldn't quite identify.

Neal cleared his throat, as though to speak, his gaze now focused on the dimming flames of the fire instead of the object in his hands.

"Three days ago, a young man arrived with the satchel in his backpack.... His name is Uri, and he is friends with your son, Anton."

At this unexpected declaration, everyone, including their host, perked up.

"That's right," Nikolai confirmed.

But Neal didn't seem to hear their host, his own words continuing to spill out, slowly at first. "A gentleman in a market stall gave it to Uri a week ago, who had then brought it straight here. The man in the market received it from a late-night visitor the night before, who had stopped by the man's home, unplanned. Although they knew each other, it was an awkward exchange, money changing hands."

Oriel caught on quickly. Neal's descriptions of places and people were a timeline in reverse, describing where the bronze object in his hands had been.

Neal paused, stuck; fumbling with his words, as though struggling to describe what he was seeing in his mind. It didn't take long for the others to catch on either, each tossing out helpful hints to Neal as though they were playing charades. Oriel fought to keep from laughing at the absurd scene unfolding in front of her for fear of disrupting the inquiry.

But the voices posed too great a distraction, drawing Neal from his trance-like state, eyes blinking and refocusing on the present.

Oriel got up and took a seat next to Neal, his eyes watching her apprehensively, extending the wand of bronze in his hand, hoping she would take it from him. He looked uncomfortable at being the center of attention, but she shook him off, refusing to take it.

"Can you try it again, please?" Oriel asked, placing an encouraging hand on his arm.

He wasn't sure why she was asking, or why he was willing to do it, but he nodded and did as she requested. His breathing slowed, gaze growing less focused on the present.

Neal pictured the scene where he had left off, his vision gaining a sharpness he hadn't seen before. When the chatter around the fire threatened to bring him out of the trance again, he eased open his eyes to see the cause of the commotion. He was greeted by two scenes, though, the one physically around him and the other, which had only just existed in his mind, had merged a mix of realities. Frozen in time, a table containing several objects appeared in the same space where their dying fire sat, ghostly men, unmoving.

As Neal shifted his focus from the world in which he sat, to the one found only in his imagination, it became more solid in appearance.

Oriel lurched to the side, almost losing her grip on Neal's arm when the phantom room around them spun ninety degrees and a figure who had been frozen in the vision's doorway, stepped into the space, dropping the familiar bronze object on the imaginary table.

Neal watched in amazement, not fully believing his own eyes. He was just as enthralled as the others who were sitting around him on the patio. The scene had only lived inside his head, more like a memory or a movie he had watched, but here and now, it almost appeared to be solid to his touch if only he reached out for it.

"Keep going," Oriel encouraged, urging him to continue.

The ghost with the artifact retreated from the stone structure, those in Gamsutl following the artifact.

"No, wait, go back!" Rosario cried out, climbing to his feet.

The scene did so, continuing backwards in time.

"No," Felix corrected, also jumping up, "Back forward. Can you go forward a bit? Back in the room we were just in?"

Neal rolled the scene forward until both Rosario and Felix called out at the same time.

"Stop!"

Per their request, Neal stopped the scene, freezing it in place.

Felix and Rosario shifted around in the scene to get a better look at the table in the vision, which held several objects, including the one they had just examined. Getting too close to the actual fire, Rosario danced back and swatted at his pant leg, never taking his eyes off the phantom scene.

"Is that what I think it is?" Felix asked, pointing at another object in the odd collection.

"I was thinking the same thing," Rosario answered, animated.

"Relevant to the search?" Lily asked matter-of-factly.

The two men turned, confused at first, were so enticed by the prospect of what they saw they didn't immediately understand her inquiry.

"Come again?" Rosario asked.

"Is this relevant to the search for the tree?"

"She's right," Felix admitted, deflated. "Time for this later, my friend. For now, we need to confirm our object's origins."

Reluctantly, Rosario turned, watching the individual in the mirage pick up the object and walk backwards out of the room, the scene changing swiftly.

Oriel could almost feel the Librarian's pain as she watched Rosario turn, trying to keep his eyes on the quickly retreating structure.

The views moved faster now, not only in time, but geographically. Working backwards with increasing speed, the handoff from person to person continued until an individual could be seen burying it at an archaeological site.

There it sat, day after day, season after season, years, decades, centuries, undisturbed.

"Can you go faster?" Felix asked, still on his feet.

Faster and faster, the seasons whipping by; the scene never really changing.

As though hitting pause on a remote, they could see a dark form huddled over a shallow hole, rain pounding down on the scene, trees whipping wildly. Although it looked like the individual was burying the object, they were actually retrieving it and leaving, in reverse, time continuing to flow into earlier eons.

Slow down, speed up, slow down again. Snow and ice became more prevalent, people changing gear, swapping lighter clothes for furs. More night than day. Northern lights blazing overhead, wiggling, the black sky mirage above blending with the actual sky above Gamsutl.

Boats replaced footpaths and horses. Forest trails and open grasslands became rugged coastline and open water. The scene slowed as the artifact bearer stooped low and ducked backwards into a small cave opening.

The imaginary movie that Neal had been producing and Oriel was projecting, ground to a halt.

"I can't follow it," Neal admitted, baffled. "This hasn't happened before."

"I think they created it there," Felix explained, pointing towards the natural cleft in the rock face. "Can't follow something that doesn't exist."

Neal nodded in understanding. It made sense to him.

"The entrance to *the* garden?" Rosario whispered, staring in awe.

"As in the biblical place? The Garden of Eden?" Neal asked, his brain grasping at the impossible, while he struggled to hold the phantom scene together. He was pretty sure that had Oriel left him to his own devices, the vision would have already evaporated.

"The actual Garden? Probably not. Inspired by the original? Perhaps." Lily clarified. "Even if you find it though," she continued, "it's not really a place you want to visit," she warned. "Or so the story goes."

"Can you edge the scene forward a bit, Neal," Felix asked, "so we can get a wider look at the view?"

Neal wasn't sure of anything now, but he tried it, focusing on the crack in the rock, urging the lone figure to emerge again. Within seconds, the artifact bearer strolled forward into view until Neal stopped him or her in their tracks.

Everyone on the patio turned to look in all directions, but it became painfully clear that there were no recognizable landmarks to give them an idea of where the mysterious opening might lie.

"Perhaps the morning will bring more revelations," their host declared, standing. With the spell broken, Oriel pulled her hand from Neal's arm and the scene faded from view, only still running in Neal's head. Nikolai said goodnight and had his children show each of the visitors to their accommodations.

The group members exchanged glances, nodded, and then retreated to their respective rooms, each branching off of the small courtyard, fire and light fading.

"What in the hell is going on?" Oriel asked herself aloud, lying down on a thin mattress that had been pushed into the far corner of her small stone room. There was nothing here, save for what she had carried in herself. Spartan didn't come close to describing the space, but it was dry and it was clean. With a heavy blanket pulled across the doorway, she found herself in total darkness, illuminated only by the vivid memories of the evening. Even after all her years and after seeing so much, what she saw Neal do tonight had been surreal. "Amazing," she remembered herself whispering into the darkness before her consciousness was replaced by troubled dreams.

Ch16 – Gamsutl, Dagestan

Oriel's dreams retreated, pushed aside by low voices. She had spent most of the night dreaming of this lonely little town, so it didn't take long for her brain to locate her physical form in space. With no windows, only a bit of light and a hint of chatter drifted in around the blanket stretched across the doorway of her room. Oriel listened, but none of it sounded familiar. Still dressed, she stepped outside into the intense midday sunshine. Even with a large fabric covering stretched over the courtyard above her, she still had to shield her eyes from the light.

"Good morning," Neal said from his perch upon a stone ledge which bordered the steep drop into the ravine behind him.

Oriel walked over and sat down beside him, her eyes taking in the unfamiliar sights and sounds that were absent last night. The previously abandoned city looking less forlorn this morning.

"When are we?" she asked, yawning.

He shoveled in another mouth full of scrambled eggs and goat meat, shaking his head.

"Don't know for sure. I still can't wrap my head around it," he said around his bite.

As though on cue, a woman in what she assumed to be local traditional garb stepped forward and handed her an identical bowl, wooden spoon included.

"Dyakuyu." Oriel said with a smile, which often covered her poor pronunciation.

The old woman smiled back, nodded in what could only be conceived as a welcome of sorts, and retreated just as quickly.

"And you speak Russian?" he commented, so many surprises being tossed on him.

Oriel shrugged as though it were no big deal. "Poorly," she admitted humbly. Thoughts of last night's activities on this very patio came rushing back to her. Although she could see the sun high overhead, she knew she hadn't slept that long. "Did they tell you?" She asked.

"No, but I haven't spotted anyone dressed in modern clothing or any teens staring at their smartphones."

"Not all teens are addicted to the small screens," she defended, pretending to pout as she shoveled in what qualified as lunch then and not breakfast.

"You don't?" He asked teasingly.

He had her there, Oriel thought, laughing. "Alright, maybe I'm on it a bit more than I should be, but it's research."

"Research? Got it," he said with a laugh, clearly not buying it. "And as for your question regarding when we are, I can't decide. Considering how these structures looked last night, they could have been abandoned last year or last century. Somebody lived in this village rather recently. How far we are in the past right now is hard to say."

Oriel agreed, looking around at the vibrant scene and the population going about their daily tasks, a far cry from the abandoned mountaintop location that had been here last night.

Neal continued, "My brain can't even fathom the fact that we're here, while the fact that you don't even seem fazed by any of this tells me this isn't really all that exceptional," he said, pointing at the bustling village with his fork.

"Oh, you have no idea how truly exceptional this actually is," Oriel corrected. "Not completely unheard of, but exceptionally rare. Like your ability," she added, deciding to take the leap and gently probe at the potentially sensitive subject. She watched him squirm a bit, as though trying to decide how he wanted to answer.

"Ability," he parroted, his voice trailing off, mouth turning as though the word was bitter on his tongue.

Oriel could tell that he didn't seem enamored by her compliment. "Not a fan?" She asked. Neal wasn't the first person she had met who felt that way about their talents.

He didn't answer, choosing instead to finish his meal, so she went in a different direction.

"You could answer our question, though. Dial things forward and see how long it takes."

"Forward?" Neal mumbled, setting the empty bowl aside. "It never dawned on me to go forward." He eyed her with a look of respect, admiration, the young woman clearly having a powerful grasp on their new mutual reality.

"Well, you've never technically been in the past before, I assume."

"Nor having realized it was even possible," he laughed.

He placed his hands down on the wall, prepared to take a quick peek. "Just out of curiosity, right?" he asked.

"Of course. Research," she confirmed, placing a hand on his shoulder. "May I come too?"

90

He smiled, intrigued. "How do you do that, exactly?" Neal asked, having spent a portion of last night pondering how she had made his visions a physical reality.

"It's an ability of mine," she answered, not knowing his background or what the hell he had been through to see such a gift as a curse. But she was going to do her best to change his opinion of it. "And I can teach you."

Neal was both excited at the thought, yet equally uneasy at the prospect of delving further into his abilities. But he needed to focus, so he set aside her offer and drew his attention to the task at hand. Centering himself on the wall and settling in, he let his mind wander and took in the scene as though he were watching it from a short distance. On cue, the day around them grew dim and then went dark. A flash of light followed, then winked out again. Dark, light, dark, light, warm, cold, snow, rain. Oriel swore she could actually smell the seasons as they whipped past, one after the other. Forward, their view went, not much changing in the immediate scene.

"Older than I thought," he whispered, careful to keep his focus.

The scene slowed, coming to a stop in the darkness, stars above. Around the flames sat familiar faces, Oriel suddenly conscious of the scene.

"My hair is a mess," she stated, with a mirthful laugh that told Neal that she was only kidding. Mostly kidding anyway, she thought to herself. Only a small streak of vanity was wound through her DNA.

The tousled look of her blond locks was actually quite captivating, Neal thought, but he kept that opinion to himself. "It's still unnerving to see yourself from the outside."

Oriel felt the closed doorway of his past open just a crack at that admission, and she smiled at the prospect of exploring it further.

As though stretched on a rubber band which had snapped, Neal let go of the scene with his mind and it shot backwards again. "Late nineteenth century," he declared, as they closed in on their current, temporal destination, the vision blending seamlessly with their reality. "Should we be concerned about how we're dressed?"

"Probably not," Oriel answered, assuming that Nikolai would have mentioned it had it been important.

"Not going to tear a hole in the space-time continuum?" he joked, but she didn't hear the question.

Oriel jumped fluidly to her feet, catching Neal so off guard that he nearly rolled backwards off the short stone wall on which he sat. In the bright sunlight, Neal's eyes spied a long blade glimmering in her hand as she leaped towards the center of the patio.

They had come out of the vision and, reacting solely on instinct, Oriel detected the threat and sprang into action, the ancient blade materializing in her grip with practiced ease. Its deadly tip was pointing menacingly towards a dark figure seated in the same chair she had occupied the prior night.

To Neal, the man looked strangely out of place in the ancient village, his clean, dark suit in stark contrast to the white stone buildings. Oriel edged warily closer, clearly knowing something about their unexpected visitor that he did not.

The man's eyes opened and his gaze swept over the pair, no hint of alarm at finding the young woman approaching, fiendish-looking weapon in her hand.

"You should probably be concerned," Neal warned the man, watching how familiar Oriel looked with the blade. He wouldn't have wanted to be on her bad side at the moment.

Oriel studied the man, wondering if her eyes were deceiving her, a hangover from Neal's magical ride, but when Elana appeared at the edge of the patio and then darted away in panic, Oriel knew that her that her brain wasn't playing games.

"Tell me why shouldn't I cut you down right here?" Oriel barked, hesitant to edge any closer.

The man looked more amused than fearful, and that apathetic attitude really pissed her off.

"Because I'm here to warn you."

"I wouldn't take too long to get to the point," Neal clarified, unsure what Oriel might do if things dragged out too long. He got the impression she didn't suffer fools easily.

"I am here to *help* you," the man clarified.

"Go on," Oriel growled, punctuating her answer with a flick of her sword to make it quick.

"There are those in your group who don't share in your objective and are working against you," he said, eyes shifting from Oriel's to Neal's and back again, the implication obvious.

"Why would you want to help us?" she asked, changing the subject.

The stranger looked irritated at the question, rolling his eyes dramatically. "Let's just say that maintaining the status quo helps to benefit us both."

Oriel knew better than to reason why one of the Dark Lord's would want that to be the case, so she shifted gears away from his motivation and more towards tangible facts.

"If all you have is innuendo and accusations, this is going to be a quick conversation," she warned him.

Motion in her periphery drew her attention. Elana appeared on the steps beyond, pointing in her direction. Seconds later, Nikolai, Felix, and Rosario came into view, eyes searching.

"Looks like our time is up," the man said without looking behind him. "Can't say that I didn't warn you." With a haughty wave to the new arrivals, he shifted out of phase like a cooling mirage, and evaporated from view.

"Dammit," Oriel exclaimed.

"That he's gone?" Neal asked.

"That we didn't learn anything tangible."

The anxious looking group pushed tentatively forward onto the patio. Taking stock of his team members, Felix took the lead.

"You, okay?"

Oriel nodded, feeling the adrenaline draining from her veins. "Fine." It was not lost on her that Lily was conspicuously absent once again. "I guess we have our confirmation that the darkness is regrouping."

"Is that what he said?"

"Doesn't the fact that he was here and knew what we were up to confirm it?"

"Not necessarily. Our visitor isn't one of the Sael Lords, nor even a member of the darkness," Felix confided, catching Oriel off guard.

"What was it then?"

"A lessor demon named Leonard."

"You know him?"

Felix waffled a bit, rocking his head. "Mostly by reputation, though we've crossed paths before. First time I've actually gotten eyes on the beast, though."

"Not what I expected," Oriel admitted. "Should I have been a more gracious host or cut off his head?"

Felix laughed, watching his friend twirl her sword menacingly. "Either works for me, but I'll leave that decision up to you should he unwisely choose to return."

"Problem?" Rosario inquired, as he and Nikolai stepped forward.

"Demonic visitor."

"Great," he replied, clearly not meaning it. "What was he after?"

"He said he was here to offer us his assistance. Said there were forces in our circle that have objectives counter to our

94

own," Oriel remarked, the three men noticing her stare falling on Lily and Neal, who were now seated in hushed conversation on the other side of the patio. Oriel had to admit, as much as it pained her, that they had no real background on these two or why they would lend a hand to this endeavor.

"I have made some inquiries," Nikolai whispered, "but nothing yet."

"For now, we stay the course," Felix decided, and all nodded in agreement.

"Lunchtime?" Nikolai offered.

"Yes," Felix said, leading the group back to the same seats they had occupied the previous evening.

"Who was our visitor, and what did he want?" Lily asked, her and Neal folding themselves back into the group.

"Just a lessor demon trying to stir up trouble," Felix answered, nonchalant.

Prepared to ask a follow-up question, she thought better of it, staying silent and letting it go.

"The tree you mentioned last night?" Neal asked. "In a garden, but not *the* garden of Eden. How does this tree help us?"

Oriel wondered herself how the mythical location would play into their mission objective. It appeared to be a subject which Felix felt no apprehension in talking about.

"The Tree of Tempus. A mythical object which may or may not have been an actual tree at one point. If the artifact we examined last night is actually from the tree in question, then I think we can confirm that a great magical source manufactured it. Many cultures and origin myths are centered on just such a tree."

"Like the tree in the bible?" Neal offered.

"Precisely. What we're after is likely a facsimile."

"Any chance that it's just a metaphor?" Oriel asked, wanting to clarify.

"Highly unlikely, but I don't think we can completely rule it out, even with that branch in hand."

Nikolai rose and wandered away while Felix continued. "And our tree also lives in a garden, so there is very similar symbolism. I am of a belief that both are or were real and we are looking for both of them."

"To what end?" Neal asked, as much to Lily as to Felix. He seemed to be doing fine, so Lily let him continue the line of inquiry.

"As in Genesis, it is said that the tree can allow us to know good from evil, and some myths also tell us that the tree can tell us how to defeat evil, and that's our goal."

Having heard it expressed out loud, amongst people who were only now hearing it for the first time, it sounded nutty to Oriel and she had witnessed it all, first hand. "It's true."

"And we're hoping that between you, Neal, and Oriel, we can get some additional answers. You can do it again, right? It's not like a onetime deal?" Felix asked, referring to his gift.

"All you want, no limitations,"

"That was insanely cool last night," Oriel said, much to Neal's chagrin.

"Yes, it was. I've seen nothing quite like it," Rosario added; Felix nodding in agreement.

"And if Felix and Rosario haven't seen it before, you know it has to be great." She added.

As they made their plans, Nikolai returned, looking distressed.

"The branch is gone." Nikolai said, holding the empty bag. "I can't imagine how."

"I didn't see that our visitor had it in his possession, but maybe he took it," Neal offered.

"Nor would you," Felix said, forgetting that the man in front of him had literally just been tossed into the deep-end, with little preparation. "Some people," he said, looking at

96

Oriel with a twinkle in his eye, "have a natural gift of hiding things from view." But if it wasn't Leonard, he thought to himself, then the only other options were slim to none.

"It looks like we'll have to find another way," Nikolai admitted, though he was struggling with how they might accomplish that.

"The location of the tree and garden was the one answer we didn't need," Felix offered, pacing the small area.

"No?" Neal asked, confused.

Felix shook his head. "Last night, I figured out where the cave opening lies. Or more likely, my subconscious did most of the heavy lifting while I slept."

Even Oriel could see that Felix was holding something back, the smirk clear on his face. He had such a terrible poker face that he no longer tried to disguise it.

"And Rosario? We're going to need your help to get inside."

"Really?" He asked, looking proud to be needed. "Why is that?"

"Because it will make getting into the Louvre seem like child's play."

Ch17 – Gamsutl, Dagestan

Oriel didn't sense the intrusion until she felt the physical nudge. Sliding her eyes open revealed the smiling face of Elana staring down at her, barely visible in the dim light. "Morning already?"

The young girl nodded apologetically.

"Thank you," Oriel mumbled, sitting up, groggy. When the young girl exited, a blast of bright light shone inside, proving that it was indeed morning. She got dressed and stepped outside, finding a very different scene. Instead of a lively village, only Nikolai, Felix, and Rosario were in sight, seated around the small fire.

"Back in our time?" Neal asked, stepping up beside her, still amazed that such words didn't sound crazy when spoken out loud.

"Almost," Nikolai answered, noticing the pair.

"A bit more secure, and it provides additional options for us," Felix added, confirming that the trio were already in the planning phase for the next steps.

They scooped out breakfast from the large pot over the fire and took two seats, listening quietly as Nikolai announced the day's logistics.

Hike, truck, train. Simple.

Elana appeared, looking confused. "Ms. Lily's belongings are still in her room, but I can't find her."

Nikolai didn't look alarmed, more curious. "Anton?"

"He is helping me look."

As though on cue, the young man came up the steps and onto the patio. "I've looked everywhere," he said, shaking his head.

The village was fairly extensive, but if his children couldn't find her, then it was unlikely she was still here. It was also unlikely that she had fled, or been taken from here without him knowing it.

"Problem?" Felix asked, concerned.

"I'm not sure yet," he said, turning back to his guests.

Oriel noticed Neal continued eating, nonplussed about the news of the disappearance.

He smiled at her, a confident look in his eye. "Not an issue," he assured her.

Oriel poked at her own breakfast before noticing the young woman seated on the short wall to her right, bowl in her hand. She blinked a few times, watching Lily scoop out some meat and take a lackluster bite, focusing more on her meal than what was going on around her. Oriel could have sworn that no one had been sitting there seconds ago and there was no conceivable way that Lily could have walked through here without being noticed.

Oriel looked over at Felix, and once catching his attention, tossed her head in Lily's direction.

Felix did a double-take, stunned by what he saw.

"I think we're ready," Felix declared, getting to his feet.

When Nikolai moved to protest, he spotted Lily finishing her meal. Oriel didn't know if Nikolai looked more concerned that the young woman had disappeared or that she had magically reappeared right under his nose. He didn't seem like the type who liked surprises, especially on his home turf.

"I guess we are," he said, eyeing the Lily with renewed suspicion.

After leaving instructions with his children and gathering up their gear, the group wound their way through the village and down the mountainside.

It was cute, Oriel thought, watching Neal, as he was distressed at leaving Anton and Elana alone in the village, his gaze turning back to look for any other signs of life.

"They'll be okay," she reassured him, edging closer and patting him on the shoulder.

"How can you be so sure?"

"I was that age once."

Two hours later, the trail leveled out at the bottom of the narrow valley and their first waypoint was in sight. It was a lot easier heading down than it had been climbing up there, Neal thought to himself, ready to drop into a vehicle and take a break. As their group made their way towards the road, he spotted two SUVs parked on the shoulder of a hairpin turn, driver's out, and waiting patiently. This was the same route that he and Lily had taken up to the village and if he weren't mistaken, one driver of the drivers looked familiar. He was the same man who had shuttled them here and pointed the pair up the mountain. He had been doubtful, seeing no signs of civilization in the distance, but Lily, always in control, led the way and they had found their destination without issue.

Ahead of them, Nikolai had reached the pair and was exchanging hearty greetings in a local dialect that sounded completely alien to his ears.

Although there had been no signs of a discussion, Nikolai made introductions and then had everyone throw their gear into the largest of the two vehicles, directing Neal and Lily to the smaller SUV and the new driver.

100

With no objection, Neal followed Lily to their assigned ride, and it pulled away, trailing a cloud of fine dust behind it.

Nikolai climbed up front while the other three slid into the middle seat of the ancient Yukon. The two locals conversed for a few minutes before he turned around to address the trio.

"He said that Lily offered him cash to deliver them here. They approached him at the train station, but he can't confirm that they had arrived by rail. Neal had made some small talk on the ride here, asking questions about the area, but they mostly they rode in silence."

Nikolai followed suit, turning back around and falling into silence.

"They were cautious," Rosario noted, impressed.

"I doubt anything goes on in the area without the local network knowing about it. Probably wise for us to remember that," Felix replied.

That was undoubtedly how Nikolai had heard of their arrival, Oriel thought, watching the mountains sliding by outside.

"Did you learn anything?" Felix asked, over Rosario, who sat between them.

Oriel shook her head, turning back to the window, her thoughts shifting from what lay behind to what lay ahead.

Ch18 – Chechnya, Georgia

It had taken two days of controlled chaos, starting in Hollywood, and five hours on the road this morning before Oriel could get Felix alone. The driver was working the pump, Nikolai was checking with the other driver, and Rosario was circling the station, anxious and bored out of his mind.

"What's his deal?" she asked, eyes watching the vehicle in front of them.

"Nikolai? Not too much to tell beyond reputation and rumors. Rosario would have more details."

"Give me the high-level," she said, wanting to get a bead on the man without alienating Rosario by asking pointed questions.

"Widower, two children. Descended from a group called the Avars," he said, catching her nod that she had some idea of who the group was. "Touched by the magic, he was born with some gifts nearly a century ago."

"*Some* gifts?" She asked, incredulous. "Time displacement is pretty serious."

Felix chuckled. "Yes, I agree. But the source of that ability comes from the mountain itself. Nikolai merely channels it."

Oriel looked bewildered, and Felix noticed.

"The mountain under Gamsutl has a heart of pure magic, origins unknown. Perhaps sensing its power, the first locals lived there. Or it chose them," he said, feeling philosophical. "It's pure speculation on why the villagers built on that location, so many centuries ago, but one thing is for certain: the bridge servicing the village was sabotaged decades ago. They made it look like an accident, but those in the know suspected that the government realized there was something special buried there and cut off the mountaintop from its only motorized route. Without it, those living in Gamsutl cut ties and started moving away. Beside Nikolai and his children, the only other occupant died in 2015. Nikolai's presence is the only thing keeping the wolves and their excavators at bay."

"Is it safe for him to be away, then? For the kids to be alone?" She asked, suddenly regretting her comment to Neal.

"Not really, but that's only if they find out he's gone. Anton and Elana will keep the home fires literally burning to help with the subterfuge. That's part of the reason we're leaving the area this year, rather than from our time. We can slip away more easily without tipping anyone off."

"Can we stay in the past where the darkness slumbers?"

"That would be nice, but I'm afraid not. The further that Nikolai gets from the mountain, the weaker the connection gets."

Interesting, Oriel thought, having never heard of such a thing.

Ch19 – Tbilisi, Georgia

"How was your trip?" Oriel asked Neal when he sat down beside her on the train platform.

Neal passed her some jerky he had purchased from a street vendor. "A driver that didn't speak English and a co-passenger who only speaks when she absolutely has to. When I'm the biggest talker in a group, you know you're in for some peace and quiet. I may have even dozed off for a few minutes, a miracle given the road conditions."

Oriel could guess that the driver spoke English far better than he let on, choosing, or being paid to listen, rather than to speak. No doubt Nikolai had already received a full transcript of what little had been said in Neal and Lily's vehicle. No doubt the young woman suspected such an arrangement and kept any important talk to an absolute minimum. Neal, however, seemed more like an open book, Oriel thought, save for his own personal history.

"Same here," she said, unable to place the taste of the meat he had offered her. "Should I ask?"

"I didn't."

They laughed, the sounds of a train in the distance catching their attention.

"Any idea when we are?" Oriel inquired.

"1990, if the papers I've read are accurate, though looking around, I seriously doubt this place would look any different in our time."

He offered her the rest of his snack, but she declined. "No, thank you."

Neal tossed the rest of the jerky to a dog laying a few feet away, but even it wouldn't partake.

"That's disconcerting," she said, laughing in fits that told her she was getting slaphappy from exhaustion.

"Crazy to think that we could travel in that direction," he said, pointing west, "and theoretically run into our younger selves."

"It is crazy," she had to admit, pondering the potential ramifications. Maybe she should place a call and help her slightly younger self avoid some painful lessons, but her cell phone had no bars. She secured it away again, more cognizant now about hiding their future tech from potential witnesses.

"Do you remember where you were in 1990?" he asked.

She did, and it wasn't her best year. Thankfully, the question was forgotten when Felix appeared, handing them their room assignments.

"Nikolai got us the best accommodations on the train, but that doesn't mean they're great," Felix said, pointing to their car. "It just means they're better than all the others we could have been stuck with."

This seemed hilarious to Neal and Oriel, who broke out laughing at the unintended joke. "Just a long day," she explained, waving away their levity.

Felix studied the pair suspiciously for a long moment before disappearing back inside the station.

"Let's get settled and have a bite to eat before I fall asleep," Oriel said, accepting Neal's offer of a hand to help her to her feet. Together, they strolled towards their latest transportation.

Considering the length of the day and how long they had been on the move, everyone in the group grabbed something to go for dinner and would eat it in their own rooms.

"Blagodaryu vas," she said to the train employee, who was assembling her and Neal's dinners, eliciting a smile from the young woman. "Menya zovut, Oriel."

"Sofia," the woman said, pointing to herself.

"Thank you, Sofia. Have a good night," Oriel said, as she and Neal headed back to their car, each to their respective rooms. Oriel, collapsing into the seat, almost too tired to eat, and nearly too tired to sleep, was weighing her options when a familiar form stopped in the hallway outside and knocked on her door. She slipped it open with her foot and Neal held up his own meal.

"Care for some company?"

She motioned to the seat opposite her. "Please."

He sat down and set about unpacking his dinner, clearly famished.

"How's your room?"

"Identical to this one; a couple of doors down," he said, pausing when he reached the bottom of his boxed meal, eyes staring.

"Something wrong?"

Neal held up a small package of candy, wrapped in yellow, waxed paper, obviously what was to be dessert.

"If it's 1990, no. I loved these Butterfinger B.B.'s as a kid!"

"And if it's not 1990?"

"Then these things are really old," he said, laughing. "Haven't been for sale in decades," he added, ripping open the packaging and popping a few in his mouth. He made a face that told her they weren't decades years old.

"Good?"

"Great! Brings back so many fond memories. This time, travel stuff could really come in handy. There's a coney by my house that went under two years ago. Think I could get Nikolai to pay me a visit in Detroit when this is all over?"

Ch20 – Black Sea Coast, Turkey

The next morning, Oriel entered the dining car, spotting Felix and Rosario already seated.

"Sorry we didn't wait for you," Felix said. "Letting everyone run on their own schedules this morning. Might be the last time for a while."

She certainly had no objections, having had a long and relatively peaceful night. "No issues," she said, perusing the limited menu card.

"This area of the world doesn't really do breakfast," Rosario said, offering the curious culinary note. "But they have some of the basics."

Oriel spotted their server working her way down the line of tables, coffeepot in hand. Had she not been mentally prepared for the woman's appearance, now decades older, she would have had a hard time not staring. Even being in the know, it was hard enough to wrap her head around the ramifications.

When the woman appeared, topping off their two coffee mugs, Oriel spied a long look. Although it was no doubt the same woman, she could see that the bright optimism of years ago had been replaced by a sad and tired demeanor. Any sparks all but extinguished.

"Dobroye utro, Sofia," she said, watching the woman's dower façade be replaced by something livelier.

"Dobroye utro," she replied, a smile forming on her lips at the familiarity, her eyes searching Oriel's face for any signs of recognition, but finding none.

Oriel watched her leave, a sadness weighing on them both. Time and circumstances could be a cruel bitch.

"I guess we're not in the 1990's any longer?"

"Easier to transition while you're sleeping," Felix answered, in a way of an explanation.

"And what would have happened if someone else had been in our cabins today?"

"You don't want to know," Felix replied, sipping at the bitter coffee, missing his normal gourmet roast.

"And you know I love traveling by rail, but why didn't you just beam us to our final destination, like we did in getting to Paris and Gamsutl?"

"Ha!" Rosario said, holding out his hand towards Felix, who extracted a five-dollar bill from his pocket and grudgingly dropped it into it his friend's hand.

"Oh my god, you bet on whether I'd ask that?" Oriel asked.

They exchanged looks, smirking.

"And to answer your question, we have too many people and I can't go that far north. The northern lights interfere with the process."

"What happens?" Oriel asked.

"Every see the movie 'The Fly'?"

"No way!" She said, shocked.

Rosario started laughing. "He's kidding you."

"Mostly kidding you," Felix said with a wink. "But still a no go."

The two men watched her expectantly, smirks still on their faces, silence hanging. Oriel looked from one to another, trying to figure out their game.

"I'm not going to ask it, if that's what you're wondering," she said, catching on.

Rosario passed the five-dollar back again to a triumphant Felix who pocketed it.

"You'd be surprised how many people think the northern lights only come out at night," Felix said with a laugh.

"And you thought I wouldn't realize that, Rosario?" Oriel asked, playing up her mock indignation.

"I didn't realize it," he said, good-natured, if sheepish.

Oriel's oat porridge arrived, and she ate in silence, watching the shoreline of the Black Sea rolling by outside. Eventually, the conversation at their table turned more serious.

"Have you learned anything from Neal?"

"Not as much as I would have wanted. He was born in New York, lives in Detroit, never married, no kids. Not dating anyone as far as I can tell," she said, noticing the stern look on Felix's face.

"Anything pertinent?"

She laughed, nearly choking on a thick bite of oats. "Not born of the magic, he indicated, but clearly touched by it. Has not been approached by anyone in the magical world, as far as he knows, so he's been able to stay off their radar. No easy task. Early struggles with his gift, leading to the predictable, downhill spiral until he met Lily in London about a year ago, when he found purpose and direction. He basically works for himself with select clients and contracts himself out on special projects whenever Lily needs his special skills."

"Speaking of Lily." Felix said.

"Other than she's the daughter of Jacob? Nothing. Neal doesn't seem hesitant to talk about her, it just seems like he knows almost nothing about her," Oriel concluded, watching both men closely to see if they would follow-up her statement with additional questions, but nothing else came.

It was so weird, Oriel thought to herself, that neither Felix, nor Rosario, seemed interested in who this Jacob was or why Neal would work for someone who looked twelve years old. No doubt there was some kind of magic at work through Lily, but what was her source and why was she, herself, seemingly immune to the young woman's spell? Maybe she wasn't immune to it after all, she suddenly realized, pondering the possibilities. Would she even know?

"We can't wait too long to figure out what's motivating Lily and Neal to take part in our little adventure," Felix spoke up. "I'm not the kind of person to turn away help, but we can't afford any complications."

"You think this Leonard is right? That we can't trust Lily and Neal?" Oriel asked, secretly hoping for a particular answer.

"Of course not," Felix scoffed. "But no matter his game, it's wise for us to do a bit more research, despite Lily and Neal's helpful facade."

"Why wouldn't Leonard want darkness to get the upper hand? Aren't they allies?"

Felix nodded to Rosario, who came to life, the living encyclopedia that he was switching into lecture mode. "Demons are an entirely different class of creatures; wholly separate from the darkness that we're waging war against. Both are evil in their own, unique ways, but the adage of 'enemy of my enemy is my friend' doesn't apply here. Yes, the powers of light," he said, motioning to the three of them, "are enemies of both the demons and the darkness, but both groups have opposing objectives. Darkness wants to overthrow the light and to cripple humanity and any of its allies."

"And the demons don't want that?" Oriel asked, surprised.

"No, the demonic world holds very little sway over the darkness because they're very similar. The demonic realm would lose its influence in this world if darkness reigned."

"So Leonard *is* trying to help us?"

"He certainly is not," Felix said, stepping in. "Don't believe that for a moment."

"If the light were to triumph…" Rosario started.

"*When* the powers of light triumph," Felix stated.

"*When* the powers of light triumph," Rosario corrected, "the demonic realm loses its grip on humanity. It can no longer wield its influence here without expending an exorbitant amount of energy. It prefers to take the simple route."

"Like now?" She asked.

"Precisely. All the strife and discord in the world today? Perfect storm for chaos to develop," Felix said, pushing his empty plate away.

"Thus, maintaining the status quo," Rosario added, stirring cream into his coffee to illustrate his point. "Light and darkness are in constant turmoil. Ideal conditions to play both sides against the other for their own diabolical purposes."

"What's their end-game?"

Felix shook his head. "They don't have one. Will never have one. Don't bother trying to rationalize anything they do. The demonic world lives for chaos, to make our lives a living hell, nothing more. We cut the legs out from under the Darkness, gain the upper hand, and lessen the grip that the demonic realm has on this world. Accomplish that and we can rest easy for a while."

"We *hope*." Rosario added.

"I'm *sure*." Felix emphasized.

Oriel felt like she was an excellent judge of character and felt confident that Neal, if he was involved in a plot to undermine her team's objective, was only doing so, unwittingly. She couldn't get the slightest read on Lily, however, and that bothered her.

"Just keep her here," Oriel said to the both of them as she rose to leave the table.

"Who?" they demanded, but the answer became obvious. Lily approached, taking all three of them in.

"Good morning," Oriel said cheerfully, motioning to her chair as her breakfast dishes were being cleared. "You should try the oatmeal. It was delicious."

Lily studied her for a moment before agreeing to sit and to the recommendation. "Thank you."

"I'll be right back," she said, turning and striding away quickly before she lost her nerve. Fearful of looking back, she pushed into the next car and climbed the stairs, pausing for a moment at the top. She listened for any movement but couldn't hear anything above the sounds of the train itself. Somewhere, at the far end, just around the corner and out of sight, was Neal's room and presumably he was still inside. She took a deep breath, trying to calm herself, her heart beating at an unaccustomed pace.

"Get a hold of yourself," she chastised. "What's the worst that can happen?"

With the breakfast rush over, their server was at the table only moments after Lily sat down. Going with the oatmeal, as Oriel had recommended, she placed her order and, in seconds, the table fell into an awkward silence.

"So, Lily," Felix asked, tentatively. "What do you do for a living?"

She studied the two men for a moment, eyes shifting warily between the pair. Never one to understand the need for small talk, she rarely practiced it nor encouraged it.

113

"This," she said flatly, watching them for a reaction.

"Fighting the factions of darkness for the future of humanity?" Felix asked, confused.

"Yes," she replied.

Silence returned, Felix cursing under his breath on what was taking the kitchen so long to scoop out the young woman's breakfast. With food at the table, conversation wouldn't have been required.

"Do you have a family? Children?" Rosario tossed out, trying to be helpful.

Lily studied him, looking for any signs of humor or guile in the man's disposition, but finding none.

"Do I look old enough to have either?"

The men laughed uncomfortably.

"She's got you there, Rosario."

"Yes, I suppose she does."

Silence ensued for a few more moments, but Rosario couldn't help himself. "Well, technically speaking," he said, breaking into lecture mode, "there are parts of the world, sadly, where young women your age could be engaged or even married," he stated, countering what he determined to be Felix's faulty conclusion.

"Technically, you are correct, but Lily doesn't look like the type of woman who would find herself willingly in such circumstances. Am I right?" Felix asked her.

Lily nodded, struggling to understand why people put themselves through this ordeal for the sake of socializing.

"That probably rules out kids too then, I imagine," Rosario commented.

Felix turned to his partner in crime. "That's kind of presumptuous, isn't it? Many women who aren't married have children. But again, I don't think Lily would be the type."

The two men looked at her for some kind of confirmation, but she offered none. Instead, she turned to an old and trusted response; no answer. Pose a question and go on the offensive was her motto.

"What type would that be?" Lily asked, intrigued by his statement.

Felix swallowed hard, feeling trapped, shaking his head and shrugging his shoulders.

Where had Oriel gone? Lily wondered. If she were here, the three of them could carry on a conversation without her while she tried to enjoy her breakfast.

"Where was she going?" Lily asked them both.

"Who?" Felix answered first.

Oriel took a last look around and walked hurriedly towards the far end of the rail car. As expected, she could see inside the room and it was empty. She tried the handle and found it locked.

"Couldn't be that easy, could it?"

She could walk through a magical barrier of the highest complexity, yet a simple piece of wood and a glass frame posed a challenge. After one last glance around, Oriel produced a set of lock picks and kneeled down, eyeing her opponent. They were in the past some thirty years and this rail car added thirty more to its age. They had installed the locks to give the occupants a sense of security, and not really to keep a determined person out. It was in the train line's best interest to not have people damaging their equipment.

Oriel managed the standard tumblers in seconds and rose, sliding the door aside and stepping in, chased by voices echoing down the passage. She slid the door shut, and sat down as though it was her own space, looking out the window, yet keeping one eye on the hallway.

Shadows passed, voices normal, no familiarity.

Oriel stepped to the door, glanced both ways and then carefully extracted the lone piece of luggage from what qualified as a closet. She could feel magic coursing through her fingers as she unzipped it and peered inside. Oriel poked through the contents, finding only a toiletry bag and a couple sets of clothing.

"Couldn't you have kept your diary in here, Lily, outlining your evil plans? How inconsiderate of you."

At least the branch wasn't here, she thought, knowing that in the right hands, they could easily hide it from view on their person, as she did with her sword. That took fairly high-level magic to pull off, and she still had no evidence that the young woman had that kind of power.

"But you possess at least one magically imbued item, though," she said, rummaging around with her hands until she hit upon the smooth object. Extracting it, she noted it was a stone, a deep black until she held it up to the light and tilted it, a rainbow refracting from deep within it.

"Labradorite. Nice." Although small in physical size, she could feel its immense weight in terms of magic, no correlation between the two qualities she knew.

She set the stone back inside, zipped up the overnight bag, and stowed it back in the closet, making sure she left everything as it was. No one, she hoped, would be the wiser.

With one hand on the doorknob, she froze. Someone had stopped right outside the room, their body blocking the light. She silently flipped the lock, unable to remove her hand out of fear that the movement might draw unwanted attention.

A knock on the hollow door rang out. She should have been relieved, knowing that it wasn't Lily, but with each passing second trapped in here meant the odds of her being detected were growing exponentially.

She held her breath, body pressed to the side of the door, as a second knock came.

'Nobody home,' she willed, mentally broadcasting the message towards the visitor.

If it was Neal and she was detected, there would be no way to explain her way out of it, given that she had remained concealed. If it was anyone from the rail service, she might bluff her way out. But there was no way to see who stood outside the door without giving herself away.

'Move along. Nothing to see here,' she breathed.

Lily stood, dropped her napkin on the table next to her uneaten breakfast, and made to leave. Felix and Rosario leaped to their feet, surprised by her sudden, unexpected move.

"Wait," Felix pleaded, clearly animated.

Lily paused, watching him for an explanation.

"You haven't finished your breakfast," Rosario pointed out.

She turned and walked towards the far end of the car, now physically out of reach by the two men, their only option now gone.

"Should we go after her?" Rosario asked.

"And do what?" Felix replied.

No further knocking, but the shadow still hadn't moved. Was it Neal? Was he standing there staring at my hand, she wondered, waiting for me to finally give in and reveal myself? Seconds passed, still no movement, Oriel's fingers moist on the metal handle.

Damn it, she swore under her breath, willing whomever it was to just leave.

Resolved now to surrender, Oriel gave herself up and stepped fully into view, expecting to be staring into a pair of eyes, at first surprised and then full of anger. Instead, she saw Neal's backside retreating away from her down the car's narrow hallway.

Oriel gave him a few more seconds' head start, opening the sliding door and risking a quick peek. Finding that Neal had turned the corner and was out of view, she stepped out and slid the door shut, locking it again behind her.

She thought she was in the clear, until Neal reappeared a moment later, coming up short when he rounded the corner and spied Oriel standing outside Lily's compartment. He smiled as he closed the gap.

Was he smiling because he had caught her red-handed? If he had thought someone had been inside the room when he was knocking, she would have been his only suspect.

"Looking for your boss?" She asked.

Neal took it as a statement, not a question.

"Not here," he answered.

She took it as a statement, not a question.

"Nope," she confirmed.

They smiled, both a bit confused, but in a playful way, lost in their silent gaze until Lily appeared, eyeing each of them.

"You're here!" They said in unison.

"It's been five minutes."

"Relax, Rosario. I'm sure everything's fine," Felix said, "And if it's not, my money's on Oriel."

"Mine too."

Although Felix was confident that his oldest friend could take care of any contingency, he breathed a sigh of relief when she came through the door of the dining car a moment later, casually strolling in their direction.

Lily watched the pair disappear from view before turning to face her room. She reached out and wiggled the handle, the door still secure. Examining the lock carefully, she found nothing amiss. Letting herself in, she gave the place a cursory look, but found nothing that would indicate that anyone, including Oriel, had recently been inside. She had no reason to question the woman, but neither did they have a history on which to conclusively base an opinion. Oriel, she found, was a hard one to judge. Emotions and motives clouded in a mysterious history she had yet to unravel.

She left the most likely evidence until last, opening the closet, removing her bag, and scrutinizing its contents. Everything was as she remembered it; the careful order of her clothes unaltered. Things looked a bit worked over, but considering how badly the train was rocking on the tracks, it had to be expected.

Lily found the stone in the bag's bottom right where she normally left it. It's powerful, magical properties configured to literally keep people out of her business. It was probably useless at keeping Oriel at bay, she now knew, surprised at just how easily the woman could punch her way through the strongest of magical barriers, if what Rosario had described was true.

She returned her bag to the closet, prepared to return to breakfast, when her nose detected a familiar scent. Lily turned one way and then another, working the room like a disciplined bloodhound. Closer to the door, she narrowed in on the source. The strongest smell of perfume was on the door handle.

"The *inside* door handle," Lily purred with a mischievous grin. "You cunning, little minx."

To the casual observer, nothing would have seemed amiss, but to Felix, who watched Oriel's approach, he could see that something was up, a quickening to her pace, a nervousness in the way she carried herself. She approached the table and sat down.

"I'm only a few seconds ahead of Neal," she offered in explanation of her hurried comments.

"Anything wrong?" Felix asked.

"No. I don't think so," she said, quickly filling them in on what she found and how close she had come to being discovered, her words pouring out fast in anticipation of Neal's arrival.

"Well, finding nothing concrete is something," Felix consoled, making mental notes of what Oriel had described.

"Wasn't worth the risk," she admitted, kicking herself for the effort.

"You had no way of knowing that until you did it; catch-22. Besides, you found the magical artifact in her possession."

"And that she's modified it for her own use," Rosario added. "That certainly couldn't have been easy or cheap."

"And that's certainly not nothing," Felix concluded, hands spread in supplication.

Oriel's ears heard the heavy dining car door slide open behind her. Felix's and Rosario's gaze told her that someone they knew was approaching.

"Neal," Felix whispered, confirming her assessment.

Oriel relaxed, not yet ready to look Lily in the eye and pretend everything was cool. She smiled to herself, knowing that while she had no trouble facing down a Sael Lord with a sword, a little breaking and entering was all it took to get her pulse racing.

"Good morning, everyone," Neal said, taking the last remaining seat at the table. He ordered a late breakfast while the others continued to nurse their coffee.

"So, what's the play?" Oriel asked Felix.

"We have a decision to make and only a few hours to reach it."

"Choices?" she asked.

"Take the train for another three days and get as close to the target as possible, and then a small plane into the local airport, or get off the train later this afternoon and cover as much distance as we can by air."

"Trading stealth for speed. Have a preference?" she asked.

"Coin toss. No preference either way. Both have advantages and disadvantages."

Ch21 – Istanbul, Turkey

As they approached the outskirts of Istanbul, the entire team scrambled off the train as it rolled to a stop at the Haydarpasa Station. Having reached a unanimous decision, they filed out onto the street and took up position in the short taxi queue.

"No Town Car, Felix?" Oriel asked, as she tossed her backpack onto their pile.

"Can't risk the reservation records so we're winging it this trip," he defended, casually eyeing the taxis and drivers to identify which vehicle they would ultimately be assigned. He also watched those folks in line behind them to familiarize himself with anyone who might try to follow them from the station.

"Quite the building," Neal observed, eyes looking up at the entrance and façade.

"It is rather beautiful, isn't it," Oriel replied, the ornate ceilings and carved exterior having a warmth she didn't usually find in stone structures.

"We're up," Felix called out, and the group grabbed their bags and shuffled forwards. "Hagia Sophia," he said, when the driver looked at him expectantly. The request was quite common and a great fare, so the driver closed up the rear hatch and they merged into traffic.

Oriel was watching Neal, noting that his child-like fascination had returned. He was trying to act casual, but his eyes betrayed his curiosity, darting from one impressive scene to another. Not in the paranoid, but-that's-not-necessarily-a-bad-thing kind of way, that Felix was currently exhibiting, though their leader was discretely watching traffic around them for any signs of a tail.

"First time in Istanbul?" She asked.

"Can you tell?"

She nodded and smiled. "Too bad you're going to miss one the best views."

"Why would I miss it?"

Right then, as though Oriel had timed it, which she had, the vehicle descended into a tunnel running beneath the Bosphorus strait.

"Cute," Neal laughed, his view temporarily suspended.

"You won't be disappointed in a few minutes," Oriel consoled him, grand views reappearing moments after they ascended back up and into the city above.

"You were right," he admitted, gawking up at the Holy Hagia Sophia Grand Mosque from the curb. Taking a photo, he asked if they were going inside, but his hopes were dashed when a large, black SUV with tinted windows rolled up beside them, Felix clearly expecting its arrival.

"Let's go, before Neal wanders off," Felix called out, grinning.

Ch22 – Oslo, Norway

While Oriel liked modern train travel, the smooth ride and amenities on their flight into and out of London were a pleasant change of pace. They landed in Oslo and cleared customs before making it to their gate in time for their last flight of the day. Like everyone else on the much smaller aircraft, they looked tired and equally eager to reach their final destination. No other flights were connecting in Longyearbyen, so every soul on the turbo-prop plane tonight was heading there for a very specific reason. Unable to sleep because the plane was slewing repeatedly in the violent winds, Oriel was studying each passenger, trying to picture what their story might be and why each was heading to the Norwegian coal mining enclave located well above the arctic circle.

"Engineer," Neal said, stirring from his nap.

"Which one?" Oriel asked, curious.

"All of them." he chuckled.

She had reached the same conclusion, committing their faces to memory. Her game, she knew, wasn't nearly as innocent as Neal understood it to be.

After the landing announcement came over the speakers, and the cabin lights snapped on, most everyone stirred with anticipation of being on the ground. Ten minutes later, without issue, the team's travel ended when they strolled through the smallest terminal Oriel could recall and stepped outside to catch a ride.

"They should call this place No-way!" Rosario grumbled under his breath; arms wrapped around himself against the bitter cold. He was hopping from foot to foot, trying to generate any bit of warmth, eyes staring longingly down the lonely stretch of roadway. Given the late hour, they could not get back inside the building, doors secured behind them.

"Sixty seconds," Felix called out, pulling the battery from his cell phone again before stuffing it back into his parka jacket.

Everyone turned in time to witness a large vehicle appearing in the distance, headlights flashing.

They loaded up their gear in record time, climbed aboard, and enjoyed the heated seats and warmth for the ten minutes it took to reach their accommodations. A brilliant green ribbon of the northern lights danced overhead, but only Oriel and Neal seemed to notice the spectacular display. The others, drawn by the irresistible allure of a heated room, overrode any sense of curiosity.

"First time?" She asked again, noting the look on his face.

"First time actually seeing them," he said, face craning skyward.

She smiled at his child-like appearance, mouth agape, remembering what it was like the first few times she witnessed the aurora borealis. Although the phenomenon went by various names over the centuries, and its appearance in the sky wasn't often welcome, she always felt herself drawn to them. Oriel missed experiencing new things, having seen and been through so much in her long life, so experiencing them through someone else was often her only recourse.

Neal turned and looked at her way questioningly. "Ready?" He asked, feeling like she was only remaining outside in the cold because he was standing there gaping at the sky.

She nodded, and the pair stepped inside the dormitory-style building, even the relatively cool air in the public spaces feeling great after being out in the blistering cold.

They found Felix milling on the second-floor landing, waiting to lead them to their rooms.

"Not much bigger than what we had on the train, but at least it's not rocking and it has great heat," he said, passing them their keys and wishing them both a goodnight.

Ch23 – Longyearbyen, Norway

The next evening, following an uneventful day of rest and preparations, their locally acquired truck had no trouble handling the gravel roads, Oriel once again behind the wheel. Only miles from their destination, they would be on site in minutes. In between their accommodation's and their target, the barren, gray-white, snowy landscape, was solely illuminated by the stars shimmering above. Ahead, the airport lights were just coming into view. Up the hill to their left, set against the dark horizon, Oriel spotted a glowing rectangle in the distance, its appearance so unexpected that one's eyes were naturally drawn to it.

"What's that?" she asked Rosario.

"*Wired* magazine did a story on the vault not long after it opened. The entrance, which you've noticed in the distance is, 'an artwork called Perpetual Repercussion by Norwegian artist Dyveke Sanne, a light-box containing triangles of highly reflective, acid-resistant steel, set in a ten-centimeter-deep glass niche, alongside prisms and mirrors. It casts a flickering, abstract pattern across the snow-clad slopes of Platåberget during the perpetual darkness of winter.'" Rosario quoted from memory.

"That's pretty cool."

"Enjoy it. Once we're inside, it's all business, with only a few spartan amenities."

They rode on for another minute, making a hairpin turn and continued climbing, the glowing rectangle drawing them towards it.

"Guard shack?" Felix asked from his position behind Oriel.

"No. And no guards inside the vault either, if you can believe it. The first line of security is its remote location."

"And the second," Felix followed up, wanting to prepare himself.

"Polar bears."

Oriel chuckled at Rosario's reply, but she could tell from a quick look at the man riding shotgun that he was serious.

At the end of the quick climb, the roadway leveled out into a small parking zone, no lights illuminating the area. A lone truck, even larger than their own SUV, sat in the spot closest to the entrance. Oriel parked next to it, examining their destination through the windshield.

"Cameras?" Felix asked.

"Yes, but at this time of night, and with only one or two people working, I doubt they will be monitoring them. It will feel warmer inside, but it's not. We'll just be out of the strong winds. Keep coats and gloves on and keep your face covered, as there are additional cameras once we get inside."

As cold as Oriel felt now, she wasn't sure if she would ever be warm again. And she doubted, once inside, that she would suddenly feel a desire to shed clothing. The mountain looked cold and menacing in the distance.

"Ready?" Rosario asked, trying to brace himself both physically and psychologically against the expected blast of cold air that rocked their ride. When they all signaled that they were, they threw open their doors and hurried towards the entrance, a sharp-edged concrete structure that emerged from the hillside like a razor blade.

Even as enchanting as the artwork appealed to Oriel, the brutal cold left more of an impression, her gloved hands pulling her hood down against the arctic winds. They crossed a small gully in front of the entranceway, which looked as though running water might have already undercut the concrete structure. It might have been a security feature like a moat, Oriel wondered, only a small, aluminum bridge in place to get pedestrians from the parking lot to the front door. No way that it would support anything mechanized, remembering back to the briefing where Rosario had told them that no powered equipment was used inside the facility. Risk reduction, he had called it.

Although crusted with a solid sheen of ice, Oriel could still make out the edges of the sturdy metal door, hardware functioning like you would find on the rear of most tractor trailers. Rosario pulled at the handle and thankfully, it opened without issue or audible alarm. The barrier was thicker than she would have imagined being necessary.

"To keep the cold in," Rosario yelled to her over the roar of the wind. After the small group pushed single-file inside the structure, he secured it behind them with a noticeable echo.

"Welcome to the Svalbard Global Seed Vault," he said, using its formal name, which was stenciled unnecessarily on the wall next to them.

True to his warning, and despite being out of the wind, it seemed every bit as cold inside as Rosario had warned it would be. Guess it's working, Oriel thought to herself with a shiver.

Rosario took in the space, examining the details as though seeing it for the first time.

"You were prepared for this, weren't you?" Felix inquired.

"Yes, but I've only gotten a verbal description of the entrance hall. For security reasons, you won't find any photos of this room on the Internet. My contact told me, despite having been inside once for an official event, she hadn't thought there would be a need to break in and thus, took no notes, nor any photos."

"And you trust this source?" Felix inquired, dubious.

"Mostly," Rosario replied, turning away from the entrance and towards the inner door, the entrance hall acting like an airlock between the brutal temperatures outside and the bone-chilling temperatures inside. Duct work above carried away any heat generated in the facility and dumped it safely outside.

Rosario set down his backpack and studied the reader and scanners mounted next to the inner door frame, as though sizing them up. He extracted a tablet and a flash card, a short cable connecting the two.

"Don't suppose your gift works on these types of barriers, does it?" He turned and asked Oriel with a wink.

"No, but I could kick the door in if you like," she replied with an equally sarcastic smile.

"I wouldn't bet against that," he said, exchanging a knowing look with Felix.

Magical barriers posed no resistance for Oriel. She had even gotten pretty good at working a set of lock picks if the mechanism wasn't too complex. But she was every bit as inept and ineffective as everyone else when it came to this type of equipment.

Seeing Rosario working the tablet and picking the high-tech lock seemed incongruous for a man who looked more at home surrounded by musty bookshelves. She watched as he slid the card into the reader, set his own palm upon the tablet and then mirrored the move with the reader mounted next to the doorway. He keyed in a sequence on the pad next to it and a pressurized hiss followed, the inner doors opening just a crack.

Rosario stored the equipment and took up the backpack again, turning to the group like a man that had had no doubts.

"Shall we?"

He pulled open the door and let his associates file inside. Everyone hung close by, fine with letting Rosario take the lead, their eyes staring down the long, unoccupied hallway in front of them.

To their right, a steel staircase climbed into the upper reaches of the entrance hall, but Rosario ignored it, choosing to continue forward.

He had been accurate in his descriptions so far, Oriel noted. No extravagance had been spent here, just crude, boxy, and efficient construction. It continued this way for the first hundred feet, a slight downward trajectory, before the tunnel turned circular, corrugated steel replacing concrete. A series of blue light fixtures were set out on the floor and projected upwards, giving the space an other-worldly appearance.

Another hundred feet later, the steel ended altogether.

"This isn't concrete," Oriel whispered, examining the white, undulating wall.

"No. The concrete up front is exposed to the elements," Rosario said, pointing back to where they had come from, "but here, corrugated steel was used to support the tunnel from varying temperatures and water infiltration. Ahead of us, though, the permafrost is cold enough and deep enough that it is self-supporting. If it gets warm enough here to melt the walls, then the entire point of the facility is moot."

He hadn't whispered his response, as though he had no fear of being overheard. While the rest of the group appeared surprised when a gentleman appeared from an unseen opening ahead and on the right, Rosario was clearly expecting it. The employee in coveralls and high-tech winter jacket took in the group, a confused look on his face. "Can I help you?"

"Greetings," Rosario began, stepping forward with a disarming smile and extended hand. "Dr. Dewey."

Ch24 – Longyearbyen, Norway

"Is he dead?" Neal asked as he and Nikolai dragged the employee into the work area and placed him in one of the few chairs.

"No, but he probably wishes he was," Rosario cackled mischievously, retrieving the darts stuck into the man's jacket. Unplugging the leads from the wrist fired Taser he wore, he wound up the wires and projectiles and stored them in his backpack, reloading a fresh cartridge.

"Damn Rosario, remind me to never to shake your hand," Oriel replied, seeing a side to the man she had never suspected existed. They both laughed, though to her, it felt a tad wrong to do so.

"Now comes the interesting part, finding the proposed doorway we seek."

Neal looked at Rosario, confused. "Couldn't we have just asked him?" He said, pointing at the unconscious man.

"Or threatened him?" Nikolai suggested, with a gleeful smile and a bit more enthusiasm than Oriel would have preferred. She was seeing their little team in a whole new light.

"He works for the seed vault and probably doesn't know what we're looking for."

"Probably?" Lily asked, speaking up for the first time since leaving their accommodations.

"Likely," Rosario replied, shouldering his backpack. "If we don't find it, we can always come back and do it your way."

Stepping back into the corridor, they could move no further, a much more substantial door blocking their way into the vault. Swiping the stolen employees' badge across the scanner and placing his own palm onto the pad, the lights shifted to green.

"Open says me," Rosario said with a flourish of his arms, clearly enjoying his moment.

The group slid through the airlock and into the corridor beyond, when allowed them direct accessed to the three seed vaults.

"Where do we start?" Felix asked.

"And what are we looking for?" Neal added.

"We start with that," Rosario answered, pointing to an inconspicuous object mounted on the far wall. It was set into a rounded niche maybe fifty feet across, extending from floor to ceiling.

"They carved this gigantic recess just for that?" Oriel asked, baffled by its purpose.

"Unfortunately, no," Rosario said, looking dismayed. "According to that article in *Wired*, they designed this recess to deflect explosive energy."

Oriel looked around, perplexed. "What kind of explosion?"

"Nuclear. If the blast came down the main tunnel, they figured this bowl-shaped feature might reflect a portion of shockwave back in that direction," he said, motioning towards the main entrance.

Oriel was nauseous at the thought that there were so many nukes available that one or more might even target this remote corner of the planet.

Returning to his work, Rosario stepped to the wall and examined the unusual object mounted there. To Oriel, it looked like a medieval mace but with no sharp protrusions.

The team listened as Rosario described what they were looking at. "It's a piece of art," he said, trying to unfasten it from the wall. "By Japanese artist Mitsuaki Tanabe. Stylized representation of a rice seed."

"Did you get that from *Wired* Magazine too?" Felix asked.

"I did actually; significant source of arcane knowledge."

Finding the releases he knew had to be there, Rosario removed the artwork from the wall, hefting it in his hands to test its weight. "Article claiming that it was made from stainless steel also appears to be accurate."

"Going to use it to break into our hidden space?" Neal asked.

"Nope," he said, passing it to Neal. "It's actually the key."

"What does it fit into?"

Rosario eyed Neal expectantly.

"That is where you and your unique gift comes in. We need your help in finding the corresponding lock. Hopefully, you can pin it down quickly, since this entire place has only existed for a decade."

Neal caught on, taking a moment to find a comfortable position on the hard floor, despite the chill. To assist, Oriel sat next to him, placing her hand on his knee, the four-foot-long piece of artwork stretching across their collective laps.

At first, nothing happened. The group eagerly waited for the magic to begin. Frustrated by the lack of results, Neal shifted, trying to will it to happen. Even though they were deep inside the mountain and inside a sealed chamber, the sounds of mechanized equipment and even the breathing of his associates proved ample distraction.

When Neal felt Oriel's hand shift to his shoulder and Lily's encouraging words in his ear, the outside world faded to black. A vision in his mind of the chamber in which he sat firmed up. Although he could hear the murmur of others around his physical form, he was in the zone, rewinding time. He started out slowly to get a taste of what he could expect. When it became clear that they had mounted the artifact to the wall and left undisturbed for some time, Neal pushed harder and time unspooled faster. He shot backwards past the vault's initial construction, before pausing the playback. They were under the mountain, inside the rock, within what looked to be a tiny, natural cavern.

"There," Felix exclaimed, walking towards the deflection wall where the art had been fastened. With Neal's gift and Oriel's added power, the illusion was so convincing that Felix ducked under a drop in the phantom cavern ceiling, pulling up short when he reached the real-world wall that stood in his way.

"It looks like it turns to the left," Rosario said.

Felix agreed, catching Oriel's eye and silently motioning for her to keep Neal going. She nodded, watching the two men collect their things and head towards the doors leading into the center vault. A large monitor mounted next to the vault doors showed the space to be occupied by rows of shelving filled with inventory.

"The active seed vault," Felix confirmed. "I don't see anyone inside."

Rosario tried the handle, finding it unlocked. Just inside the cavernous space, the men shifted to their right, picking up the tunnel that Neal and Oriel were still projecting. The vision meandered deeper, penetrating both a locked fence and stacks of loaded shelves, before disappearing towards the back of the room. Convinced that they knew the general location of the tunnel, Felix returned while Rosario started working his magic on the lock.

"We've got it," he said, motioning to the group. Neal and Oriel let go of the illusion, gathering their gear and following the others.

"You did great," she acknowledged, much to Neal's relief.

By the time they had all gotten inside the vault, Rosario had the gate open and had already begun looking over the rear area of the space.

"Moment of truth," he said, eyes searching.

Ch25 – Longyearbyen, Norway

"Spread out," Felix instructed. "Look for any kind of hole or depression or symbol where our key might fit."

They did as he directed, each team member examining the wall and floor in their respective areas. Several minutes passed without success, frustration and anxiety growing.

Oriel was in the center section, where a conduit from the lights above ran down the frozen wall to a switch box and outlet. Moving her hands over the area, she found what she was looking for.

"It's here," she exclaimed.

The team surged towards her, eyes searching.

"I don't see it," Felix asked, feeling where Oriel's hands had been, finding nothing.

Oriel pressed the unbroken wall with a finger and it disappeared through the magical barrier.

"This is where my abilities stop," Rosario said, turning to look at Felix, "And hers begins." He motioned for the seed, holding it out towards Oriel.

She took the stainless-steel rice seed from him, spun it around and pushed the stem into the wall as deep as it would go. The big reveal, they assumed, would happen though, didn't.

"What now?" Rosario asked.

Oriel turned to the right, running a gloved hand along the wall. A few steps later, she found the opening, turned towards the group, smiled, waved, and disappeared through the wall as though she were a ghost.

"That is just creepy," Neal commented, "But in a good way."

"Come on in," they heard a voice declare, Oriel's disembodied head poking out.

As each team member felt for the opening and braced themselves to enter, Lily positioned herself last in line, fearful that anyone behind her might witness her glee, a euphoria that she could not contain, eyes glistening. They had located the entrance and gotten inside, the unthinkable, finally within reach. She swiped at the unexpected tears, trying to compose herself as she stepped forward into the void.

Modern construction gave way to a natural cave tunnel, which then emerged into yet a larger, dome-shaped opening beyond. There they found Oriel, standing just inside the space, unmoving.

Lily emerged, her eyes taking in a view weakly illuminated in flashlight beams, her euphoria fading.

While Oriel's beam remained on a dozen bodies strewn across the floor in various states of decomposition, the rest swept the cavern, looking for any signs of what had befallen the men and women and at least two children.

"Anything?" Felix said, asking for suggestions.

With no response, Felix motioned to Neal. "Follow in my footsteps."

Selecting the closest body, Felix walked carefully to it and kneeled down.

"We need to know what we're dealing with here. Can you take a quick look?"

Neal nodded, taking a hold of the leather sleeve of the corpse, long stripped to bone. Oriel could see him struggle, wanting to rush to his aid, but was stopped in place when a blast of air and the sounds of rushing liquid reached her ears. Everyone froze, the sight of water flooding in from unseen openings, grabbing their attention.

Lily, experiencing unfamiliar feelings of fear and dread, turned back and stepped to the wall, hands frantically trying to find the hidden doorway. "Oriel! Over here," she screamed.

Already knee deep, Oriel pushed her way to the wall and felt for the opening. "It's no longer here," she explained, trying to remain calm and rational despite the cold rushing up her legs.

"They drowned," Neal called out to Felix over the roar of the freezing water filling the room. He felt silly saying it, the fact now obvious.

"There has to be a way out, keeping checking!" Felix barked!

Neal's eyes could read the terror on Lily's face and resolve on Oriel's, as the two women continued searching for an exit, Nikolai and Rosario assisting.

Neal fought off the urge to rush to them, instead reaching through the churning water and retrieving one item after another. The numbing sensation burning his entire body posed a considerable distraction, but the threat of imminent death seemed to focus his mind.

No good.

No good.

No good, he said, tossing each useless item back into the water.

It had gotten so deep, so fast, that he had to dive now and swim for the bottom to reach more artifacts.

No good.

No good.

This isn't working, he thought to himself, bursting upwards to take a ragged breath.

His chest clenched from the thoughts of his life ending here as much as the cold restricted his breathing. Steeling himself for another go, he kicked harder against the swirling current and dug for the bottom. He felt around, at first finding nothing, but then his hand tightened around something heavy. The scenes flashed through his head with a speed his foggy brain struggled to process. Neal felt his limbs growing unresponsive until a jolt of adrenaline poured into his veins. This time, the owner of the item he held didn't seem to be here amongst the dead. They had abandoned the artifact during the flood, and had moved to the far side of the room, swimming to the far wall and through an opening he hadn't noticed being there before. It had to be a way out.

Neal burst to the surface, barely able to stand, his six-foot frame keeping his face only inches above the water. By now, several others were already swimming to stay up.

"Oriel!" he screamed out, catching her attention. "Over there! Everybody, follow me over there!" he pointed frantically, thrashing in the water towards the far side of the cavern.

She heard her name and turned, seeing Neal wave and point. Oriel pushed Lily in that direction and followed, her numb limbs moving sluggishly. But the chamber wasn't that large and her will to survive propelled the team members in that direction, each wondering what Neal had found.

When the two women arrived, they found everyone else feeling the cavern wall for an opening. It didn't make sense to Oriel, but she followed suit, pressing against the area of the wall where Neal had directed her. Almost immediately, she found the edge of an opening that her fingers could see, but her eyes could not. She dove down, face feeling as though a million needles had impaled it. Kicking through the gap in the wall, Oriel fell through the magical barrier and landed hard on the other side, in the least graceful fashion possible.

"Get in here!" She yelled back towards her team. As an arm or leg appeared, Oriel would grab it and pull, helping each person out of the way to make room for the next.

Felix, Rosario, Nikolai, and Lily.

Spitting out a mouthful of water, Neal dropped last onto the floor at Oriel's feet, gulping in air. "What the hell was that about?"

"It was all an illusion," Rosario concluded, as he stood and dusted himself off.

"It wasn't real?" Nikolai challenged; not sure he had heard the man correctly. He hated the water, preferring the mountains for good reason.

"You and your clothes are dry," Felix added as evidence, barely able to comprehend what had happened to the group. "What a mind job."

"How was I swimming then? And how did I end up with a mouthful of water?" Neal asked, incredulous.

"And why am I so cold?" Lily asked meekly, eyes still wide with shock.

Although it was all just in her head, Neal removed his jacket and slipped it around her shoulders.

"Thank you, Neal," she mumbled through chattering teeth.

He nodded, looking uncomfortable at the show of gratitude.

Oriel felt the opposite, however, unzipping her jacket to test the air. It was warmer here, she concluded, the others in the group doing the same.

Having the foresight to keep her flashlight, Oriel pushed back through the barrier and had a look. "The room looks like it did when we entered it," she said with a shake of her head.

"And it looks like there is only one way forward," Felix noted, pointing his own beam across the room and upward toward the ceiling, where the only exit appeared. "And despite the answer being obvious, in theory, I'm not sure these steps are going to help us get way up there."

Oriel laughed out loud at the absurdity, the sound echoing harshly in the barrel-shaped space. "Let me give it a go."

The steps in question were actually two sets, one left, one right. Each climbed upwards, following the curved walls, both finishing in inverted fashion where they came together at a platform identical to the one they were standing on.

"Be careful," Neal warned, though he didn't try to dissuade her from attempting the feat.

She went right, the first few steps mostly normal, each only slightly tilted to the left in relation to the prior. After a dozen such steps, the tilt had grown so extreme that Oriel was sure that gravity would peel her from the wall and toss her to the ground. But it didn't happen. In fact, she didn't even feel a pull to either side despite her eyes telling her brain a far different story. She looked at her team members, finding a mix of surprised faces watching her progress.

"It's fine," she said, completing the journey. Once on the far platform, she turned back, seeing the others watching with fascination, their bodies appearing as though they were hanging down from the ceiling. "It *was* a total mind job," she mumbled, using Felix's term. "Come on up! It's easier to do it with your eyes closed," she advised.

They each tried it in succession, with varying levels of success, until finally, arms flailing, the last reached Oriel's location.

"This place is really messing with my head," Neal admitted, suddenly tired. "Though once up here, it seems perfectly normal again."

"I couldn't agree more," Oriel said.

"Hey, I think we made it!" Felix called out in a hush from down the next tunnel. A weak source of light had drawn him in that direction.

Everyone followed, stunned at what was revealed. They exited from an alcove set into a cliff face, and emerged into the open. A flawless twilight sky stretched out above them.

"Is this all an illusion, too?" Nikolai asked the group, his mind unable to grasp the enormity of what he was seeing.

"I don't think so," Rosario answered, making a note of every detail. Centered in front of him, drawing all their attention, was a tree of bronze, growing up from the ground, elevated upon a stone dais.

"Is this where our branch came from?" Neal asked, the group edging closer.

The entire tree, as Nikolai had done with the artifact, glowed brightly with glyphs, save for one branch, which looked diminished. Neal stepped onto the dais and fingered the end of the limb, inspecting the tip. He couldn't know for sure, but it looked like someone had hacked the bronze artifact from there. His eyes turned to Felix and Rosario, both of whom looked pale and anxious, eyes darting around the area. They looked as though his transgression upon the platform might have triggered some kind of trap, but nothing seemed amiss.

"Everything alright?" he asked, suddenly cognizant of the potential danger.

"Appears to be," Felix said.

"You're not sure?"

"We didn't know for sure what we would find here," he admitted.

"But this is what you were expecting, right?" Neal asked.

"More or less, but only at a high level. Details were fuzzy."

"Fuzzy. Good to know," Neal replied. "You didn't think we were going to make it, did you?"

Felix made a waffling motion with his head. "I thought we would find this place, but Rosario and I just weren't sure what was true and what was myth."

"Fair enough. I'm not sure I would have believed you, given what all we've seen today."

Neal took a survey of their surroundings. Nikolai was circling the dais, eyeing everything with suspicion. Oriel had ventured as far as the dais would let her, even her gifts at punching through magical barriers being no match for this place, it seemed. The stone walls of the alcove crowded in so close to the ring of stone surrounding the tree that she couldn't skirt around the edges and move beyond the immediate area. Lily, still wrapped up tight in Neal's jacket, sat on a small bench under the tree, looking lost and forlorn. Like Oriel's, her eyes were also searching for something, gaze pointed off into the distance beyond the impenetrable barrier.

Neal noted Lily's precarious state and wondered how much longer they would be here.

"Now what?" he asked Felix and Rosario, who were carrying on a quiet discussion amongst themselves.

"We're not sure of the *what*, but we were pretty sure that the *when* has already passed," Felix said, disappointed.

Neal wasn't sure what the cryptic remark meant, but the look of disappointment on the men's faces told him that something they expected to happen here hadn't.

Turning from the discussions, Oriel's eyes continued to scan the immediate surroundings, convinced that they were being watched. But she caught sight of no one beyond the barrier. Then her senses sprang to life, the feelings of danger radiating through her body, limbs tingling.

Neal turned towards Nikolai for any answers, but the man simply shrugged. No idea what they were doing here. He turned to Lily next, who looked small, tired, and beaten, the fight out of her for the moment. When he turned to see what Oriel was doing, he noticed the glimmering sword in her hand, head swiveling in his direction.

"The ropes of death surrounded me; the floods of destruction swept over me. The grave wrapped its ropes around me; death itself stared me in the face!" Rosario declared in a loud voice, quoting King David, as he back-pedaled franticly towards the dais, fumbling blindly in his backpack. The darkness of the alcove seemed to solidify and slough away before the man's eyes, crashing towards him like a wave about to slam into a break wall. Rosario's heel caught the short rise of stone surrounding the dais and as the shadows surged towards him, gravity pulled the man downwards onto the unforgiving platform, the air exploding from his lungs at impact.

The darkness loomed over him, the threat real and closing in. Rosario held the backpack to his chest like a shield, hand inside it, but no longer searching for a weapon. His eyes widened, knowing that this evil entity would not be denied. The dark beast, lunging forward to swallow the man, Rosario now resigned to his certain fate.

Time slowed as the librarian watched the evil advancing towards him. "Delivery me, Lord," he whispered, calling on God for a miracle, eyes searching the heavens above for a savior. What the man's eyes saw at first confused him, a fluttering of material in motion. Sailing silently overhead, shimmering sword grasped in one hand, Rosario's eyes followed the angel he had prayed for as she drifted over him and towards the enemy. As Oriel neared the beast, its gaze spying on her approach, she grasped the weapon in both hands and drew it back, ready to unleash a devastating blow.

Flying within range, Oriel swung her sword downwards with maximum force, slashing the blazing edge down and through the belly of the beast. The magic of light erupted from the enchanted blade, the dark, evil mass exploding backwards towards the alcove shattering into a million jagged splinters.

Even without physical form, the dark mass roared in frustration at being denied its prize. The ground shook and the cliff face above shed a bit of stone and dust, as the energy unleashed by Oriel and her sword, directed at the Dark Lord, radiated outward in all directions from the blast, a spherical wave of rippling energy rushing outwards.

It roared again, rushing forward as it tried to reassemble itself from its broken remains. But the beast didn't immediately seek retribution, the unexpected ferocity of the attack causing it to pause. Another fierce roar hammered Oriel, but she stood her ground, refusing to be drawn deeper into the shadows and away from the magical garden and tree.

As the darkness milled about, angrily trying to shake off the effects of the attack, it seemed to notice the sword in the woman's hands and it slowed its movements, a realization settling in, a painful memory returning from its past.

Oriel sensed it too, history from a different time enveloping her. Gone was that young woman from the battlefield. Replacing her was an entirely different person. Though hardened from years of experience, she had learned so much more since her last physical encounter with this beast.

"Still limping after all this time?" She mocked, noticing its lurching movements. "You should really have that looked at, Shard," she said, using the name that ancient sources had identified. Her knowing that simple fact and declaring it out loud seemed to antagonize the entity, its smoky form shifting in indecision.

147

Although her tone was lost on the phantom, she could see its form rippling with recognition. It shifted, taking stock of its opponent. Although it had been centuries, the passing of time since its first encounter with this woman seemed like only days ago. The sting of defeat bounced around in its memory while the familiar sight reminded it of its previous encounter. Although it couldn't feel true pain, it knew that Oriel had diminished it and that she was the one responsible for its lessening.

It turned its single, working eye, a dark void now in the center of its jagged face, examining the others in the group. Although not as bitter, the beast recognized Felix from the lineup. A different sort of longing fueled the hate buried deep within in its psyche.

Felix looked on in horror as the Dark Lord focused its gaze on him. The desire for it to shred his flesh and consume his bones seemed to radiate outwards from the blackened mass that drew more solid by the minute. Felix's brain told him to flee, but the fright he was experiencing had frozen the man in place. The only avenue of escape was back through the tunnel, and that meant drawing closer to the enemy. Oriel, he knew, had stayed the course and held her ground, but while she had done so voluntarily, he was locked in place, fear keeping his muscles from recognizing the impulse to move that his mind was generating in large numbers.

"I like what you've done with your eye," Oriel teased, waving a hand over her own face to indicate what she was referring to, the beast apparently incapable of understanding her meaning. "Moving it over to the center of, I guess, your face was a nice touch. And the scar next to it?" She said, running a hand down her own temple to indicate its injury. "I hear chicks dig them. Not this chick, per se, but some do, I suppose." Oriel then broke out in maniacal laugh, deep, sincere, and reverberating, which caused the others in her group to exchange nervous glances amongst themselves.

"Should you be antagonizing it?" Felix questioned.

"Gimpy here?" She asked over her shoulder, keeping at least one eye squarely on Shard. "I doubt I can fill it with any more hatred than what it's already holding for us, can I?"

"Point taken," he said, clearly not meaning it.

While distracted, with the unwitting help of Felix's question, Oriel had edged forward again, closer to the reconstituted darkness.

"En garde," she whispered, racing forward and landing another slashing blow before stepping back again. Although it lacked the punch she had delivered earlier while at a full sprint, the beast was driven back again on its heels, reeling in disbelief at the audacity of the mortal who dared attack it for a second time. Though it no longer appreciated the subtle nuances of human emotions, it knew it didn't like what it was experiencing and that it was all because of the infernal woman standing right in front of it.

"Oh shit, it's about to go down," Felix warned, seeing the Sael Lord rear back in preparation.

"Come on!" Oriel screamed at it, smiling, waving a hand to egg it on, challenging it to attack her, focus all its attention on her. The words, as much as the wide grin, infuriated the beast, which could no longer contain its collective fury. It surged in all directions before pulling back again, as though trying to decide on a form to take. It broke up into several distinct but still connected clouds of darkness, one mass at the center, larger than the rest. Then it surged towards Oriel.

"That's more like it," she growled, raising her sword again and racing to close the gap before the monster was ready to defend itself. She delivering another solid slash at Shard's core, before dancing back to avoid the beast's ragged claws.

Nikolai and Felix rushed in and grabbed Rosario, pulling him to his feet and back from the melee.

149

"She is the Angel of Auschwitz," he croaked, eyes wide in euphoria, as he watched Oriel hack and slash at the entity with brutal efficiency. Though she attacked her enemy like a true berserker, Rosario could see that there was a discipline to her movements. The onslaught was all one-sided in Oriel's favor, but he felt no pity for the Dark Lord, which savagely took every blow that Oriel could muster.

Shard reeled at the viciousness of the unrelenting attack, trying unsuccessfully to counter the blows. It shed off bits of its form, trying to surround the woman, but she seemed to anticipate its every move.

"We need to help her," Neal said, frantic, unsure of what to do.

"Here!" Rosario called out to him, tossing Neal a hammer from his backpack. The man was pretty good with his fists, but the solid wooden handle in his hand felt more promising. He shot a glance towards Lily, who looked shocked and appalled at the brutality on display, but was still sitting on the bench and safely out of harm's way. He checked their flanks and, finding no immediate threats, stepped to the edge of the dais to join the others.

To Neal's eyes, the alcove and cliff face seemed to brighten, as the shadows continued to be drawn up and into Shard's phantom form, before breaking into more and more distinct pieces. Whether on its own or because of Oriel's relentless assault, he had no way of knowing. To keep the enemy from surrounding her, she made a controlled retreat, dropping back toward her allies. She was grinning from ear to ear, thoroughly enjoying the retribution she was doling out, pent up fury unleashed.

"Any tips on fighting these things?" Neal asked, noticing the darkness condense to the right and left of the Dark Lord as it advanced towards them, giving up its hesitation to approach the tree and the dais on which they stood.

"Treat it like flesh and blood," Felix offered. "Lash out as though you're expecting to hit something solid, but be ready when your swing goes right through it. Don't worry about that though, they'll feel it. And stay away from the big one," he said, "It's the core of the beast, where the largest threat lies."

Oriel had chosen the Sael Lord for herself and he had no qualms with her making the first selection. She was more than holding her own; the entity beaten back time and time again, its continued roars of frustration echoing at her audacity.

"Their attacks on you will pass right through you," Rosario added, finding his voice again, "but you'll eventually feel it, so try to avoid getting too close. And hold the line here," he added, "close to the dais and to the tree itself. They're weakest in the light and when close to powerful magic, mainly everything here."

Neal nodded. "Got it. Nikolai? Any advice?"

"Don't die," the man offered succinctly, revealing a nasty-looking dagger in his hand.

"I'll try not to, thanks."

With those words, the darkness reconfigured and advanced again towards their line. True to the team's strategy, Oriel held her position, driving the Dark Lord back again and again and again, never chasing it towards the darkened alcove. Push forward, inflict damage, piss off the beast, retreat and repeat.

Combining its multitude of different forms into fewer, but larger creatures, it charged forward, attacking the small group, trying to get in behind it despite the tree's proximity.

The darkness pushed the group into a tightening knot, back-to-back, trying to overwhelm the enemy. Each member gave better than they got, unleashing blow after blow on the darkness.

Oriel was focusing all of her energy and attention on Shard itself, which seemed intent on saving its fury for her, memories of the battle of 1204 still fueling its revenge. She was more than willing to accommodate the beast, barrage after slashing barrage, causing catastrophic damage to its misty flesh, bits continuing to fall away and evaporate. Screams of rage only fueled the woman's relentless lust for phantom blood.

The Dark Lord's smoky appearance resolved into more finite form, hulking arms with slashing claws sweeping towards Oriel, but she danced fluidly around the danger, slashing at each limb as it swung ineffectually past. It lunged forward, only to be repelled by the magic infused into the tree and dais, and would be driven back again as Oriel cut her way into any portion of the beast's body she could reach.

"You've gotten soft!" Oriel chided the Dark Lord, a look of glee upon her face as she first taunted and then pummeled the evil one repeatedly. She had known many periods of pain in her life, driven by the evil of this world, and she was more than up to the task of converting that rage into retribution at the only outlet available to her at the moment.

Under Oriel's relentless attack, the beast was forced to draw in more energy from its minions. The fury firing Shard's attack on the woman had become its sole focus. As it grew in size, and became more substantial in physical form, the damage it could inflict grew more deadly. But in doing so, Oriel knew, it had also opened itself up, sustaining more significant damage from her unyielding assault. She could see its shifting blackness growing less spectral, parts of the beast's body appearing almost solid. Those were the areas where she concentrated her strikes, the magical blade sizzling as it cut deeply into the ghostly flesh. She would not be denied, her arm flowing dangerously, her weapon an extension of her hand.

Although it appeared to Neal that he too was holding his own against the darkness, it was disappointing to not know if he was inflicting any actual damage on the enemy or merely playing with it. This kind of intense activity was never a part of his physical regiment and he began to tire, his arms turning to rubber from swinging at thin air. It would have been easier and far more rewarding if he could have felt a connection to the target instead of having to launch and then try to stop his momentum.

He quickly learned two things from the battle, though; that a round-house launch of the hammer was less taxing, and that he had apparently taken several hits during the melee, sore spots registering on his body. Although the enemy's attacks had passed through him, with little disruption, one blow finally rung Neal's bell, knocking him to his knees, stunned. The darkness, sensing the weakest link, shifted its energies to Neal's side of the battle line and tried to surge in that direction.

"Neal!" Rosario cried out, drawing the team's attention.

Oriel, seeing him down and under attack, leap to his defense, slashing at his attackers without mercy. Her magical blade and the proximity to the dais and the tree had weakened the enemy on that end of the battle line, multiplying Oriel's ability to inflict extensive damage, splinters of darkness rained down from Shard's body, dissipating into thin air as it struck the enchanted ground around it.

"Enough!" Lily screamed, having crept forward, her demand echoing in the alcove and from the cliff above the garden. The unexpected noise frightened her friends almost as much as the enemy, the bulk of the smoky beast fading from view.

As the others helped Neal to his feet, Oriel turned, sword raised and pointed it into what would have qualified as the face of the Dark Lord, a lone black void for an eye, studying Neal's vulnerable form, a palpable hunger radiating outward.

"C'mon!" Oriel yelled, challenging the darkness to draw closer and continue their fight, but it eyed Lily, and then her, and thought better of it, the shadow of its remaining form dissipating from view.

Sensing that the evil had fled and that the enemy had withdrawn, Oriel hid away her sword and turned to her team. Massaging her right shoulder, she was pleased to see that everyone was basically unhurt. Neal had suffered the only actual injury, his fingers gently testing a sore spot on the back of his head, a welt forming. It had been a century since Oriel had last fought that hard, her arm weary, the blows that Shard had landed finally registering as pain. Her eyes caught Felix's and she could see that he had already reached a decision.

Before anyone got comfortable, he voiced his opinion. "Let's go before the beast returns with reinforcements," Felix suggested. "We've gotten the answer we were seeking, just not in the way we thought we would."

Before turning and leaving, Oriel took one last look at the area, wondered what mysteries the enchanted garden held.

Ch26 – Longyearbyen, Norway

Lily, who had returned Neal's jacket and had selected a single seat on her side of the aisle, was wrapped in a blanket, staring blindly out the window into the black, moonless night, absorbed in her own thoughts.

Nikolai had selected the seat behind Lily, and as he was often apt to do, slept soundly, head leaning against the fuselage.

Neal was nursing a lump on the back of his head and a dull headache with an icepack a shot of Scottish whiskey. He had selected a window seat, Oriel resting her head on his shoulder. She was asleep before the wheels were up, even the take-off not waking her. He could tell by her movements, though, that she was having some kind of fitful dream, not a surprise given the day they had been through. He finished his drink and was soon fast asleep as well.

Behind them, Felix had picked the rear row, no one outside their team within earshot, so he and Rosario could review what they had learned today. But following the skirmish and Rosario's close call, the man had been uncharacteristically quiet and disengaged. Felix looked at his friend, concerned.

"Great job today, Rosario. You were well-prepared and executed the plan without incident." He said, trying to draw the man out.

Rosario nodded in response. "Thank you, Felix. It went well," he admitted proudly, but still reserved, eyes staring ahead of them, Oriel's blond hair visible between the seats.

They fell into a silence again, Felix thinking their conversation had ended, when an exhausted Rosario spoke again. "It's really her, isn't it?"

Felix knew what he was asking. "The Angel of Auschwitz?"

Rosario nodded, eyes still locked on her sleeping form, head still visible as it lay on Neal's shoulder in the row in front of them.

"Yes," Felix acknowledged.

"Until today, I didn't think it was possible," Rosario said, words catching in this throat. "But now I am wholly convinced that it's true." Silence ensued again as a rush of emotions raced through the librarian.

"Would you like to talk about it?" Felix offered, though he was never entirely comfortable with such personal conversations.

"Another time perhaps."

Relieved, Felix patted his friend on the arm. "Let me know when you're ready."

"Thank you," he answered, switching gears. "I wanted to talk to you about today, though, in a different capacity."

"First time facing down evil?"

"No," Rosario answered cryptically, "but it's the first time I've gotten a look at an actual Sael Lord. Are they all like that?"

"They're all basically the same. Some are more motivated that others. Some larger, some darker, some more devious."

"And the one today?"

Felix chuckled, knowing exactly what Rosario was getting at. "Not the biggest, but he certainly has a mean streak that sets him apart."

"Are they individuals?"

"Not in the way that humans are. The evil operates as a collective of sorts. You saw how they fought independently but were still one body, each anchored by the anger and fury that the Sael Lord feeds them. Their attack is coordinated, but it's also a weakness. They don't feel pain, per se, but an attack on one damages and distracts the rest."

"Were they waiting for us?"

Felix shook his head, munching on a granola bar. "No, I don't think so. Wouldn't be hanging around the garden for too long."

"Maybe one of the outer chambers? Seed vault itself? Guarding the entrance?"

"It doesn't sound like their M.O. to me," Felix said, wondering where Rosario was going with this.

"Are we sure the garden would repel them? You saw how it attacked us right up to the dais and in sight of the tree." Rosario challenged. "From what I've read, I assumed they wouldn't have been able to do that."

"It doesn't seem plausible, but I have to believe that they wouldn't or couldn't have been anywhere in the chambers or seed vault itself, for any length of time," Felix said, wondering if what he was about to say would provide solace or anxiety for his shaken friend. Deciding that knowledge was power, he pushed forward. "I know it must not have seemed like it, but the Sael Lord and his shadow warriors were greatly diminished today. I can only assume that it was due to them being in the garden and in proximity to the tree."

"That was diminished?" Rosario asked, staring at his friend, alarmed.

"Not a lot," he said, backpedaling. "But enough to tell me that the garden was the real deal and still holds great power."

"How did they find us, then? I thought we had done a pretty damn good job of covering our tracks. We've been on the run for days and off their radar."

Felix could hear the uncertainty in the man's tone; today having been a close call, first with their infiltration, then the flooded chamber, and finally the attack. He had forgotten how formidable their foe could be, even in their weakened state and in small numbers, inside one of the most magical of mythical locations. The darkness had returned in force and was regrouping, Felix thought, no doubt left in his mind.

"But we beat them back yet again," he said, offering Rosario some encouragement.

"Could we have done more, though?"

Felix heard the 'we' in the question, but could tell from the resigned tone that Rosario was asking if he, alone, could have been better prepared.

"I don't think we could have," Felix answered, taking on the burden for their group's mixed success today.

Rosario nodded slowly, wanting to believe it was true, but still clearly shaken.

Ch27 – Oslo, Norway

Oriel awoke, tired and sore, but not alarmed at the unfamiliar surroundings. She stepped to the bathroom, stripped and took stock of what she saw, turning in various directions to get a good look at herself. It wasn't pretty, but as the expression went, it was the price of admission; a badge of honor. Various shades of yellow and blue bruises were spread over her entire body, concentrated on the more vulnerable areas around her shoulders and upper legs where the enemy had focused their attention. But she smiled, knowing that she had inflicted far worse on Shard, memories of the yesterday's delicious melee dancing her head.

She turned around to survey the rest of her body, her eyes spying a trio of reddish welts cutting parallel lines across her back. They didn't even break the skin, she noticed, so they were of little consequence, unlike the nasty single slash that cut in the opposite direction, from right shoulder to her left hip. Although that injury had eventually healed, it had left a permanent scar, the white line visible across her pink flesh. It had been there a long time, and while it didn't cause her pain, the tightness of the skin when she stretched served as a reminder to never let her guard down.

Oriel stepped closer to the mirror and inspected her face and neck. Although never one to be vain, she thought she looked great for a woman of considerable age. She could see the weariness in her eyes reflected in the flesh surrounding them.

She pushed herself away from the mirror and climbed into the shower, dialing back the heat. Oriel stood under the hot water, trying to wash away the weight of the world. There was hope that the impending tide of darkness had all been an illusion, but it was coming back with a vengeance; changing both its tactics and how it went about corrupting humanity. She knew it wasn't all resting on her shoulders, but being in the know and having been fighting it for so long, Oriel knew she owned a piece. The world she envisioned, under the control of evil, was not one she wished to inhabit and if she had to keep fighting, she would.

Washed clean and a rosy pink from the hot water, she stepped from the shower, motivated by a different sense. Her nose picked up the wondrous smells of food cooking, her growling stomach encouraging her feet to follow.

When she reached the landing at the foot of the stairs, Oriel found Felix at the stove, preparing enough food to feed a dozen or more. Eggs, toast, bacon, hash browns, and some kind of baked treat that was still inside the oven.

"Are we expecting visitors?" She asked with a smile, only half teasing, given the amount of food on display.

"Good morning," he replied, looking sheepish, as he poured and passed her a cup of hot coffee, black. "I'm not sure what anyone wanted, so I've prepared several options."

"Nathaniel said you had become quite the chef de cuisine." Under the most oppressive of situations, Oriel knew Felix always walked and talked with a sense of confidence and bravado. In the kitchen, though clearly capable, he seemed self-conscious.

He laughed at the suggestion, her comment as much a compliment to his cooking prowess as to his management style and need for control.

"Load up a plate and have a seat. No set time for breakfast today, but since I was hungry and the one doing the cooking, I got things going early. We'll have to figure a few things out today," Felix sighed, clearly not happy with the situation.

"Not looking forward to it?" She asked through a bite of thick bacon.

"Frankly, no, because I have no idea how it's going to go. Too many variables in play."

He made himself a plate and sat down opposite her, hoping to enjoy his meal before the others arrived. Felix took a bite, silently eyeing the woman across from him.

"What?" she asked, not looking up from her plate.

"You've been formidable in the past, but yesterday?" He said with a shake of his head that conveyed a feeling of disbelief. "That was impressive. An entirely new level."

Oriel smirked, eyeing her friend suspiciously. "Last time you complimented like that, it was about my flexibility."

He laughed, clearly remembering the occasion.

"I ended up free-climbing the Cliffs of Moher, trying to reach an opening in the rock that you said held a repository of magical items."

"Those were the days," he laughed again. "We did fish you out."

A few moments of blissful quiet ensued before Felix spoke again, his tone more solemn.

"Seriously though, you were our savior. Without you, Rosario for sure, and the rest of us most likely, would have been screwed."

She pondered a smart-ass retort, her usual M.O. when complimented, but the seriousness of his words and the way he delivered them made such a response seem cheap and crass. Not that she was above cheap and crass, but the occasion felt like it deserved a higher road. "Thank you. I've picked up a few new things over the years," she added, modestly, feeling weird about it.

"Want a refill?" Oriel asked, grabbing the old-fashioned enameled coffeepot from the stove.

He nodded, extending his matching coffee cup.

Oriel had to admit that Felix had done well. The farmhouse he had rented as their HQ, isolated on the outskirts of Oslo, was fully stocked.

"You didn't think they were waiting for us?" She asked, switching gears back to business.

Felix poked at his breakfast, having already eaten too much.

"Heard that, did you?" The man should have known better, since Oriel had always been the best at obtaining information. "No, I don't. I told Rosario as much," he continued.

She nodded, knowingly.

"That means they knew we were heading there."

It was his turn to nod, sipping at his coffee as he eyed her with a conspiratorial look.

"But you don't think they followed us there either, do you?" She asked.

Felix's smile answered for him, and she agreed.

"That means that someone in our party tipped off the enemy to our plans," Oriel said, eyeing her friend. "Or you're wrong."

They both laughed, releasing their built-up tension.

"I'm never wrong," Felix said.

"Hello? Cliffs of Moher?" Oriel countered.

"I'm sure the cache *had* been there at one time."

162

"Uh-huh," she said, turning to the sounds of footfalls on the wooden staircase. A few seconds later, Neal appeared, eyes falling on the feast spread out across the top of the antique, white, porcelain stove.

"Help yourself before it gets cold," Felix told him.

"Don't have to ask me twice. To whom do I owe my thanks?"

Oriel laughed, "It certainly wasn't me."

"Looks great, Felix, thank you."

"Welcome, Neal. How's your head?"

"Fine, I guess. Can't really find the spot this morning unless I go searching for it."

"I don't know, Neal. Voracious appetite is a symptom of a concussion." Felix said, a look of concern on his face.

Oriel studied Felix and noticed that he too must have picked up a few new skills himself, no telltale sign of deception on his face. She laughed, playfully slapping at Neal's arm. "He's kidding you."

Neal winced, not feigning his reaction. "Tender all over," he admitted. "Just a boatload of craziness yesterday."

"Welcome to life behind the magic curtain," Felix said, rising to clear his dishes and attend to the scones still in the oven.

"I bet you're doing fine this morning," Neal said to Oriel. "Why is that?"

"You totally kicked ass yesterday. Absolutely amazing."

"That's what I told her," Felix added, eyeing Oriel as he popped a plate of hot orange and cranberry scones in the middle of the table. "No heavy cream, though. Sorry," he warned.

"Thank you both, but it was a team effort, as you just testified with your injuries," she countered, hearing more footsteps approaching. If Neal could see the deep bruises she wore on her body, or knew that she had just popped four

163

aspirin before coming downstairs, he wouldn't be so complimentary, Oriel thought.

Neal nodded and smiled, agreeing in principle to dial back his enthusiasm. "Can't make any promises, though."

She didn't mind the compliments from Felix. After all, they were well-founded, knowing what they had faced yesterday and the potential consequences. Nor did she mind hearing them from Neal, though they were well received for different reasons. Oriel just didn't appreciate the responsibility that came with such praise.

"You'll have to suffer through it at least one more time, I fear," Felix warned her, Rosario emerging first into the small kitchen.

"Good morning, everyone," he said, grabbing a plate. "Good morning, Oriel."

Knowing her discomfort, Neal stifled any comments, but Oriel could tell by the wide smile on his face that he really wanted to pipe in.

Oriel drew in a slow, calming breath, eyes locked on Neal's. "Good morning, Rosario."

Ch28 – Oslo, Norway

Everyone ate and then everyone chipped in to square away the kitchen and store away the cookware.

"As appealing as the option appears, we can't afford to stay here," Felix said as the group moved to the living room where a fire was already burning in the corner stove.

"Reason to think they've found us?" Nikolai asked.

"I think we have to assume the worst and keep moving."

"What's our next move?" Neal asked.

Lily sat quietly, more than willing, it appeared, to let Neal lead. But Oriel could tell that the young woman was fully engaged, eyes and ears taking in everything. Oriel suspected she missed very little.

"We have some decisions to make first," Felix began, eyes finding Oriel's.

Let the fun begin, she thought, as their leader laid out his case like a prosecuting attorney might. To Oriel's surprise, nearly five minutes passed before the first objection was raised.

"Hang on one second," Neal pushed back, getting to his feet, finger pointing. "We came here to help!"

"And we're grateful for it," Felix said, hands up defensively.

"It sure as hell doesn't sound like it. It sounds like you're accusing us of something!"

Oriel suspected Neal wasn't the type to turn on the team, but she had no factual basis for that feeling, having only known him for a few days.

It wasn't a strong case. She should be speaking up, but didn't know where she stood, only happy that if this conflict had to occur, that Felix had taken it upon himself to air all the dirty laundry himself. That still didn't make it any less awkward, though. The look on Neal's flushed face pained her to see.

"No one is accusing anyone of anything, Neal," Nikolai assured him, trying to defuse the situation. "We're just trying to figure things out, right?"

Oriel could tell that he was frustrated and was anything but convinced.

Observations had fingers pointing. Accusations had temperatures rising.

If this was all part of Felix's plan, it was going great. But to her, it looked like their quest was coming off the rails.

When everyone, save for Lily and herself, were on their feet, nose to nose at the center of the room, it looked like their team was going to come to blows. They were going to accomplish the enemy's work for them.

And why the hell was it so hot in this room, Oriel wondered, suddenly needing to flee from her seat.

"Take five," she barked, interrupting the scrum that was about to take place. "That's an order." When she had, at least temporarily, thrown the spirited discussion off balance and bloodshed was no longer likely, she turned and stepped outside.

Oriel stood alone on the front stoop, staring out into the cold, overcast afternoon. A few flakes fluttered to the ground. Like in Longyearbyen, a spotty layer of drifting snow blew across the hardened landscape. Here, however, their hideout lay in a shallow, but wide valley, the land used for short growing seasons. Plowed earth, ready for the next crop, crept up on their rental house from all directions, save for a thin ribbon of gravel that allowed access to the property.

She breathed out, watching the vapor rise skyward, taking some of her body heat with it. Her eyes watched a small murder of crows land in front of her, milling about at the demarcation line where the plowed field ended and what qualified as lawn began. A few more of the black birds circled down and joined the group, a cacophony of complaints as they jockeyed for position around one mammoth crow, darker than the rest, which seemed to be the leader. Its beady back eyes studied Oriel with interest as though it were waiting for something to happen.

More and more birds circled overhead, coming down like snowflakes from above. She heard the door open behind her and someone stepping out. Oriel didn't bother to turn; she would know who it was soon enough. The crows' complaints rose in volume at the intrusion, but not a single one of them flew away, dark eyes watching.

"Even colder here," Rosario observed tentatively, referring to their hideout, as he saddled up beside her. He had clearly not planned well, exiting the structure without a coat as she had done.

For those prepared, she knew, the cold could be an ally, as the Germans, on the wrong end of the lesson, learned during World War II. Her mind had drifted away, back to that time, until Rosario spoke again.

"About yesterday, Oriel," he began. "I didn't get a chance to thank you properly last night for saving me."

Oriel nodded, but didn't look his way. "You're welcome," she mumbled, gaze still on the birds milling about. Although her fury had been carried off on the bitter breeze, she still housed plenty of agitation. As though expecting some kind of bloodshed, yet more birds arrived, their collective volume growing. The leader, standing at the edge of the plowed field, however, continued to watch the exchange in silence.

Rosario waffled, clearly wanting to turn from the cold and go back inside, but didn't want to squander this first genuine opportunity to approach her. "About that," he stammered, unsure of how to proceed.

"Don't mention it," she said, hoping to nip his inquiry in the bud.

Was Oriel being humble and didn't think it worthy to discuss? Or was she warning him not to broach the subject? Rosario was torn about what to do when he became distracted, noticing the group of birds looming only a few meters away.

"What are they doing?" He asked rhetorically, looking around for some ideas, but finding none. "Did you throw out something for them to eat?"

"Not yet," Oriel said, watching the leader of the crows continuing to linger, as though listening in on their human conversation.

Unable to contain himself, he blurted out, "Are you…?"

"Yes," she replied, cutting him off coldly.

"May I ask you about…?"

"Not now," she said, silently kicking herself for leaving the door open to future discussions.

He nodded, satisfied for the moment that her answer wasn't an unequivocal no.

"Not a good omen," he continued, watching the crows continue to gather.

If he had been watching Oriel close, he would have caught the sinister grin forming at the corner of her lips, eyes narrowing with a twinkle. She agreed, but not for the same reasons. It all depended on what side you're on, she thought darkly to herself, a delicious shiver running through her that was far more than from the wintry afternoon temperature. Her eyes watched an innocent scene playing out in front of her, but her mind raced back to an earlier time, a similar place strewn with her fallen enemies, crows carrying away the dead, bit by bit in their beaks.

While the birds' unexplained congregation had put Rosario on edge, Oriel found their presence comforting.

"I'll see you inside," Rosario said, turning quickly from the cold and the unsettling scene.

As though disappointed in how things had failed to develop, most of the birds, save for their leader, took to the air in noisy agitation.

Oriel gave a subtle shake of her head. With a squawk of disappointment, the large, jet black crow took flight, flying towards her.

"Don't go far," she called up to it as it drifted overhead, "the day's not over yet."

When Oriel stepped back inside, she found them all in their previous seats, waiting for her to return. This time, though, Lily spoke.

"Thank you, Felix, for laying everything out as you did earlier. It was very interesting, and you would have to agree, Neal, that if the shoe was on the other foot, that we would be every bit as suspicious. Am I right?" Lily said calmly, no hint of emotion in her voice. "After all, we only joined the party a few days ago."

Neal nodded, the fight visually draining from the man. "Fair enough," he admitted.

"Thank you, Lily," Felix said, appearing genuinely relieved.

"I would add, though, that if not for Neal's considerable gift, that the team wouldn't have located the garden, our primary objective," she said, in their defense.

"Very true," Felix, Rosario, and Nikolai conceded.

"And if we were trying to stop the mission, arranging for the enemy to attack inside the garden, where they would be at their weakest, would be a very poor choice on our part."

All the men, including Neal this time, nodded in agreement.

"The flight into Longyearbyen, at our hotel room, or even on the open road to the vault, would have provided a much better point on which to attack us, wouldn't you agree?"

They clearly agreed, Oriel thought, watching it all with rapt fascination. She also agreed with Lily's logic, but did she really, or was it just Lily's apparent gift at play? Would she even know it if she were compromised? That Oriel wasn't sure was perversely disconcerting.

Ch29 – Oslo, Norway – Afternoon

Lunch, Oriel thought, was far more subdued than breakfast had been. To be expected, given the emotional bloodletting that had just occurred, a thousand accusations cutting deeply. But unsurprisingly, Lily had suggested they all sit down around the small kitchen table to share their meal and no one seemed to object. Oriel considered taking her meal into the living room and eating by herself, just to see if she could actually do it, but thought it petty and instead complied, sitting down with the rest of the group.

Felix had prepared everything family style and set down several large bowls and plates in front of the group.

"Swedish meatballs?" Nikolai asked dubiously, not because of what was in them, but that their team was currently sitting in Norway. "Are we going to get in trouble eating these here?" He teased.

"Bite your tongue, Nikolai. These are Kjøttkaker and they're very much integral to Norwegian life."

"Are you sure they aren't Swedish meatballs?" Neal asked. "These taste like the ones I get at Ikea." Although Oriel sat between him and the Felix, she could only do so much to protect him if their chef retaliated. Fortunately, their leader took it all in stride, assuming correctly that it was just playful banter and not an actual critique of his cooking.

"You're lucky you're not all getting sheep's head," he said, returning to the stove for the last of the food.

"Potatoes?" Oriel asked, eyeing the bowl hopefully.

"Have to have them when you're in Norway."

"And this?"

"A brown cheese that is manufactured to regional tastes, called brunost."

Always one to try the local fare, Oriel broke off a piece and popped it into her mouth, appreciating its sweeter than expected flavor. "I like it."

Felix nodded at her comment, appreciating his efforts.

"I did not have time, nor the ingredients, to make tilslørte bondepiker for dessert, but I did whip up some lefse, with butter and cinnamon sugar on top."

He sat down and fixed himself a plate, enjoying the silence of happy diners eating his first formal foray into Norwegian cuisine.

"Much better than Ikea," Neal mumbled through a mouthful of meatball, taking another bite.

The group laughed, the tension easing. Food really could have that effect, Oriel thought, as she finished her first plate and tried to move the conversation forward. "Okay, Felix, what's our next move?"

The man cleared his throat, ready to respond. "I think we can agree that the forces of darkness are, in fact, regrouping and will pose an imminent threat, correct?"

Everyone nodded, Neal joining in once Lily had made her decision known.

"I would propose then that we proceed immediately to step two; the recovery of the crown, which we will need to access the portal system."

Oriel looked alarmed, leaping to her feet. "You don't, have it?" She exclaimed!

Sheepishly, he admitted he did not. "No, I don't have it."

"But you know where to find it, right?"

"I have a pretty good idea where we can find it."

"Why did we risk raiding the seed vault if you don't even have the crown?"

"Until we knew for sure that the darkness was regrouping, we didn't need it. No reason to put the cart before the horse."

"Where is it?" She asked, conceding his first point while moving onto the second.

Felix wobbled his head, looking sheepish.

"Oh my god, you don't know where the key is?"

"Not exactly, but I suspect I know who has it."

Oriel starred at him, motioning expectantly.

"Captain Alvarez has it," Felix said.

When she bared her teeth and squinted hard at the man, he thought better of his answer.

"*Had* it, technically," he corrected.

Oriel took a deep breath and paced the kitchen, but it was only a half-dozen steps from one end to the other.

"Can we call him?" Neal offered, trying to help.

Oriel almost laughed at that, but she was too pissed to enjoy it.

"He's dead," Rosario clarified, diffusing the situation without revealing too much, too soon.

She expanded her pace radius to include the slightly larger living room, Oriel letting her mind drift back to 1204 and the day of that fateful battle. Felix placed the crown on the kid's head and sent him into the portal, where it's magical powers instantly broke every single atomic bond holding the boy's molecules together. With nothing physical to hold it up any longer, gravity took over and the delicate-looking gold crown tumbled to the stones. With the closure of the portal, and the threat to their existence eliminated, the darkness departed. The good captain had walked past them laughing, crown tilted jauntily on his own head. Oriel assumed incorrectly that Felix must have retrieved it from the man at some point, but hadn't, the magician's morale broken by his miscalculation of the prophecy.

"We no longer needed it," Felix defended gently, stepping into the room.

Oriel nodded in understanding. The aftermath of that day had been a major shit-show. Hundreds of deaths and nothing to show for it. Those who had funded their expedition, in the form of goods, gold, or mercenaries, wanted Felix's head on a spike for what he had advertised as a simple expedition.

"Is it going to work this time?" She asked.

"I believe it will."

"No guarantees?"

"There are no such things. And if I guaranteed it, you'd call bullshit."

She smiled, knowing he was right. "You're right, I would have. Next step?"

"We pay a visit to one of the nearest observatories to the battle and try to get a line on what happened to Captain Alvarez."

"Observatory?" Neal asked, confused, the rest of the team hanging in the doorway.

"I'll explain later," Oriel answered, turning to Felix. "Which observatory."

When Felix didn't answer, she had her answer, and it was the last place she wanted to visit.

"Shit."

Ch30 – Marazion, Cornwall

"Why did I think this place was in France?" Neal asked Oriel, as he stared out across the water from the small, upstairs window of the Abbey Stone Coffee House. They watched the last of the forecasted sprinkles blow down the shoreline and out to sea.

"You are correct and incorrect. This is the St. Michael's Mount here in the UK, while you're thinking of Mont St. Michel's. That one is two hundred miles in that direction, on the French coast," she said, pointing out into the channel past the island that Neal was referring to. Oriel was tempted to slide into tourist guide mode and dazzle the man with all kinds of facts and figures about both places, but it seemed better to just sit together in silence and enjoy the moment before they were scheduled to 'storm the castle'.

"Have you been here before?" he asked, turning from the scene to study the woman seated next to him, her face bathed in the bright sunlight.

Although Oriel appeared relaxed, it was all an act. A tempest was churning just below her calm surface. She took a sip of her tea, hoping the warming brew would steady her nerves as she contemplated how best to answer his question.

It should have been the easiest thing in the world to do and yet she threw out the only reply that would demand more details. "It's complicated," she said, a mischievous smile that couldn't be entirely hidden behind her teacup as she took another hit. Not that she wouldn't have minded talking about her history here, with him, but it wasn't the best time for it.

He smiled, turning his attention back outside, drifting clouds blocking out the blinding brightness. 'If you want to keep a secret, you must also hide it from yourself,' George Orwell wrote," he said, turning back to find Oriel's hazel-colored eyes studying him.

"He was right." Oriel knew, having just opened herself up for more scrutiny with the answer she gave. She hoped Neal would persist until she had told him all about it. Maybe it was a test for her to gauge his interest. She could tell by the playful expression on his face that he was probably thinking the same thing. If the opportunity presented itself, she would tell him the story. Not all the literal, gory details, but just enough of the truth to convey what had happened to her here. She wasn't sure that human language could express the complete truth, though it seemed like Neal had seen some pretty dark stuff himself. Maybe that was why she felt a certain kinship with the man, like he might relate to her through his own history.

Outside the window, a lanky arm appeared, waving to get their attention. That was the signal.

"Ready?" He asked, busing their dishes.

"As I'll ever be," she replied, truthfully.

They joined the back of the line of adventurers moving through the wrought-iron gate and starting down the flagstone causeway, the path arching out into the water before terminating in the distance at their destination. You got on at one end and got off at the other. There were no other options, save for dropping off the edge and into the water. With the pleasant weather in the forecast, a decent line of tourists joined them for the half mile stroll to the island.

"Up for this?" Felix asked Oriel, dropping back in line beside her. As long as he kept the inquiry light and ambiguous, there was no reason for anyone to suspect why he was asking. After the prior day's dance with Shard and his minions, it would be only natural for him to inquire.

She nodded, but felt herself slowing down as they neared the island, not from the incline in the causeway, but from the weight of this place bearing down on her soul.

Ch31 – Marazion, Cornwall

The group pushed onward; the path climbing slightly on the last section of the causeway. To their right was a tall, stone wall, which bordered the small harbor that served the island when the footpath was under water during high tides.

Entering the grounds proper was like stepping back in time. Although it was old by American standards, the commercialization of the buildings made Neal's cynical mind assume that they were reconstructions. In reality, though, many were centuries old, repurposed to serve and sell food and trinkets to the excited folks who wandered over to the island.

"Try to look like harmless tourists," Felix instructed.

"No problem," Neal replied, his head on a swivel, taking everything in, camera phone at the ready.

Although Oriel had tried long ago to put this portion of her past behind her, memories of the place continued to surface as they walked towards the castle in the distance. What she saw today was a far cry from how it had been. The island was open, inviting, clean, bright, and full of hope. Everything it wasn't when she was here last.

It was a sanitized playground for families who, despite taking several of the tours, would never hear about the genuine horrors which had occurred there. It was a place that had also offered refuge to those in trouble, but she had no experience with that side of the equation.

Their group, Oriel knew, had no interest in the touristy bits even though many were housed in outbuildings that existed during their time of interest. So, they continued up the ever-steepening path towards the fortifications, hidden from view by the treetops, which cut across the center of the small island.

As they approached the castle, a young nun was standing in the doorway as though waiting for their arrival. Felix led the group forward, smiling at the woman as they drew closer.

"Good morning," he said.

"Good morning to you, too. Here for the tour?"

"We are indeed," he answered, passing the young woman their tickets.

"If you'd like to come with me, I'll be taking you behind-the-scenes today, to the places that are normally off limits to the public."

We'll see about that, Oriel thought to herself, a devious smile on her lips.

"We're excited to see it. Please lead the way," Felix said.

They set off, starting with the more heavily traveled public spaces. Although the woman was running through the stats on the island and its history, no one was really listening save for Oriel, who bristled at the glossing over of the location's dark chapters. Oriel wrote off the narrative, assuming they had provided the nun with the script to use on the family-friendly tour. She did her best to drown out the tour-guide altogether so she could recall the layout, looking for their intended target. She knew the place from experience and Rosario had prepped them all on what to look for, but so far, the tour had failed to turn up the entrance to the observatory they sought.

"Family vacation?" the woman asked once they had reached the midpoint of the tour. Even Neal pausing his photography at the odd inquiry.

The question baffled Felix, staring at the odd group of folks with him, wondering how she could have reached such a conclusion. Force of 'habit', he assumed, finding his pun quite funny.

"College reunion," Oriel offered, continuing to poke her head into the odd assortment of doors that opened into areas she didn't remember. "Has there been extensive reconstruction work done in this area?"

As though surprised by an inquiry she hadn't heard before, the nun thought for a moment and shook her head. "Not that I'm aware of, but I'm relatively new here. I know there was some work done in the family's quarters, but nothing in this area."

"Is that area on the tour?" Oriel pressed, trying to sound casual.

"Oh no. Strictly off limits, I'm afraid. I've worked here for nearly five years and have only been in there one time. Shall we continue?"

The nun didn't wait for an answer, the bulk of their group following closely at her heels as the others continued to explore.

"Could the observatory be in the family spaces?" Felix asked.

"Not big enough," Oriel replied. "From what we've seen so far and what I remember, that area couldn't contain what Rosario described."

"I agree," he said. "The size of the collection would take up a pretty large space. Unless it's carved out of the island itself, it has to be located in this end of the building though."

"Not under us, unless they've cleared the crypt," Oriel added, likely ruling out such a location.

"Could we be heading towards it?" Felix indicated with a nod of his head in the direction the others had gone.

"Only thing down there is the chapel, and I doubt they've repurposed it. There could be an entrance or clue in there, though, so we should take a look. It will help us rule more of the castle if we don't find anything."

The trio caught up with the tour, about the time the nun had become concerned, her ability to backtrack blocked by Nikolai and Neal, who filled the width of the narrow stone-lined hallway.

"Our apologies," Felix said, waving a hand at Rosario and Oriel, "but these two were debating on whether they manufactured the castle of tourmaline or biotite muscovite granite, and I couldn't get them moving again. I'm sure you know how kids can be," he said, sharing a knowing glance at their tour guide, who seemed confused.

"I still say I'm right," Oriel challenged.

"Not on your life," Rosario retorted.

The nun nodded, happy to keep things moving along. "Shall we take a look at the chapel?"

They wandered into the open space, peaked ceiling, small pews, and stained glass behind the altar. It was all very much like Oriel had remembered it, having fled through here during her time on the island.

Waving her over, Felix asked, "Is this you?"

A bronze angel, sword in hand, was standing over a defeated demon, waiting to be run through by a thin blade.

"No," she chuckled, a wintry smile on her lips and a deadly twinkle in her eyes. "They certainly wouldn't be commemorating my visit here," she whispered.

Felix felt a shiver tickle his spine at seeing the look which came over his friend's face. Oriel had never fully confided in him what had gone down here so many years ago, but if half of the rumors were true, it had ended poorly for her captors.

"Well, the heirs probably sang about it," Felix offered, trying for some levity, but getting no response from Oriel.

"I think that's supposed to be St. Michael, the namesake of the island," she said, stepping closer to the small artwork to get a better look.

The woman who had frightened Felix only moments ago had transformed back into the woman he knew.

As all excellent tour guides do, they could hear theirs relay the pertinent details of the priory chapel, pointing out many aspects of the space from its earliest history. Other than finding most of the doors locked, their team was running out of places to search.

Rosario, sensing that time was short and that their options were thinning, gave a knowing glance at Felix, who pondered the unasked question for a few moments before nodding in agreement. The time for subtly had ended.

"Thank you, Sister Isabelle," Rosario began, passing the young woman a very generous tip for her time. She took it graciously and thanked them for visiting. He wasn't about to let her off that easily, though. "I have one last question, though. A request actually."

Their entire group was watching, Isabelle noting that each person was far more attentive now than at any time during the tour.

"Yes?" she asked, curious.

"We need to speak with your director."

"Director?"

"Yes, Director of Special Acquisitions," he clarified, watching the nun for any reaction. He was not disappointed.

"Special Acquisitions?" she replied, poorly feigning ignorance.

Rosario smiled, seeing the hint of recognition on the young woman's features.

182

"We need to speak with your Golden Hat," Rosario clarified.

Ch32 – Marazion, Cornwall

"Brother De León." The matron said, as the group was ushered into her office. "Welcome!"

"Thank you very much. I'm sorry that we haven't been introduced previously," he said, strolling forward with his hand up.

Oriel watched the hand shake with more interest that usual, wondering if their librarian was going to taser his counterpart. She was disappointed when no barbs were launched in the exchange.

"Me too. I'm Sister Anne," she said, rising to her feet.

Rosario came up short, pausing.

"Not *the* Sister Anne?" He asked, eyebrows raised in recognition.

Her wicked smile told him he was right. "Most of it's true."

"Is that right?" Rosario replied, intrigued, a smile growing on his own lips.

Another sister, Beatrice, cleared her throat, interrupting the moment.

"Now then, who came with you today and what can the Observatory of St. Michael's do for the esteemed Golden Hat of Paris?" Sister Anne inquired.

"These are my colleagues, Felix, Oriel, Nikolai, Lily, and Neal," Rosario introduced, only hitting the highlights of each person. "And we are in need of some information."

"Can we discuss the specifics over dinner? The evening meal is always ready at five."

"We'd hate to impose."

"Not at all. We're always prepared to accommodate hungry guests."

"In that case, we accept," Rosario said, on behalf of the team.

Sister Anne led the group to the dining hall where the smells of a meal reached them. "Please grab a bowl of soup and have a seat."

Following some unseen arrangement, each member of the team was corralled towards a seat. At one table, Sister Anne sat with Rosario, Felix, and Nikolai. While the others joined Sisters, Beatrice and Isabelle.

'Kid's table,' Neal mumbled to himself as he dug into the seafood stew.

Despite the matron's remarks, it was clear by Beatrice and Isabelle's reaction that visitors here were an actual rarity. The pair reveled in having company. And when they heard how Oriel spoke French, they hung on every word.

Even Neal, surprised yet again by the woman seated beside him, listened intently as the words rolled off her lips, an old-fashioned accent apparent to even his untrained ear. The trio were conversing in French and from what Neal could deduce from Oriel's hand gestures, she was entertaining them with a history lesson of their island.

Suddenly conscious of Neal's exclusion, Oriel returned to English. He seemed pleased by the change, smiling at her consideration. Lily, who sat on the other side of Neal, enjoyed her soup, seemingly indifferent to the entire situation.

"It really is a beautiful room," Oriel noted. Decorative plaster walls with dark wood accents matched the beams that spanned beneath the vaulted ceiling. Requisite paintings of local dignitaries lined the walls in true local fashion. Though a far cry from what she remembered, there was enough here to jog even her distant memory.

The women seated across from her were obviously proud of the place, and weren't responsible for the dark chapters in her life, so she saw no reason to throw shade at their enthusiasm.

From the doorway to the kitchen, an impossibly old woman shuffled in, tray precariously balanced in both hands. Fearing that she might drop it, Neal pushed back his chair and went to her aid, relieving the server of the load. She smiled up at him, thankful for his help. Instead of providing him with directions, she simply turned and left the room.

"Pasty anyone?" Neal asked.

"Familiar with these?" Sister Anne asked, clearing a place in the center of the table for the tray.

"Yes, ma'am, I grew up in Michigan," he replied, passing out the plates.

"Finnish-style pasties are fine, but you haven't lived until you've tried our Cornish variety," she said, throwing down the good-natured gauntlet. "And we have neither gravy nor *ketchup*," she warned Neal, with emphasis.

He eyed the plates, sans condiments, dubiously, but was willing to give it a try.

Sister Anne nodded to Isabelle, who said grace.

"Buon Appetite," Sister Anne finished in French, having heard the earlier conversation at the other table. Neal didn't need a translator for that popular phrase.

The pasty was delicious, Neal thought to himself, dissecting each distinct flavor, noting the usual suspects, but there were a few others he didn't recognize. Taking another bite, he looked up to see Sister Anne observing him, a smile on her lips as if to say, *I told you so.*

In answer, he shrugged as though he had had better, but wasn't convincing.

Conversation slowed as the meal continued, and had turned to more mundane topics. When they had finished, Sister Anne had one last instruction for the group.

"You may start your research tomorrow, right after breakfast. Tonight, please accept our hospitality."

Despite Felix being the de facto leader of the group, Sister Anne had posed the question to Rosario, who nodded his acceptance on behalf of the group. With the situation settled, Sister Isabelle showed each of them to their quarters for the night.

"You don't believe them, do you?" Sister Beatrice asked their superior once the pair had returned to Sister Anne's office.

"I've certainly heard of Mr. De León, by reputation only, of course, but anyone who knows the history of the Golden Hats and our charter could easily find out his identity."

"You're not planning on letting them into the observatory, are you?" Sister Beatrice challenged further, looking nervous at such a potential breach in protocol.

"Of course not. We'll play the perfect hosts and then tomorrow, we'll show them to the regular library while I make some quiet inquiries."

Last in line, Isabelle showed Oriel to her room, pushing the door open to allow her guest to step inside. Isabelle didn't step in, so neither did Oriel. Too many times in her long life, had she fallen for such a ruse and was hesitant to add to that list again tonight.

Oriel's eyes searched the space for any signs of duplicity, but could find none. By all accounts, it was a beautiful room. A room that anyone would have been more than happy to sleep in. This part of the castle hadn't even existed during her last visit, so it didn't carry any kind of dark association with her past treatment. That still didn't mean she unwittingly stepped into every offered room without careful consideration.

With enough light still coming in from outside through a pair of southward facing windows, Oriel could see that there were no visible bars installed that might prevent a quick escape. They could have covered the openings in some kind of high-tech, modern plexiglass, she noted dryly, but that was just her cynicism rearing its ugly head.

"Is something wrong?" the young nun inquired, looking uneasy.

"It's lovely," Oriel replied, trying her best to emulate Lily's sing-song accent, but from the look on her host's face, it clearly wasn't convincing.

Not knowing what else to say, Isabelle said "Good night," and retreated down the hall.

Oriel watched until the nun turned and descended the stairs before edging forward and inspecting the door. It was made of solid wood, but thin, for indoor use. There was no lock installed, she noted, happily. Likewise, the windows both opened easily, only flimsy screens in place to keep her from leaping the few feet down to a section of roof beneath the room.

Still anxious about staying on the island and the memories of her confinement, she elected to keep both windows cracked, accepting the forecasted chill for some peace of mind. Wedging the lone desk chair under the doorknob, she got undressed and slipped into bed.

Ch33 – Marazion, Cornwall

Oriel awoke later than she could have imagined, nearly nine a.m., to the smell of a light rain drifting in through the still cracked windows. She got ready, grabbed her gear and went down into the non-public spaces of the castle to find her entire group, and the four nuns, having breakfast. She made a plate and ate in silence, beyond offering her cheerful, and accurate, assessment of a very peaceful night.

When they were finished, they were shown into the library, and the nuns retreated, leaving them to their research.

After an hour of fruitless searching, Felix shut the last book from his stack in frustration. Rosario was still going through the shelves, making mental notes of all the volumes and artifacts he was finding on the shelves, but seemed frustrated and confused as well. Oriel was flipping through volumes, but likewise, wasn't getting anywhere. Nikolai was leaning back in his chair, apparently asleep, but the lack of snoring made his status tough to judge. Neal was spending his time picking up each book and rewinding the clock in his head to look at the tome's history, out of pure boredom more than anything else.

189

"What's his story?" Neal asked, putting down the last book.

Felix follows his gaze and could see that the man was talking about Rosario.

"He is the Master Librarian of the Parisian District, a member of a network of such libraries. Known formally as the 'Golden Hats', charged with acquiring, restoring and maintaining knowledge of the world and everything in it," he said, waving a hand at the room they were in. "Touched by the magic, but not born of it, his gifts aren't as dramatic as your gift, but he's experienced some of its benefits, like a longer than normal lifespan, and both a memory and curiosity that borders on the divine."

At this, Oriel perked up, not realizing that Rosario was one of the touched, something she normally picked up on when she spent any length of time around someone. "I thought that those put in charge of the libraries couldn't be of the magic."

"There are no hard and fast rules, but the order that runs the network found that those with magical abilities often got lured away by a life that found favor in their respective skill-sets. Although it's not a glamorous, nor normally an exciting life to be sure, it has a draw for the right individuals," Felix said, his eyes watching his friend work his way through the collection. "It is not so much a life as it is a calling for those who excel at it and Rosario is right there at the top of the list. Almost irreplaceable, really. It's not a position that you can train anyone for, as the value of each librarian grows with his or her own personal knowledge and experience."

"He's even started referring to our small group as 'the coalition'," Oriel noted, an endearing smile on her face at the statement of intimacy.

"That's what Rosario does best. He's in charge of cataloguing, classifying, and categorizing everything he comes across. Only logical that he would organize us into his

190

taxonomy." Felix said, rising from his chair and stepping over to his friend to see how his task was going.

"Born of the magic?" Neal asked, eyeing her.

She smiled and looked at him, the naivety written on his questioning face. He had a gift, but no one to guide him. It was no wonder he seemed lost in this world, she thought. Oriel felt a strange stirring to help him, something that wasn't inherently part of her own normal, social skill-set, weeded out of her over centuries by a growing cynicism with humanity.

"Most people are born into the world, in the traditional sense. A mother, a father, and a biological urge that sometimes leads to a child," she said, enjoying his awkward laughter and uncomfortable demeanor.

"Is this going to be about the birds and the bees? I might be beyond that now," he said, catching himself as their eyes met. "But if you'd like to cover the basics, I'm open to it."

It was Oriel's turn to smile, the double meaning hanging there for a few moments that warmed her soul. She cleared her throat and continued, trying to regain her composure, a heat spreading across her cheeks. "Children come in two varieties. Those who have gifts powered by the magic of the world, and those that don't. If you have them, you have them. And if you don't, you don't. No rhyme or reason on who has them or what they are. Lineage and parentage don't seem to have any effect, nor a pregnant mother sleeping outside under a full moon, for instance. Complete coin toss as far as anyone can tell."

"Sort of like Harry Potter and the muggles?"

Oriel laughed. "*Yes, just like Harry Potter!*" she called out, her voice carrying throughout the large room.

Without looking over, Felix reached back and flipped her and Neal the bird, eliciting even more laughter from the pair.

"He hates any reference to Harry Potter; calls it an affront to the realm of actual magic," she explained. "Where was I?"

"Babies," he said, playfully watching her more intently.

"Oh yes, them," she said, feeling the flush returning. "They grow up and with it, their gifts can become more pronounced. There are those of us around the world who keep any eye out for such things."

"Then off to wizarding school?" He asked.

"Not quite, though there are those who find mentors or small guilds of like-minded folks to help them understand their gifts and to give them an idea of how best to use them."

"And those *born* of the magic?"

Oriel squirmed a bit, hoping he hadn't caught that subtle nuance and would assume that the magic simply touched both him and her and leave it at that. In for a penny, she thought, steeling herself for the big revelation.

"Those born *from* the magic," she said, watching him carefully, "are adopted into their family. They don't know or remember what came before."

Neal looked skeptical, and was about to comment when he thought better of it, seeing how serious she had become.

"You were adopted, but don't know who your birth family is?" He asked, more gently this time.

She nodded. "They literally left me on the doorstep of a couple who took me in and raised me as their own."

"No questions asked?"

"They didn't know who to ask, even if they wanted to. And I was the first of their children, raised on a farm in the middle of nowhere, so there was no one to question my sudden appearance. I had siblings, you could say, and they never questioned who I was or where I had come from." Dancing around the subject made Oriel feel bad, but she wasn't sure that Neal was ready to hear just how long ago this had happened.

"So, who are you, Oriel? And where did you come from?" he asked softly, a gentleness in his voice, knowing he was touching on a very sensitive subject.

Oriel shrugged, her eyes dropping momentarily to the hands in her lap, as though they might hold the answers. "I don't know the answer to either of those questions," she said, eyes rising again to match his, which carried a pain in them she might have worn herself. But so much time and life had gone by that she rarely gave it any thought, and certainly never talked about it. "Lily isn't the only one with a gift of helping people talk about their insecurities," she admitted

Neal smiled, and in that moment, Oriel wanted nothing more than to reach up and touch his beautiful face, but an unexpected interruption broke the spell.

"At least you two could spend your time on better pursuits; perhaps discussing the historical accuracy and metaphors found throughout the *Lord of the Rings*?" Felix said, dropping a boxed edition of the books on the table in front of them before storming off with a humorous glint in his eye.

Ch34 – Marazion, Cornwall

Lily strolled into the room, without explanation of where she had been or what she had been doing. No one, save for Oriel, seemed to care or take notice of her strange coming and going. She took the seat that Oriel had occupied minutes earlier, watching the scene with a detached gaze that seemed to take in everything. Oriel couldn't quite per her finger on why the mood in the room had changed, but clearly knew that Lily's appearance had that effect on her, though it appeared to have the opposite effect on Neal, who seemed to relax whenever the mysterious young woman was within reach. She felt an uncharacteristic edge of envy cut at her, but shook it away, concentrating on her own investigation of sorts, an anomaly on the bookshelf in front of her.

Neal, feeling a need to engage with Lily about what they had found, or more correctly, what little progress they had made, only took a few seconds.

Silence-filled tension hung over the room.

Oriel finally caught on to what her subconscious mind had been urgently pointing out, nagging at her, trying to get her attention. Six familiar items lay on the shelf, but were sitting out of chronological order. Once she realized the issue, a compulsion in her character requiring them to be correct, it was easy enough to line them up properly. The built-in shelving unit upon which they sat swung silently away from her, the unexpected movement catching her off guard for a beat.

"Huzzah!" she exclaimed, turning to the others, who were looking on with interest. The commotion had even awakened Nikolai, who stretched, eyes searching for the source of the disturbance.

Beyond the opening, automated lights glowed dimly from unseen sources, cabinets of high-tech design lined the walls and were filled with all kinds of objects, both large and small.

"That's more like it," Felix said, both he and Rosario rushing forward, only to be stopped by an unseen force blocking their way.

So focused on getting inside, Rosario continued to push against the barrier as though his insatiable desire might overcome the impenetrable magic.

Felix, however, was more pragmatic. He stepped back and nodded to Oriel, indicating that it was time for her to do that 'thing' of hers.

Although reluctant to relent, Rosario also yielded the doorway to their teammate. If he harbored any reluctance that she might overcome the security arrangement here, his desire to get inside was stronger.

She made a move to enter, but like Rosario and Felix, was also stopped short, hands feeling the air for any explanation. Oriel put on her mime act, going way overboard in the motions, looking absolutely absurd. She looked first at Felix, who was only rolling his eyes at the unnecessary delay, but then at Rosario, who looked unconvinced, the skepticism palpable. Neal looked confused.

"Hilarious," Rosario said. The librarian didn't look upset at the fakery, rather that her deception was slowing him down, his eyes turning to the wonders just out of reach.

"Can we get on with it?" Felix asked, impatient.

Oriel turned and strolled into the hidden room as though passing through any other doorway.

"Hey, you need to invite us in," Rosario reminded her.

"I can do that?" She said playfully, pretending that she might just keep all of this for herself.

"If you're inside, yes, anyone can," Rosario repeated, unnecessarily.

"Veuillez entrer."

Rosario nearly bowled her and Felix over to get inside, as he moved from cabinet to cabinet, eyes searching eagerly.

Neal paused just inside the room, at the first case in front of him. It was a tall object, slender and cone shaped, of highly polished gold sheeting, inscribed with symbols and glyphs, many of which he didn't recognize, but could tell that they conveyed information. "An actual Golden Hat?"

Nikolai nodded. "Yes. They give each member their hat upon ascension to their ranks during the coronation ceremony into the order."

"Should I watch the door?" Oriel called out.

"Don't bother. They already know we're in here. They've been watching us all morning," Rosario answered without looking up from the cabinet he was inspecting.

"How can you be sure?" She asked.

"I would be, if I had let someone near my observatory."

Rosario had been correct. Oriel turned to see Sister Anne and Sister Isabelle perched in the doorway, the elder matron looking baffled, while the younger sister looked on with frantic eyes at the trespass.

"How did you get in here?" Sister Anne demanded.

Before anyone else could answer, Rosario took the initiative so everyone in the room would hear. "I think we'll be keeping that to ourselves," Rosario declared, "at least for now."

Ch35 – Marazion, Cornwall

"We're all very glad that you came," Lily said, walking up to face their two hosts. "You could really help us make sense of all this and narrow down our scope."

The two women looked around as though it seemed a reasonable request.

"Won't you come in and sit, so we can ask you some questions?" She continued, Lily taking each by an arm and leading them towards the large workspace in the center of the tall room.

They sat down, compliant but looking uneasy.

"Isn't that better?"

The two sisters admitted it was, though their body language seemed incongruous.

Oriel watched the exchange with a mix of amused interest and horror. The three men looked on as though nothing untoward was happening. Felix and Rosario seemed downright pleased at the prospects of the two women helping in their research, given that it was their library.

"Now gentlemen," Lily prompted, "What is it that you are searching for and need to see?"

Rosario was literally rubbing his hands together in anticipation, while Felix looked around the room, trying to gather his thoughts.

"Let's start with Alban's History of the Iberian Peninsula Vol 2," Felix offered.

"And do you have Marquette's Treatise on Northern European Fiefdoms?" Rosario asked.

They did, each nun moving into the racks to retrieve the items in question. When they returned, seemingly more eager to help, the two guests rattled off another half-dozen sources they wanted to review. When they seemed satisfied for the moment, Oriel posed her own question, asking if this library also housed an observatory, having noticed the familiar-looking ceiling above?

"Oh, yes. Would you like to see it?" Sister Anne asked.

"We would," Oriel said, motioning for Neal to follow.

Lily didn't rise, choosing to remain there in the mix, the side excursion having nothing to do with the mission. So much the better, Oriel thought, as Sister Isabelle lead the way up the spiral staircase to the highest level.

"Wait until you see this!" Oriel said in anticipation.

Thirty minutes passed before the trio came down the staircase and back to the table. The sisters looked pleased by her guest's reception of their observatory, Neal looking overwhelmed by the experience and Oriel thrilled by Neal's reception.

"Any luck?" Oriel asked.

Shakes of their heads told her that progress had been slow.

Felix and Rosario asked for their next requests as the two women departed to retrieve the books and documents.

"Perhaps your inquiries haven't been specific enough?" Oriel said, deciding to test her theory upon their host's return.

"Ladies, we're looking for any historic reference you have regarding a former Moorish Captain named Abah Alvarez, who lived in the early to mid-thirteenth century, here in northern Europe."

Instead of searching her memory, Sister Anne responded immediately.

"He's here."

Felix and Rosario exchanged confused glances.

"Like, here, here?" Rosario asked.

"Yes. He's interred here, under the castle, in our catacombs."

"Why would he be here?" Felix asked, more to himself than Sister Anne, but she answered it, anyway.

"He was one of the castle's patrons and because of his service to our order."

Oriel seemed pleased that she had gotten to the answer before the pros. Even Lily acknowledged her success with an appreciative nod.

"Do you think it could be with him?" Rosario asked.

"I think we have to assume it is," Felix confided, given it was close, and they had no other leads. "If not, we can return to the records here and see if there is anything in them."

"Agreed."

"So, we're…." Neal asked.

"Yes," Felix answered.

"And we're going to…."

"Yup," Rosario said.

"Oh, boy…."

Never one to beat around the bush, Lily turned to Sister Anne and focused her attention squarely on the woman. "You're going to need to show us where he is."

"I can't," she stammered, "I would if I could, but I can't. There was a collapse in the tunnel leading below the castle. The owners had an engineering firm look into it, and they determined it was still unstable."

"And there are no other ways into the catacombs," Felix asked, feeling frantic that they had gotten so close, only to be denied now.

"None," she said, looking apologetic.

No way that Sister Anne knew of, Oriel thought, studying the woman and finding no hint of deception.

Felix caught Oriel's eye, silently asking if it was true. He only knew an inkling of the story, but knew that she had spent an extended amount of time here.

"What about the top entrance?" Oriel asked Sister Anne, brimming with confidence that she knew the information to be accurate, but hesitant to speak about how she had acquired it.

All eyes turned to Sister Anne, who looked confused. "Top entrance? There isn't one."

"I'll show you where it is," Oriel answered, reluctantly getting to her feet. "What time is it?"

Ch36 – Marazion, Cornwall

"Okay, it's 9:25," Felix confirmed. "Now what?"

Oriel shook her head, looking down at the wide expanse of patio under their feet. It wasn't always a place for tourists to enjoy their snacks and thankfully, the site was not yet open for business. "See here, this chimney and associated stonework?"

They all nodded in agreement, though none knew where this was going.

"See the shadow it's casting here?"

The group took several steps back and examined it, Nikolai speaking first.

"It looks like a fist with a finger extended, pointing."

"And any ideas what it's pointing at?"

"I would guess it's pointing at a hidden entrance to the catacombs?" Felix wagered.

"Yes, a very well-hidden entrance. There used to be a large flagstone here," Oriel said, stepping on the tip of the shadow's extended finger. "When was this covered over?"

"Last year," Sister Anne said. "It was part of the ongoing repairs and improvements. The family had several inches of concrete poured over this entire area so it could be opened up to the public."

"Of course they did." Or they did it to close off access to anyone who might have been looking to get under the castle, Oriel wondered darkly.

"No way we're getting through this," Felix concluded.

Sister Anne answered, thinking he had posed the question to her. "I didn't even know about this entrance."

Everyone waited patiently, Felix eyeing his friend as she considered his inquiry. "Any other way in?"

"Only one entrance left, and it's through the family quarters." Oriel said, clearly not happy. "Are they here?"

"They won't be back until next week, but we're not supposed to go in here unless it's an absolute emergency," Sister Anne pleaded.

"I think this qualifies," Felix added gently.

After traversing the castle, they made their way through the structure to the far wing where the family retained ownership. The group assembled before an impressive-looking doorway.

"The family's private quarters," Oriel clarified, for the benefit of her group. "In 1954, they turned most of the island and its buildings over to the National Trust, who would open it to the public and maintain what was here. They kept a lease, though, for the next millennium, and maintain private quarters here for themselves and select guests."

Sister Anne nodded in agreement, not understanding how this young woman knew about the underground portions of the castle, which she herself did not, after leading the order on the island for the past twenty years.

It took another dose of Lily's encouragement for Sister Anne to produce and use the key to open the way for them. When they stepped inside, it looked far different from how Oriel remembered it. The rooms were opulent compared to the nearly bare room where she had literally been kept prisoner.

The tiny interior room where she had spent the better part of her time on the island had been converted into a closet serving the new master bedroom.

"I think we should go, and call the family first," the head nun protested, but didn't get a response from her guests. She didn't turn to leave either, clearly intrigued.

The space was even smaller than she remembered, the racks of clothes and a chest of drawers taking up most of the room. Where it had been a perfectly square space previously, now it was not. Oriel moved to the back wall and poked her head through the racks of skirts and slacks until she found what she was after. Very nice, she thought, momentarily distracted. Shoving the hangers aside, a keypad became visible.

"Don't suppose they gave you the code in case of an emergency?" Oriel asked, turning and locking eyes with Sister Anne. The woman shook her head.

"Let me," Neal offered, stepping forward and taking her place. He closed in on the panel, touching it gingerly. Although the nuns didn't understand what was happening or why the gentleman wasn't pressing any buttons, the rest of the group knew the score and didn't interrupt.

"Paranoid much?" Neal grumbled, loud enough for them all to hear, but not caring.

"What is it?" Oriel whispered, eager to continue moving forward and get out of the room, despite its modern, civilized trappings.

"Anyone have some paper? The code is fifteen characters."

Oriel smiled, stepping closer. "Is it 3141592653358979?"

"Great guess," he said, looking impressed.

"I was right?"

"No, not even close."

"Can we get on with this, please?" Felix asked, anxious himself to keep this going, before the dark forces, or modern security folks, made a move against them, the nuns only being able to help if the latter condition arose.

"Tell me what they are; I have an excellent memory."

"We might only get one shot at this," he warned, "And even then, it might trigger some kind of response."

"I understand. But we have to try," she replied, taking the responsibility on herself.

Neal whispered the code just loud enough so Oriel could hear, and then she repeated the digits on the pad. There were no lights to blink and no audible sign that anything had happened, but when she leaned against the wall, it gave way under the light pressure she applied.

Oriel snapped on a small flashlight, stepped onto the cold flagstones and was transported back in time, the discomfort of the place laying heavily on her. But this room hadn't defeated her then, and it certainly wasn't going to today.

Shining the light on the floor, she could see that the stones, which had originally stood over a rudimentary hole, had been busted up and tossed down into the space below. Although the opening had been squared off a bit using modern tools, the stone wall to her right still bore the scratches she had dug into the rock during her imprisonment. Additional marks had also been added, showing that others had been held here following her escape. She shuddered under the revelation, but shoved it down inside her for contemplation later.

Feeling the pressure of time and bodies behind her, she shook off the memories and continued down a set of modern, wooden steps which had been erected to allow easy access. Shining their lights about, they fanned out inside the space, searching every corner.

"Oh my," Rosario exclaimed in the darkness, all lights swinging in his direction.

They found him studying a row of darkened shelving, not containing books or scrolls, but dusty bottles of wine. "History in liquid form," he noted, "and much of this is ancient indeed."

Rosario turned, knowing enough not to leave any telltale fingerprints behind that would betray their visit.

"Wine connoisseur?" Oriel asked him.

"Purely for research," he said, with a smile they shared.

"Over here," Felix called out.

They moved into a side chamber, domed, and maybe fifty feet in diameter. Stone arches reached upwards, supporting hundreds of tons above, clearly ancient.

In sharp contrast, modern tables ringed the room and held the most modern of equipment. They lifted some covers, none dusty in appearance, and took a quick peek. The computers and monitors were easy enough to recognize, but the array of scientific equipment was lost on them. Oriel studied a few of the maker logos and model names for later research, but it wasn't the reason they were here.

While most of the group studied the modern additions, save for the nuns who stood off to one side looking anxious, Felix and Rosario had collectively come together at the center of the space and were examining almost imperceptible markings on the floor.

"Look like a portal to you?" Felix asked his friend, who kneeled beside him.

"I believe it is."

"We might have killed two birds with one stone," Felix said to his companions.

"But we still don't have the key," Oriel replied. She remembered stepping into this space during her previous visit, but had quickly ruled it out as there appeared to be nothing there she might use to escape. Back in the main chamber, she stood, staring at the stone wall in front of her. "There used to be an opening here." She pointed.

"Are you sure?" Felix asked, walking along the surface, fingers feeling for any signs of an opening. The stone and mortar looked ancient, and very unmoving, but he knew looks could be deceiving.

Offering his assistance again, Neal stepped forward and placed his hand on the wall, hoping to find out when it had been constructed or how long ago an opening might have been sealed. He moved from spot to spot until he got a hit and was close enough that he could zone in on the wall and its history. What he was seeing, though, wasn't promising. As far back as the original construction of the first fortress here on the island, it appeared to be a solid, unimpeded wall of supporting rock. His scan was racing forward again in time to confirm that he hadn't missed anything when he literally leaped backwards.

"Whoa!" He said, looking around him as though something large had just scurried past him and crawled up a pant leg.

The group, which had become lulled and discouraged by a lack of further exploration, jumped around anxiously, unsure of what was happening.

Neal burst out laughing and, feeling somewhat embarrassed, tried to shake it off.

"What is it?" Oriel asked.

"There doesn't appear to have been any openings in this entire expanse of wall."

"I've been through here before," she countered, hands feeling along the stone.

"And I just saw a small child pass right through here," he said, indicating one narrow section of the stone barrier.

Her hands pressed harder against the illusion, before feeling the magic finally collapse under the pressure of her assault. She smiled at Neal, gave a hearty wave, and then disappeared through the rock barrier.

Impressive, she thought, looking for any threats on the other side, but finding none. The room had no natural light, but from the flashlight in her hand, she could make out a collection of crypts in her immediate vicinity. On the nearest one, next to the head on the carved lid, sat a brightly colored, stuffed animal, certainly modern and woefully out of place.

Seeing no threats, she reached one hand through the wall and motioned slowly with a finger like the phantoms in the movies used to do. "Enter," she called out to the others, allowing them access.

Each team member passed through; Felix excited, Rosario holding his breath, Lily trying, but failing, to appear underwhelmed. The nuns came next, more pushed than encouraged, and finally Neal, who winced as he emerged as though fearing he was about to run into an actual stone wall just on the other side.

"What was that?" The leader of the order asked, looking at them for answers.

"Long story," Oriel said, trying to catch up with Felix and Rosario, who were moving along the lines of tombs and carved lids. She wondered about the boy that Neal had witnessed, pondering if he had created the illusion himself, or like her, had the power to brush most of them aside with little effort. Force fields were easy to produce if you had the touch. Strong fields? Much more difficult. Sustained fields that felt solid, even to her? Unthinkable. The barrier in the garden had been of a type which was extremely rare. This barrier under the castle joined that very exclusive club. Although she had tried to appear calm and collected, even Lily seemed unnerved by the stuffed toy, off balance that a mere child might possess that kind of power.

"Here he is," Rosario called out, drawing them all to his position.

Although no legible writing existed on the stone box, the carved effigy on the top was unmistakable; the artist having known the man in real life.

"Captain Abah Alvarez," Felix said, in a way of confirmation, downplaying any potential connection to the man long since dead. If the nuns knew of their history or the longevity of some in the group, they were very good at hiding that fact. Though now, he noted, they were looking shell-shocked at everything that had been revealed.

"The only one down here that looks likely," Rosario replied, pointing out various aspects of the tomb's decoration.

"It's him," Sister Anne confirmed, trying to contribute something during such a solemn moment.

"Got anything in that backpack, Felix, that's going to help us here?" Neal asked, knowing what they were about to do, but still wanting to be respectful.

"I didn't expect us being so lucky."

"You aren't planning on opening his crypt, are you?" Sister Anne asked, catching onto the drift of what was about to go down.

Lily stepped forward, facing the sisters, and spoke softly and encouraging. "I'm sure with all the maintenance work going on around here, ladies, that there must be some pry bars or other tools we can use to take a quick peek, right? It will be okay."

While Sister Anne didn't look convinced. Sister Isabelle seemed far more open to the exploration.

"It couldn't hurt to take a peek, though? I'm sure they'll be gentle, right?" Isabelle asked.

"And respectful," Lily said, nodding, which seemed to melt the last of Sister Anne's remaining resistance.

"Yes, I suppose a quick peek would be alright, like you said, Sister Isabelle." Sister Anne looked almost relieved at having reached the well-received decision.

"And we'll have to keep all this to ourselves," Lily stated, hooking her arms into Sister Anne's and Sister Isabelle's, and leading them deeper into the crypt towards the collapsed exit that was unpassable. "Coming?" She called back to Oriel and Neal.

"I thought we couldn't get out that way?"

"I think I know what she's thinking," Oriel answered.

Neal laughed. "Then you're one up on me in that regard."

Ch37 – Marazion, Cornwall

"Found what we needed," Neal said, holding up the hardware.

"The sisters calling the police?" Rosario asked, noting their absence.

"Lily is keeping them company and seems to have them on board."

"On board?" Felix asked. "With this?" he asked, thumbing towards the crypt that they were about to desecrate, respectfully or not.

"It's what she does," Neal said with a shrug, passing the tools around.

Felix and Rosario exchanged knowing looks, reflecting on how they had gotten here, wondering if they too had been unduly influenced recently. They both shook it off, dismissing the silly notion.

"Were you able to get out that way?" Felix asked, changing the subject.

"Yes," Oriel answered, continuing to work a chisel along the sealed crack. "It was also an illusion, solid to the touch."

"Fascinating and scary," Rosario said, working the corner with a flat-head screwdriver.

Attacked on all sides, the lid gave up its hold, popping from the pressure. They freed the stone lid with group effort, and spun it ninety degrees, a slow billowing cloud of dust reaching up into the still air. The group edged closer and shined their flashlights inside, the collective beams revealing a nearly empty space. Only some bits of cloth and bone remained.

"Hello Captain," Felix said solemnly, staring through the narrow gap.

Lying in the middle where the chest had originally been located, an impossibly delicate crown lay among the debris, unblemished, its golden surface glowing unnaturally under their lights.

"Can you reach it, Neal?" Felix asked.

"Why me? Is it cursed or something?"

"Why would you think it's cursed?" Felix inquired.

"I've seen a lot of crazy stuff this week. Not out of the realm of possibility, I would think."

"Don't be silly. Nikolai, you grab it." Felix offered.

"I'm not touching it."

"See? Nikolai thinks it's cursed too." Neal retorted, pointing.

"I don't think it's cursed," Nikolai defended. "I just don't want to touch it."

"Rosario?" Felix asked.

"Don't look at me. If they don't want to touch it, I'm not going to touch it."

"They don't have a valid reason not to touch it, is all I'm saying."

"And you want me to pick it up?" Rosario asked.

"Yes, that's why I asked you." Felix said.

"That's what I thought," Rosario replied, but made no move to reach in and lift the ancient artifact.

A pair of arms pushed past and reached in, lifting the crown out. Oriel held it up to her eyes to examine the glimmering object. Memories of its past were revealed even without Neal's gift. It was even more beautiful than she remembered.

"I win," she said, placing the coveted prize on her head, a perfect fit.

Ch38 – Penzance, Cornwall

"Be careful, Oriel," Felix warned.

"Yeah, yeah, I know." She slid the golden object off her head and held it close while the four men returned the stone slab to its previous position.

"We'll take these back," Nikolai and Rosario said, gathering up the tools and making for the collapsed entrance.

"I'll show you where I found them," Neal offered, leading the way.

Oriel and Felix slipped back through the magical gap, pausing at the side chamber long enough to notice the glow. The crown in her hand shimmered in the darkness, its proximity to the portal powering the transformation, while Felix edged closer to the chamber, closely studying the floor.

"Anything?" she asked.

"No, we're not that lucky. It's closed."

"Think that's what this equipment is for?"

"That they're trying to reopen it?"

"Or that they don't know it's closed."

"Anything's possible," Felix admitted. "Let's get the hell out of here."

Because of high tide, the causeway was underwater for the next few hours. They opted for one of the shuttle boats to get them all back to shore, dusted off their clothes and entered the first restaurant located just outside the gate. They sat at a table overlooking the bay, storm doors pulled wide open to allow the salted breeze to drift inside.

"Think they're still watching us?" Neal asked the group as he sipped his coffee.

"No doubt," Nikolai said in agreement, biting into his crispy squid. "We just coerced our way into their facility, co-opted their leadership, invaded the owner's private spaces, and broke into an ancient crypt. I'd be watching us too." Noticing Rosario watching him eat, he offered the man a portion of his meal.

"That's not why I was watching you," he replied, with a shake of his head, declining the very gracious offer of dining on the flesh of such an intelligent creature. Rosario lifted his wineglass and toasted the team.

"Cheers," he said, taking a sip.

Oriel thought he looked quite natural holding the rose-colored glass of wine now that she knew more about of his fascination with the industry. "Good?" She inquired.

Rosario nodded. "When in Rome, do as the Roman's do. But when in Cornwall, drink their wine," he said, referring to the deep pink, local vintage. "Very good, actually."

Lunch arrived, with Felix sweeping into the room in the server's wake as she headed for their table.

"You call that inconspicuous?" Oriel laughed, referring to his purchase, as he sat down and placed the bowling ball bag between his feet.

"We certainly won't confuse it with anyone else's hand luggage," Felix defended.

"No doubt about that." Oriel said, digging the crown out of her bag and passing it to Neal without thinking. She paused, regretting the move, expecting a blast of history to materialize around them, the other diners getting a show they weren't expecting. But as Neal examined the golden object in his lap, nothing happened. He rubbed the delicate pattern of polished metal, eyes soaking in its fine detail. Then he passed it discreetly to Felix, who stored it and zipped the bag, before digging into the burger that Oriel had ordered for him.

"Excellent choice, thank you."

"You're welcome."

After lunch, the coalition, as Rosario referred to their loosely affiliated team, piled into two cabs for the short ride around Mount's Bay, to the train station in the neighboring town of Penzance.

Pointing at the sign, Neal turned to Oriel to ask the only logical question that came to mind.

She smiled, "Yes."

"I knew it wasn't just a play."

"A brilliant play," Oriel said. "I caught it just up the road in Paignton." What she failed to mention, however, was that she caught its very first performance.

"I agree. I starred in it in high school,"

Oriel didn't even try to hide her reaction. "Really?" She said, not knowing if she should believe him or not.

"Don't look so surprised; I killed it," Neal said, striking a pose.

"As the Major General?"

"Pirate King!"

"Of course you were!"

With an hour until departure, they took turns either patrolling the station or sitting with the gear. This round, Neal and Felix had drawn guard duty, the young man frequently breaking into song.

He wasn't half bad, Oriel thought to herself, joining him occasionally for the portions of the songs that she remembered. They even convinced a few others passing through the station to join them, most unaware of the connection between the location and the musical.

Returning to the group, Neal had to ask their de facto leader. "What if we didn't find it? What then?"

Felix's eyes drifted to the bowling ball bag between his feet, mind turning. "There are other keys, probably."

"Probably?"

"Most likely," he said in a serious tone.

"But it's better that we found this one?"

"We know they made other keys. A few sources over the years have even mentioned them by name. They were careful never to give a detailed description of who had them, where they went, or what they looked like because of their great power. It might sound melodramatic, if you were to ask Oriel, but they took great pains to ensure that they didn't fall into the wrong hands."

"Good thing we found it then, and no one had melted it down."

"Lost and hidden away where we'd never find it? Sure. Melted down? Not a chance with special items like this one, Neal. Only the very hottest fires in this world would stand a chance."

"Like with the terminator and the steel mill?"

Felix could tell from the smirk on his young associate's face that the kid was just trying to yank his chain. "I'm from Hollywood, so I understand the reference. And yes, that would probably do it. Maybe."

A train whistle in the distance called the group back together, and they assembled, gear in hand.

"Felix seems to prefer train travel. Doesn't like to fly?"

"Several reasons," Oriel said, walking with Neal. "Security isn't as tight. Last-minute ticket purchases don't raise suspicions or leave a digital trail. And it's far safer for everyone, in case we're attacked."

He nodded, seeing the logic. "Makes perfect sense when you put it that way."

"And he hates not being in control."

"I heard that!" Felix declared over his shoulder as he climbed aboard.

Since this was a quick day trip, there were no overnight accommodations, and no assigned places where they could hole up during the journey. They carved off a corner in the lounge car though and set up camp, a round of drinks acquired.

"We have the crown, but aren't you forgetting something?" Oriel asked.

"I'm working on it," Felix replied, no hint of desperation in his demeanor.

"But aren't we getting ahead of ourselves? We don't even know where an active portal lay."

"I would normally agree with you, one thing at a time, but the search for a Chosen One can't wait. Nikolai already has feelers out to all the right people. They can search for he or she, while we try to locate the right place to make all this happen."

Ch39 – Exeter, England

"Can I get you anything else?" the rail car's attendant asked the group, clearing away their empty drink glasses. The curious-looking group shook their heads, and the man retreated to his station, wondering if it was wise to sneak in a quick break given that his new boss seemed to have it out for him, reason unknown. With everyone on the train satisfied for now, he threw caution to the wind and took the winding staircase down to the lower level. He slipped into the employees only area, through the last car and onto the small, rear landing where he could catch some fresh air. What he really wanted was a smoke, a filthy habit he was in the middle of quitting again for the last time, but figured he couldn't risk it given that his new supervisor was on board and he didn't need a valid reason for the man to dislike him.

He checked his watch and confirmed that his self-appointed break was already winding down. Not willing to push his luck, he stepped back inside and slid the solid door closed behind him.

"There you are."

"Just heading back," the man defended, trying to sidestep around his supervisor, but his boss held his ground. Clearly it had become some kind of pissing contest, though he still had no idea why he seemed to be the man's preferred target. Nothing he had done should have provoked such a response.

"For a man who keeps telling me he needs this job, you don't seem to act like you do."

"I just stepped away for a moment, sir," he said, hoping a bit of deference might buy him some latitude. He made to push past the man and return to his post, but his supervisor didn't make it easy. Yet another contest of wills he had to suffer through. With no response from his boss, he thought he had survived another potential demerit, but his optimism withered when he tried the door, finding that it wouldn't budge.

My God, he locked it.

The attendant stood there, eyes closed, pulling long, deep breaths through his nose to calm himself.

"What's the matter?"

Motioning, he huffed out the obvious, unable to keep the frustration out of his voice. "You locked it."

"I didn't lock it; try it again."

The attendant did so, with the same result. Train style doors didn't have traditional handles that could be forced open by hand, but given his circumstances, the man wondered if throwing himself off the train might be a better career move that remaining where he stood.

"Let me try."

The attendant swapped spots, his path to the rear platform now clear.

Tempting, he thought to himself, a dark grin on his lips.

His boss pressed the large button a half dozen ways, having no more success than he had. There was a certain satisfaction in this despite the ramifications of being trapped here with the insufferable man, ten years his junior in age and nearly fifteen years his junior in experience.

The lights went out; the attendant could not even make out the silhouette of the man standing a mere three feet in front of him. He knew he was still there by the huffing of irritation that his boss was generating.

The attendant turned, eyes searching for the rear exit again, if only to get outside. There didn't appear to be an issue with the train as it continued to pitch and roll at normal speed, nothing seemingly amiss.

But.

"Why is it so dark in here?" He asked, eyes having trouble finding the barest hint of light inside the long railcar.

"Because the lights are out, dummy."

Ignoring his boss, he felt his way towards where he knew the far door lay. "I get that, but why isn't any light coming in through the window in the exit door?"

His boss turned, clearly thinking his employee must be an idiot, but paused when he found his eyes staring into the void. Even with an unexpected storm, though none had been in the forecast, some light should have been visible.

"What's happening?" The supervisor asked, confused.

The other half of the two-person team working the rail car, was staring around in confusion, wondering where her counterpart had gotten off to, when she saw him come up the stairs from below.

"Thank God, you're back. Willoughby was just here a minute ago, and I got the impression he was looking for you, Roger. He didn't look happy," the woman said. Having never seen their boss look happy, the additional observation seemed comically unnecessary to her.

"Rot," the attendant growled, lips curled, eyeing her with unconcealed disdain.

"Don't let him hear you say that; you're in enough hot water with him already," she noted, the smile on her face fading.

"You."

"Me? What about me?" She said, loading up her tray with customer orders. "I'm not the one he's after."

When the sounds of footsteps echoed from below, the woman assumed correctly who was coming this direction and smartly dashed away.

Willoughby reached the top of the stairs and looked up and down the length of the car.

"Where?" the possessed man demanded.

The attendant, pupils full of darkness, turned and stared towards the far corner of the car, nodding in that direction.

His boss' gaze focused on the group, memories of the past converging with the present. They converted all of their shared history into insatiable rage, which fought to tear its temporary, fleshy host apart at the seams. "Destroy," it hissed.

"Key," the attendant growled in dissention.

"Destroy!" the boss demanded; eyes locked on its foe to the exclusion of everything else.

"Key," the darkness occupying the attendant, challenged, knowing what was to be done.

A torturous noise radiating outward that no human could generate, escaped from the human box formally known as Willoughby. Dark primal urges fought to overwhelm his primary assignment, revenge fueling its motivation. As though reaching some kind of compromise, he turned to his minion and steeled him with his dark gaze. "Key. Destroy," he hissed through bared teeth, sweeping away drink glasses and empty food packages from the bar top next to it.

The commotion drew everyone's attention, but in seconds everyone had turned away. Such was the human attention span, Oriel thought to herself as she watched the scene unfolding before her, hairs on end. "Problem?" She asked, looking over at Felix.

"Maybe," he replied, watching as the two rail employees began moving in their direction. As though sensing the coming storm, he tapped Oriel on the leg as he got to his feet.

By design, to accommodate the maximum number of passengers, the narrow row between the seats was tight. Forced into a single file, Roger and Willoughby moved at a lumbering clip, though not fast enough to draw unwanted attention to themselves.

It showed a surprising amount of restraint, Felix thought, as he watched the pair charging in his direction. Like players on a chessboard, Felix thinking himself something of a white knight moved into the aisleway, the two dark pawns denied a clear path forward.

Behind the gray-haired obstacle in their way, the bag holding their prize sat in the open, its magical draw nearly irresistible despite its repulsive manufacture.

"Key," Roger hissed.

"Destroy," Willoughby replied, from behind him.

Two bodies, one mind, a single objective, not to be denied.

When the gray-haired man closed to within a few steps, he stopped instead of yielding, a few faces watching the light-hearted predicament unfold.

"You shall not pass!" the tall man declared, a smile on his face, but an undercurrent of a command present in his voice as he waved his arms theatrically.

Those seated nearby laughed at the unscheduled entertainment.

"Weg," the boss hissed through bared teeth, black eyes drilling into the man who dared prevent them from completing this vital task.

"You shall not pass!" The man repeated in an even more boisterous tone, everyone in the car now amused at their exchange. No one here, save for the coalition members, knew the true consequences in play.

The boss' black eyes shifted when he spotted movement ahead. The infernal woman, the one who had inflicted pain on his flesh and mocked his very existence, was moving towards the far exit, attempting to steal away with their prize, bag in hand.

With the Dark Lord and its minion distracted, the gray-haired man struck a power pose and shot out with an open-handed jab, driving the attendant's body through the air and into his boss. Both men, driven backwards by the force, tumbled to the worn carpet of the walkway.

Smiles of the spectators quickly faded, the playful scene evaporating before their eyes.

Felix turned and ran after Oriel before the two possessed souls had landed in a heap of twisted arms and legs. They scrambled to their feet in pursuit.

"Destroy," they both cried out in unison, driven to catch their prey, primary objective temporarily forgotten.

One second, Neal was resting in his seat, the train calm and rolling smoothly down the tracks northeast of Exeter, when he notices Felix climb slowly to his feet, Oriel stirring. The next, the enigmatic man is confronting a pair of railroad employees heading this way. Then a melee ensues and all hell breaks loose. What in the world was happening, he thought, snapping fully awake, body surging with energy.

Without waiting for the employees to hit the floor, Felix spun on his heel and was racing back in their direction, Oriel already on her feet and opening the connecting door, the precious bowling ball bag in her hand. She slipped through just as the door fully opened, Felix scooting through just as it closed.

Neal wasn't sure what was happening, but he knew which side he was on and leaped into the aisle just as the two rail men rushed forward. Instead of his weight and speed nudging the men off stride, they seemed ready for the mild inconvenience, lifting Neal off his feet and throwing him back in the direction he had come from like he was a ragdoll. Although the large windowpane of the passenger car would likely have remained intact and kept Neal from flying off the speeding train, it was Nikolai and Rosario who absorbed the brunt of the collision.

"What's going on?" Rosario asked from the bottom of the pile.

"I don't know, but we need to help them," Neal said, pulling himself free and scrambling for the exit.

Ch40 – Taunton, England

"I'll go up," Oriel called out.

"And I'll go forward," Felix replied, charging ahead into the next train car.

Only seconds behind their prey, the attendant and his boss also split up, Shard choosing to climb after the woman, while his minion scrambled after Felix.

Reaching the closed door, the attendant slammed the open button and raced ahead, stumbling between the cars and repeating the procedure to let itself back inside.

Emerging into the space, it paused, confused. There was no way to go upstairs in this car, he knew from the man's memory he possessed, and the far door couldn't be opened without a key that his prey did not possess. Yet there were no concealed places for the gray-haired man to hide. Where had he gone?

The car had gone silent, twenty teen pairs of eyes all pointing in his direction.

"Where?" the attendant growled, an inhuman bellow radiating from the man's heaving chest. "Where are you?" He demanded, lurching slowly forward, examining each face as he went. Every one of the scouts in turn, attired in their uniforms, watched the visitor with fear-fueled attention.

"Sheep," the attendant said, mouth barely working. "Wolf among you," it hissed.

The man seemed to devolve with each awkward step, shoulders hunched over, fists clenching as he bared teeth at anyone who dared to stare at him. "Death," he whispered to the wide-eye teens, a promise in his tone. "Where... is... he?"

The grotesque figure, noting one particular youth shifting uneasily in his seat, drew closer, face to face. Involuntarily, the youth's eyes darted to his right, to another individual sitting just across the aisle from him. Having given away the ruse, despite not knowing the significance, tears welled up in the young man's gaze.

Felix had wrapped himself in an illusion to make his appearance look similar to the other scouts, though it was not convincing enough to trick the dark-filled entity pursuing him.

"Eyes," the evil form hissed through a hideous, crooked smile.

While Felix's magic could transform his appearance for a time, the evil darkness had spotted one of the Achille's heels in the deception. "The eyes are a window to the soul," Felix commented dryly, "but you wouldn't know about that, would you?" He teased, unfolding himself from the seat and rising to his full six-foot height. The other issue with the magic spell was that no matter what illusion he employed, he couldn't make himself appear any smaller.

The dark beast took a swing at Felix, but the magician, who looked every bit like the unusually tall girl scout he had meant to portray, was ready for it. He easily slapped it away, repeatedly, as the darkness pressed its attack. Felix stepped into the aisle and continued to parry the blows as he backed away from the innocent group.

"Stay in your seats," Felix ordered the troop as he neared the far end of their car. When he could backup no further, his casual defense changed, and Felix shifted to offense. While he might have looked less intimidating in his current guise, the magician launched blow after blow at his opponent, the girl scout beating the beast relentlessly.

"Damn," the scouts declared in unison when they witnessed the effectiveness of Felix's attack.

No matter who was dishing out the pain, or what they looked like, the ease with which it was happening drove the darkness mad, a growl turning into a howl escaping its twisted lips.

"Any time now," Felix said calmly.

The beast paused, confused by the statement. The answer arrived in the form of a pair of darts, trailing thin, nearly invisible wires. They struck the attendant squarely in the back, the lightning bolt following a microsecond later.

While powered by darkness and motivated by evil, the frail human form encasing the minion had no defense against the voltage dancing down every nerve fiber in its body. When the discharge faded, the twisted form collapsed to the floor of the railcar, consciousness abandoned.

"That's a new trick, isn't it?" Rosario asked, noting Felix's appearance, as the librarian retrieved the wires and darts and wadded them up into his pocket. Nikolai arrived a second later, taking up position and looking around for any signs of further danger.

"I'll tell you both about it later. Right now, we need to find Oriel," he demanded, fishing the key out of the attendant's pocket. "Go back one car and head upstairs. She went up when I came forward. I'll go this way," he said, pointing at the door behind him, "and meet you in the middle."

Although the bag was light, it still made her climbing of the narrow, corkscrew stairs awkward as she raced to get their prize away from the darkness. She could hear a commotion only seconds behind her and knew that the threat was closing fast. Oriel needed to find some open space where she could operate, not entirely looking forward to the confrontation. Willing, but not happy, that she might have to kill or severely injure another human being who was guilty of nothing more than being in the wrong place at the wrong time, the corrupted entity commanding its human host to do its evil bidding.

Oriel laid in wait at the top of the stairs until the meaty face of darkness appeared. She leveraged her height advantage, stepped up onto the tips of her toes and then drove her right fist down into the twisting cavity, squarely striking the train boss' nose and cheek, surprised eyes widening at her unexpected attack. While inflicting hefty biological damage on the poor man gave her pause, the sickening crunch of bone, in denial of the evil's dark objective, was extremely satisfying.

Even while the employee's body had been driven unconscious, slumping down the stairwell, the eyes of the beast continued to stare upwards, anger and fury fueling its thirst for revenge. Before Willoughby had even hit the bottom step, Oriel was on the move, running the length of the car, searching for her next point of attack.

Desiring to keep the fight here, in the unused passenger car, she feigned her exit by working the door release and then ducking into one of the bathrooms, careful to leave the door slightly ajar. Her ears picked up every sound, but even over all the noise generated by the train, she could hear her opponent coming. No interest in stealth. It cast its shadow into the small space through the crack in the open door, Oriel's eyes watching for any hit of detection, but her enemy lumbered past her hiding space. The beast continued forward, mangled hand reaching for the train car's door release, but it paused, head turning to the left and right repeatedly, sampling the air even through its shattered and blood-filled nose.

In the mirror, Oriel could see the dark form stop. When its arm slid away from the door release and its body turned, she knew her ruse had failed. Trying to throw open and wiggle past the accordion-style door took far more time than she would have liked, exiting the small room in time for the possessed form to lunge in her direction. She repelled its attempts to grab at her with several carefully targeted blows as she backpedaled into the center of the car. Oriel left the bowling bag in the toilet, assuming it was safer there than trying to continue this fight with one hand tied behind her back. Unable to see through its bloodlust, and not realizing that the prize had been left unattended, the form charged towards Oriel, attempting to close the gap.

"Weak," it taunted, through bloodstained teeth. A deep gurgle that might have been something akin to human laughter hissed from its destroyed mouth.

"Shard? That you buddy? I'm surprised you're back so soon after that whooping I put on you back in the garden. Figured after that embarrassing episode and running off with your tail between your legs would buy me a few centuries of peace."

Hunched over, fists clenched, dull eyes stared at Oriel, the monster prepared to pounce.

"Kill," it hissed, saliva trailing from its loose jaw.

Oriel knew she wouldn't survive the encounter should she get taken down, but the threat of bodily harm had a way of sharpening her senses, slowing down time. She should have drawn her sword and cut away the flesh from the threat, but even though the man's mortal remains were even beyond magical repair, she still couldn't bring herself to do it. The nightmare recognized her hesitation, no such restrictions on its own actions.

Oriel knew her opponent shouldn't take her pity as a sign of weakness and smiled coldly at the beast. Pity for the man didn't mean, however, that Oriel was going to go easy. Shard showed up again, and she was more than up to beating the darkness out of the unfortunate railroad supervisor.

When Oriel ripped the fire extinguisher from the wall bracket, she turned in time to see a look of recognition in the monster's eyes, knowing that the key had been abandoned and was unprotected. Preparing to turn, but realizing too late that the despicable woman was daring to press her attack, it raised an arm in time to block the swinging, bright red tank, its arm bone shattering from the impact. While the darkness didn't register the pain, it registered the fury that came from its continual denial of the prize.

Surprised by the lack of response her attack yielded, Oriel had drifted in too close and received a backhanded blow, driving her to the floor. Seeing an opening, Shard charged forward, trying to land repeated kicks, each glancing off Oriel's body as she scrambled to her knees, hands blindly working the extinguisher for what it was designed to do. She let rip with the chemical spray directly into the face of her opponent, eyes, nose, and mouth wide open, each taking in large volumes of the foam. Although it's physical eyes and lungs were no longer working, and the senses of the beast were unaffected by the spray, the liquid temporarily blocking its vision.

Sensing that its time in this host body was growing short, Shard gave up the fight and turned, charging for the toilet and the bag containing the key. Oriel scrambled to her feet, throwing aside the extinguisher, and gave chase.

"Hell no, you're not," she sneered, catching up as the employee's shattered body ducked into the toilet, arms snatching at the bag. Reversing course, with the prize

231

wrapped in its twisted arms, Oriel was pulled forward and then slammed backwards against the opposite wall, the beast charging into the narrow hallway.

The door at the end of the rail car opened, Felix and Neal's forms stopping short, alarmed by the monstrosity they saw lumbering quickly in their direction. From the stairwell, Rosario and Nikolai emerged, equally distressed by the nightmarish vision.

With one hand wrapped around the handle of the bowling bag, refusing to yield her grip, Oriel was being dragged along for the ride. The evil entity was running on broken legs, only the darkness within providing enough support that the physical form could even still function. It gathered all its remaining strength and channeled it into one last move, swinging Oriel around with enough force that the inertia finally overcame her grip and she flew free, her body striking the floor and rolling until the wall beneath the windows halted her momentum. With a final bellow, Shard roared in fury and then launched itself through the window just above Oriel, her hands too slow to grab for the key.

Although the glass didn't shatter, the emergency frame gave way and the body of Willoughby, along with the bag, cleared the edge and rocketed from view, the train racing onwards. Even if the emergency system detected the loss of the window and the train was stopped, they would still be a mile down the tracks, likely too late to retrieve the crown.

"Shit," Felix mumbled, the air blasting him in the face as his watering eyes searched for a landmark to show where the bag might have fallen.

"Maybe its body is too broken to move," Rosario offered over the roaring wind.

Felix shook his head, more at their bad luck than at Rosario's observation. They turned in time to see Neal helping Oriel rise gingerly to her feet, all eyes searching the woman for any discernable injuries.

"Is this blood yours?" Neal asked.

"Not mine. I'm okay," she lied, more sick from the implications of what had just happened than the melee itself.

"Can you walk?"

She nodded, she could. Together, the team circled the stairs and retreated down to the populated spaces below.

Ch41 – Castle Cary, England

"Rosario, how fast is the train moving?" Felix asked as the group returned to their seats. He had checked the time on his watch and was keeping count. "Any idea what our next stop will be?"

"Castle Cary," Lily said matter-of-factly, seemingly unconcerned by all the commotion.

Felix pondered the absoluteness of the statement and nodded. They would confirm it shortly, he knew.

"Thirty kilometers an hour," Rosario answered, after questioning a conductor. He hadn't bothered to point out to the man that the train had lost an entire window upstairs, because stopping their ride now would be worse for their search than continuing onward to the next stop.

"Anything broken?" Neal asked, as he watched Oriel ease herself into her seat.

"No," she said flatly, more in denial mode than an accurate assessment of her injuries. Her face was still flush, more from the anger at failing than from the physical exertion.

Neal took his own seat between her and Lily, who continued to sit quietly, unperturbed by the loss of the crown.

How could she just sit there and act like nothing had happened? Oriel thought to herself, tossing a sideways glance at the young woman. Even if Lily hadn't realized the bowling bag, with the crown inside, was missing, shouldn't all the running and fawning over her elicit some kind of interest?

Just plain odd.

Oriel shook off the thought and pulled her backpack onto her lap, knowing that she had some aspirin squirrel away for just such an occasion.

"How long since he jumped?" she asked Felix.

He confirmed on his watch, "Eight minutes even… now."

Four kilometers, she estimated, but her mind got distracted when her hand became entangled inside her backpack. Eyes searching, she paused, disbelief at what she was seeing. Oriel looked up and then around. Her team, save for Lily, lost in their own thoughts. The teen enigma, however, was studying her, a small grin present on the normally prim young woman's face, their eyes meeting.

Oriel looked down again, just to make sure what she was seeing wasn't an illusion, fingers feeling the filigree. It was real, and they still had it. How had that happened? She looked back to Lily, who looked at each member of their small group, then back to Oriel, before shaking her head. The unspoken message sent. Then she turned her gaze back to the book in her hands and continued reading, the smirk still present.

"Problem?" Neal asked, noting a change in Oriel's demeanor.

"Not anymore," she said, extracting the pill bottle and popping the lid.

235

They had indeed pulled into the Castle Cary station ten minutes later, just as Lily had predicted. Once there, the crew discovered the missing window, and they completed repairs with British efficiency. The train cleared to continue. Although half of the team was eager to exit the train and begin the recovery phase of the project, Lily, with alarming ease, had convinced Felix and the rest of the team that they should instead continue on to their destination. Once moving again, the point now moot, everyone settled in and grew quiet. Oriel spent her time, eyes closed, replaying everything that had just happened and its potential implications.

Three hours, and several quick stops later, the train reached the coalition's destination, though their enthusiasm was noticeably subdued.

Paddington Station, on the outskirts of London, held a certain charm, but only Oriel and Lily, who shared a secret, seemed to notice. No one else, save for Oriel, even noted the familiar bronze bear statue as they walked towards the exit.

They all filed out onto the sidewalk and queued up, looking for transport. When their turn came, Lily flagged down a second vehicle and made a declaration.

"The girls need some time together, so we'll follow you," she said, steering Oriel, still stiff from the battle, towards their own ride, a black Mercedes car for hire in an adjacent queue. Oriel wasn't sure who was more surprised, the gents or herself, as she climbed aboard their transportation.

"Just follow our group," Lily said, indicating the cab next to them. The driver nodded and did as she instructed, pulling out and merging into traffic.

They rode in silence before Oriel broke the silence, careful in how she phrased her question, considering the lack of barrier between them and the driver.

"Did you think that there were others on the train who didn't have our best interests in mind?"

"Not entirely implausible," Lily answered, as though ready for the question. "But I didn't see any such signs."

"Then why the subterfuge?"

This time, Lily seemed to ponder the question. "I suppose I just like to see how people I work with react to adversity."

There was no 'suppose' about it. In Oriel's mind, Lily's eyes watching her. She didn't particularly like the idea of keeping the crown a secret, but went along with it for now. Maybe she, too, was equally influenced by the young woman's gift.

"For what purposes do you watch?" Oriel asked, cutting to the chase.

Again, Lily seemed prepared. "I would say that I am a fair judge of character; a recruiter of individuals with unique talents."

"You weren't going to let me in on the secret, either, were you?" Oriel questioned, already knowing the answer.

"I wasn't going to, but you foiled my plan," she said, laughing, the sound so unnatural coming from the teen because of its scarcity.

"So, you were also watching me?"

"Specifically, you," Lily answered, eyeing Oriel closely.

Oriel didn't know whether to be unnerved or flattered. "When do we plan on making the big reveal?" she asked, watching Felix emerge from another hotel lobby. With a shake of his head towards their taxi, their small convoy pulled back into traffic.

"As soon as we get where we're going."

"And where is that?" Oriel asked, wondering if the enigmatic young woman meant their lodging for tonight or the endgame location, as yet to be determined.

"Wherever Felix decides," Lily answered, not really providing clarity to her question.

An hour later, Felix gave a thumbs up. The team unloaded and carried their baggage to adjoining, connected suites deemed sufficient for their needs. They dropped their gear into their appointed rooms and drifted back into the common area, unsure of what came next.

There was no recrimination in his words or demeanor as Felix laid out their case. "I'm not going to sugarcoat it. Without the crown, we're screwed. Our chances of finding another key, if we can even get a lead on one, is slim to none and it will take months, if not years, to accomplish."

"No other way to activate the portal?" Neal asked, not knowing the history of how this entire system worked.

Felix shook his head. "Not that I'm aware of."

"We need to go back and search the tracks," Rosario offered. "It could still be out there. Without the darkness powering the flesh, there's no way it could have carried off the crown," he said, avoiding the ghoulish implications of what they might find. "It will be dark soon, and it's unlikely that anyone else will stumble across it tonight."

No one looked thrilled at the prospect of spending hours backtracking their route, though they had a pretty good idea where Shard and its human host must have landed.

Oriel, backpack between her feet, eyed Lily, signaling that it was time for the big reveal and if the young woman didn't do it, she would. Lily shrugged, nonchalant, so Oriel continued. Oriel cleared her throat, drawing everyone's attention. She opened her bag and reached inside. Pulling the crown from its new hiding place, she held it up. A sliver of evening light coming through a crack in the window shades radiated off its golden surface.

"How?" Felix croaked, mouth agape at the unbelievable revelation. "How?"

She smiled, keeping that bit between her and Lily for now.

"The quest continues," Oriel declared. "What's the next step?" She never thought she would ever see Felix and Rosario dance, but she was wrong. Both were on their feet, jumping around like they couldn't contain their enthusiasm.

"Let's eat and we'll figure that out later," Felix answered, both appetite and hope returning.

Ch42 – London, England

"This place is amazing," Neal said, eyes scanning the Great Court.

It was inspiring, Oriel thought, relaxing in the sunshine as it radiated down through the glass canopy above them. Seated off to one side, just outside the café, they watched as the foot traffic poured past and into the British Museum.

"How does it work exactly?" Neal inquired of Oriel, switching gears. "Somebody puts the crown on and just steps into a portal? Gets whisked away somewhere? To the same place?"

"You're full of questions this morning," Oriel observed with a playful smirk.

"It's the tea," he replied, toasting her with his cup. "And I feel like we're running a marathon and I'm miles behind."

"Not just anyone," Oriel corrected.

"Huh?"

"Your question about who gets to wear the crown? It's complicated, but there are some restrictions on who can travel via the portals. Residual bloodlines, magical gifts, and such," she said, sipping and staring at her own tea, much better in a porcelain cup than the cardboard variety. "You're right. The tea is even getting me to talk about things I really have no interest in discussing. This is normally Rosario and Felix's bailiwick."

"Does this mean I can ask you anything?"

"It's not a truth serum, Neal. That would be whiskey. Very good and very *expensive* whiskey."

"Good to know," he chuckled, making a mental note.

Felix and Rosario were coming down the stairs, around the central exhibition tower, faces full of anticipation.

"We've got it," Felix said excitedly, waving a printout in his hand.

"Maybe," Rosario added.

"Let's go," Felix encouraged, rushing towards the exit.

Some unusual shopping and three hours later, the coalition members stood shoulder to shoulder, just outside the ropes.

"Anything?" Felix asked Oriel.

She slid open her backpack a crack and peered inside at the crown.

"Glowing slightly."

Felix and Rosario were scanning the area, trying to figure out where the portal might be located.

"Does this mean we're going to be attacked again?" Neal asked, only half kidding.

"Anything's possible," Felix said, eyeing a tour bus suspiciously as it disgorged a load of senior citizens. "Stay on your toes."

"Is the portal in the center of the megaliths?" Oriel asked, ready to duck under the cordon and spring inside the giant stones to get confirmation.

"No need to get arrested this time," Felix reasoned. "Besides, it's not here. It's over there," he said, pointing off to their right, away from the primary site.

Felix led the way around Stonehenge and off of the paved walkway, which provided the closest approach that tourists could hope to legally get. As they stepped onto the crushed gravel and then circled around to the south side, a small gap appeared in the low berm and ditch.

"The portal is located just on the far side of the swale, to the right of the gap," he announced, slipping nonchalantly out of his windbreaker, Oriel doing the same. Underneath, both wore a reflective construction vest which they hoped would provide them enough cover as long as they didn't make for the stone rings themselves, which were more closely monitored by the security staff. If all went as planned, they would climb inside the ropes, walk a handful of steps towards the site itself, get confirmation, and then retreat with no one the wiser.

"Ready?" Felix asked.

Oriel nodded, and the pair slipped through the railings and sauntered slowly towards the famous landmark. Felix pretended to point out several features while she consulted a clipboard in her hand, jotting notes. When they reached the small ditch and stepped inside the berm, they stopped.

So far, so good.

"You've picked up a pair of eyes," they heard Rosario's voice whispering from their ear buds.

They didn't bother to look around, trusting that the librarian would keep them informed.

The pair turned, Felix pointing out a minor feature on the ground, imperceptible to the naked eye unless you knew what to look for.

"Security heading our way?" Felix whispered into his microphone.

"No, but he's still interested. He's not speaking to anyone, nor is he coming your way."

Felix nodded and kneeled down, carefully examining the ground in front of him.

"Anything?" She asked. "Crown is glowing brightly in my bag."

"Nothing," he sighed, frustrated. "Even in these overcast conditions, we should get a huge reaction being this close. It's closed. Let's go."

They turned and began working their way back towards the group, which had already started off along the gravel path, taking the long way around the site.

"They didn't look happy," Neal observed.

"No, they don't," Rosario answered.

The four of them reached their rental first and climbed inside, Neal behind the wheel, this time in case a quick getaway was needed. In the distance, they watched as the pair slid back into their light jackets, joining the line of tourists walking away from the attraction. Five minutes later, they climbed inside and Neal drove away.

"No luck," Felix announced, though everyone had already concluded as much.

"Was it there?" Rosario inquired, out of professional curiosity.

"Yes, but it's closed now. Probably years of digging around it."

They rode in silence for several minutes before a decision had to be made. Felix turned and directed his question to their professional researcher.

"What do you think, Rosario? Budapest? Zurich?"

"Dublin," he said quickly, no indecision in his words.

"Dublin it is."

"Another hidden library?" Neal asked.

"Yes, under a college campus," Rosario confirmed.

Neal moaned in an exaggerated way. "Couldn't you hide at least some of these places under a brewery for a change?"

"Like under the Guinness factory?"

"Exactly!"

"Technically, it could go anywhere, I suppose," Rosario concluded, pondering what the restrictions might be for such a facility, as though Neal's inquiry had been legit.

Ch43 – Dublin, Ireland

Their SUV rolled off the ferry in Dublin and made the mid-morning trek through town without incident. They parked, and the team strolled across campus, mingling with students and tourists, blending in with the thousands of others doing the same. Felix purchased their tickets and passed them out as their group lined up outside the exhibit.

"There are many people here," Nikolai noted, walking next to Felix.

"Both a blessing and a curse," he replied, trying to play it off as nonchalant, but he had been thinking the same thing since they emerged into the courtyard of Trinity College.

"Think they would try to attack us here in such a public place?"

"After appearing on the train, Nikolai, nothing would surprise me. If they're here, though, I'm not sensing anything."

"The hidden entrance is through this exhibit?" Nikolai asked.

"No, we need to see what page they're displaying today. It instructs us on how to access the repository."

"It's not a library?"

245

"Technically, it is, but it's unmanned, so Rosario and his associates classify it differently. It's available to the right people, for research purposes."

"On your page, or mine?" Oriel asked, stepping up to join the pair.

"Page?" Nikolai asked.

"Felix and I were in the area when they were fabricating the Book of Kells. We each added a few doodles to some pages while the monks weren't looking." Oriel and Felix both laughed at the absurd memory. "You and your rabbits," she said.

"Me? You just doodled serpents everywhere."

"I told you I can't draw."

"Good times," Felix commented.

"We're just taking bets on whose page they'll have on display today," she said.

"The book itself acts as a key. The exposed page controls access. It was designed that way years ago when they put in the access automation. They created this exhibit so that the book and a page would always be on display. It reduces the complexity and potential damage to the book itself."

"Clever," Nikolai had to admit.

Felix, Rosario, and Oriel breezed through the exhibit, having seen it multiple times before, while the others took their time. They regrouped on the other side of the gift shop, where another treasure sat waiting.

The scene looked familiar, Neal's eyes soaking in the view.

"I never thought I'd actually see this place," he said, smiling at Oriel.

"It's breath-taking, isn't it?"

"And this is where we need to go?" Neal asked, noting the large amount of people gawking at the incredible space.

"Oh no, this is actually one of the *college* libraries," Rosario said, "not the repository. This way," he said, leading them through the shelves of books and back outside.

They continued past the queue of tourists and around Liberty Square, the famous bell tower known as the Campanile, standing in the distance.

"Isn't someone going to see us go in?" Oriel asked, noting the large numbers of students walking around.

Rosario checked his watch. Ninety seconds to go.

"When the bells go off on the hour, it's unlucky for students to be caught underneath. Folklore says they'll fail their exams."

Knowing the magical significance of the tower, Oriel had to wonder. "Any basis for that?" She asked him, eye-brows raised?

"I never took the chance when I went to school here," he cautioned, a smile on his lips.

As though repelled by the place, Oriel detected a decidedly large drop in pedestrian traffic as though the tower were actively chasing away the students.

A man standing off to one side watched with interest as a half dozen tourists, certainly not students, coalesced around one corner of the famous tower's foundation. But they weren't taking photos or really looking around, he noticed. A member of the group was doing most of the talking, potentially a guide, not unknown on campus, but the man couldn't get a good look at him. Suspicious, he began moving in that direction.

Rosario stepped to a door in one leg of the tower and placed his hands on two specific locations on the stones. Releasing his grip, he turned to the handle and pulled open the heavy door. Peeking inside to confirm that the spell had worked, he stepped aside and ushered the coalition members to enter.

Lily, Neal, and Nikolai had already passed by and took the only route available to them, a spiral staircase down, when a shout reached the rest of the team.

"I think we've been observed," Oriel commented, the three of them watching a lone individual hustling in their direction.

"I recognize him; local maintenance guy that I used to go to school with," Rosario replied, relaxing. Ushering his final two guests inside, he gave the man a wave and then followed, slamming the door shut behind them.

The maintenance man, in his early sixties and out of shape, watched as the group disappeared inside the structure. He didn't know who they were, but he knew they didn't belong in there. He tried the door, finding it locked. Using his key, pulse racing, he stepped inside. There was no one here on the ground level. Only route open to the group was the spiral staircase up, which led to the bell chamber itself. He gave chase, launching himself upwards, fueled by righteous indignation.

Reaching the last turn, he pushed open the door at the top, ready to face the intruders. A few pigeons perched nearby, surprised by the unexpected intrusion, flew away frantically.

"Did they jump?" the man wondered, finding the open space under the bells, empty, nowhere to hide. He went from opening to opening, looking for them, but found nothing. Gone.

Emerging into the cavernous underground space, Oriel got the impression of a tomb or even a water cistern, like those found in Constantinople. As ancient as the stone space felt, the air was crisp and clean, no signs of particles drifting in front of the high-tech lights which hung above them. Even more incongruous in the room was the wall of black glass between twin limestone pillars at the far end. Here, there was a more typical security device, a hand scanner, positioned next to what appeared to be a matching glass door, also blacked out.

Stepping to the scanner, Rosario placed his hand on it and the borders turned green. With a pneumatic hiss, all the glass shifted from opaque blackness to crystal clear. Beyond, the visitors could see cutting-edge storage cabinets filling the compartment ahead.

As one group, they pushed into the space between the inner and outer doors, feeling a noticeable draft of air blowing over them for a solid thirty seconds. When it subsided, Rosario pressed the door release, and the team filed through.

"Way cool," Neal remarked, geek at heart.

Brimming with pride, Rosario let the team mill about while he went looking for the materials of interest.

"Hey, Felix," Rosario called out, pointing into one of the dimly lit glass cases as he strolled past. "They've added Vindolanda tablets to the collection since we were here last."

Moving their noses closer to the case, the illumination grew within, allowing Oriel and Neal a better view of the wooden sheets bearing the faded Roman ink.

"Some of the oldest, written records in Britain," Oriel said, for Neal's benefit.

With no observatory at this location, most of the team either sat quietly, milled about nervously, was looking at the materials in cases, or was sleeping, like Nikolai.

An hour later, Felix declared, "I think we've found a location we need to check out."

"Where are we heading?" Oriel asked for the group.

"Berlin, but we need to make a stop first."

The team headed back through the airlock, Rosario securing both doors behind them.

"Aren't you worried that a welcome party will be waiting for us outside?" Oriel asked, nodding up the stairway.

Rosario shook his head. "Never go out the same way you came in, the guidelines say," he said, leading them down a different tunnel towards their exit.

The group sat at a single high-top table in the back corner, a mix of different emotions on their faces.

Oriel, guarded.

Nikolai, tired.

Neal, delighted.

Lily, confused.

Rosario, content.

Felix, amused.

How their little coalition must look to all these people, if any of the witnesses here had bothered to give them more than a cursory glance when they had arrived, Felix wondered.

"Greetings everyone? How are you today?"

The group looked at one another, baffled by the question. The server, used to such a response in the most touristy spot in Dublin, naturally assumed it was a language barrier. "Wie geht es Ihnen?"

Felix, noting the confusion, answered for the group. "We're doing great, thank you."

The server nodded to him, thankful that the tour guide spoke English. "What would everyone like to drink?" She asked, handing Felix the drink menu.

The coalition members, thinking this must be some kind of test, looked to one another for the answer, but found none amongst them.

"Three pints of Guinness, two pints of Smithwick's, and one Coca-Cola," he said for the group, much to the server's relief.

She nodded and drifted away to the next table.

Oriel, even knowing that their words would be lost in the din of the loud and rowdy crowd, leaned in and whispered to Felix. "Are we being tailed? Did they follow us from the repository?" She asked, wondering what they were doing hiding in the back of the bustling establishment.

"I certainly hope not."

"Then why are we here?" Lily challenged, her eyes continuing to search for answers.

"Because we needed a brief break to catch our breaths and regroup."

Their server returned, tray in hand, and set the Coke down in front of Lily, before eyeing Felix for instructions.

"Anywhere in the middle is fine," he instructed.

Lily eyed the tall glass with distaste, as though Felix might have been trying to poison her. The others were far more eager, making their selection at his signal. Taking the remaining pint for himself, he raised it to toast his team.

"Sláinte."

Ch44 – The Broken Tooth – Berlin, Germany

"I can see why it's called the 'Broken Tooth'" Nikolai said, staring at the tortured structure.

Looking up at it from the curb, having just climbed out of the subway station, no one in the group could disagree with his assessment. The column of stone had clearly seen better days.

"Best part is, we don't have to break in this time, or use subterfuge to check it out," Felix said, leading them to the ticket line.

"Just not the same," Oriel replied, in mock disappointment. A visit going to plan would be an agreeable change, she thought.

Nearing the door, Neal grabbed a pamphlet and read through the highlights.

Formally known as the Kaiser Wilhelm Memorial Church. Mostly destroyed during World War II. Remnants shored up and turned into a memorial to the war.

"Would an angel or dragon mosaic on the floor be a clue to where the portal may lie?" Neal asked Felix and Rosario.

"We should start there, but there's not necessarily any connection. Chances are, it would be unmarked and in an obscure corner somewhere," Rosario answered.

"And fortunately, we can rule out the new, connected buildings and what's left here from before the war isn't very large," Felix said. "Anything so far?" He asked Oriel.

She feigned looking for her wallet, peering down into the bag strapped across her shoulder. She shook her head, pulling out a five Euro note and dropping it into the donation box, garnering a smile from the woman at the counter.

They slipped inside, splitting up, each briefed on what to look for. But Felix and Rosario could tell that the search would be unnecessary. The entire space couldn't be more than three or four-hundred square meters in size. Fortunately, there was only one tiny alcove walled off for private space, small enough that the crown could tell them if a portal lay within just by edging towards the door marked 'employees only'.

Felix had reminded them all to act like tourists, casually taking in the sights, but Neal had no problem playing the part, his eyes examining all the beautiful mosaics. He had more of a problem trying to remember that they were there for a specific purpose, so he failed to notice a half-dozen individuals, seemingly uninterested in the structure and its history, draw closer to the coalition team members.

Oriel had stepped directly on top of the floor mosaic, which Neal had mentioned, and looked down again into her bag. The crown sitting at the bottom sat dark and unchanged. She moved off to the front corner of the room to begin a systemic search pattern, Neal coming up beside her.

"If the portal is here, will it be bright enough that others will notice?"

She looked up from her bag. Yet another negative reaction. "Not really. If I'm standing on it, there might be a glow, but I'll step quickly away. With the lights and mosaics in here, people will assume it's just a reflection."

"Does it glow brighter if someone wearing the crown is standing in the portal?"

She grimaced before answering, her mind racing back into the past. "When it goes bad, there's no mistaking it. I've never seen it work, so I can't answer that one." Oriel could still remember the spots temporarily burned into her vision from the intensity of the blinding flash, like lightning exploding in front of her face.

"Is it a problem if we're on the portal and you have it with you?"

"Only if the portal is still active and the people in the portal at the time are made of or contain any darkness," she said with a smile. "You're not, are you?"

"Not that I know of."

"Only one way to know for sure," she said, feigning to pass him her bag.

Neal acted like it was radioactive and waved her off, stepping back with a laugh. "Better safe than sorry."

Felix and Rosario emerged from a side alcove, no sign of a portal. He was watching Oriel and Neal working the room, when he turned and bumped heavily into an individual coming towards him.

"Sorry," he mumbled, apologizing, when he registered the familiar face. "Nathaniel?"

The young man didn't answer, nor looked into his eyes, but Felix could tell that his friend was in distress, shuffling nervously from foot to foot.

"What are you doing here?" He continued.

Still no answer.

"He came with me," a familiar voice said from behind Felix.

"What's he done?" he asked Nathaniel, stepping closer to examine the young man, who turned away from the inspection, looking embarrassed. It didn't take a great sleuth to deduce the answer. When Felix whirled on his feet to face the threat, he growled at the specter. "What did you give him?" He demanded.

The demon smiled, enjoying the moment. "Nothing he didn't want, Felix."

"I'm sorry, sir," Nathaniel whispered gently. "I wasn't strong enough."

"It's alright, son," Felix said, placing a hand on the young man's shoulder. "You have nothing to apologize for. Leonard, on the other hand," he said, turning his gaze back to their unexpected visitor.

"But I told them," he said, faltering, focus failing. "I had to tell them."

"Tell them what?"

"That she had come to see you," he mumbled, as though it took great effort to speak the words.

The gears slipped into place. "Oriel," he answered, glimpsing the bigger picture. They had co-opted Nathaniel into being an early warning system, of sorts, in case she had ever made contact. Felix knew he should have been far more careful, chastising himself silently, but centuries had passed and he had let his guard down. Worst of all, he felt as though he had let the young man down, leaving him precariously positioned between himself and the enemy. Felix knew he must have been radiating anguish and grief, because another voice joined the conversation, speaking up from behind the demon.

"And I came with him," Oriel said, burying the point of her sword through Leonard's jacket and into his unholy flesh. He didn't seem to feel the pain, unphased by the piercing of his evil, physical form.

Although the small group was wedged between two garment racks, holding a collection of souvenir clothing, people in the vicinity were catching on that something was amiss.

Keeping the demon theoretically at bay with her blade, Oriel looked casually around to see the score. A few unfamiliar faces, clearly associated with this dark threat, had edged closer, surrounding them. Having finished their own circuit, or detecting something was wrong, Rosario and Lily edged closer, trying to look casual and unconnected, but failing miserably.

Although it looked like a stalemate, the forces of darkness, either demons or victims, closed the circle tighter, unconcerned about the consequences.

"Just give us the key and you can go back to living whatever lame lives you had before," Leonard offered, cutting to the chase.

"I don't have it," Felix said, defiantly.

"I wasn't talking to you," the demon said, looking over his shoulder at Oriel.

"I don't have it either," she lied, pressing harder with the tip of her sword to emphasize her point, literally.

But Leonard could feel the crown's radiant energy assaulting his unholy flesh, the only true discomfort he was feeling.

Tired of the game, the demon gave some unspoken signal, and two men, one on each side of Oriel, launched a coordinated attack. The man to her left leaped for the bag on her shoulder, but Neal launched himself to her defense, both he and the attacker going down hard on the mosaic floor. The man on her right brought his arm up, gun in hand.

A flash of silver preceded Oriel's sword, freeing both the hand and firearm from the evil puppet, a single round blasting through the front window, shattered glass falling to the sidewalk. People, inside and out, scrambled in all directions for safety.

If they weren't going to get the crown, Leonard thought, he would put a kink into the team's mortal plans. Drawing a long knife of his own, he lunged forwards towards Felix, determined to the cut the head off the threat.

Seeing the deadly blade heading his way, Felix tried to backpedal, but struck something firm, preventing his ability to dodge the demon's strike. At the last second, Nathaniel, ushering all of his energy, launched himself into harm's way, the unholy weapon piercing his heaving chest. He seized Leonard's arms and held on with all of his remaining strength.

Oriel made a move to strike down the demon, but Nathaniel had gotten in too close. Had she known the young man had been mortally wounded, she would have gone in for the kill.

Rosario and Lily, seeing more opponents pouring in through the side entry door, grabbed Felix and pushed the distraught man towards the shattered front window. Neal pulled a defiant Oriel into their wake.

"Let me go," she demanded, fighting his grip.

"Another time, on our terms," he offered.

The five of them emerged into the sunlit afternoon and ran, Nikolai joining them as they fled.

"What happened?" He asked, eyes searching the sidewalk behind them.

"Bus!" Rosario cried out, vocalizing his plan.

Just as the coalition members jumped aboard, the doors closed and the large vehicle rumbled away.

"Don't bother sitting down," Rosario continued, eyes looking through the rear window to see if they were being pursued. So far, it didn't appear so. "We're getting off at the next stop and moving off the street as quickly as possible, got it?"

When the bus stopped a minute later and the doors opened, all six, in various emotional states, stumbled down to the sidewalk and scrambled into the alley opposite the bus stop, edging deeper into the shadows, waiting.

The team watched as the public transport pulled away before relaxing a bit, adrenaline still coursing through their veins.

Oriel, still gripping her sword, raced a few steps forward, slamming a surprised Nikolai into the brick wall with surprising force.

"Where the hell were you?" She demanded, one hand on his chest, the other pressing the tip of her sword upwards, just below the man's rib cage.

Neal's eyes widened in surprise at the speed and ferocity of her attack, fearful that if the man so much as smirked, she would run him through before anyone could stop her. But he needn't worry, Nikolai showing the right amount of fear, eyes wide.

"Small space," he stammered. "A small place, so I looked outside. To keep watch."

"You did a shitty job of it!" She snarled, the sword still in its deadly position.

"Inside. They must have been inside!" He defended, beads of sweat forming on his brow.

"Oriel," Rosario whispered, edging tentatively closer. "Leonard would have gotten in, unseen, and it's possible that the others could have just walked in. Nothing really to tip us off to their true intentions," he reasoned.

For several seconds, nothing happened. Rosario was pondering his next words carefully, when Oriel pushed off of Nikolai's chest and backed away, exhaling a deep, pent-up breath, and stowing her sword away in the folds of her jacket.

Nikolai shrank a few inches as he came off his tip-toes, smoothing out his clothes and trying to gather himself.

The sounds of approaching sirens reached their ears.

"We need to keep moving," she said, leading them deeper into the alley.

Ten minutes later, and Oriel had them back on the subway, racing from the scene.

"Are we heading in the right direction?" Neal whispered to Rosario.

The librarian was slumped in the seat next to him, holding Felix upright. Since boarding, neither man had spoken.

"With our current objective to simply get away, any destination will do," Felix answered robotically, stirring temporarily from his grief-stricken stupor.

That wasn't how the expression went, Neal knew, but he wasn't about to argue the point.

Their group fell into a prolonged silence, tensing less with each successive subway stop. They were racing away, kilometers at a time, successful in their escape, it seemed.

"Discover anything?" Felix asked, finally sitting upright on his own.

"No," Oriel said, eyes full of concern for her oldest friend.

"Portal closed?"

"Closed or broken," she said, knowing that if it had never been there, the trip to Berlin, and the death of Nathaniel, would have been for naught.

"Probably damaged during the bombing," he reasoned.

Oriel didn't know if it was true or if the comment was just a way of dealing with the guilt, but she was willing to run with it, having no evidence to the contrary.

Ch45 – Berlin, Germany

Two transfers later, the team purchased tickets at Berlin's Central Station and boarded a train heading south without incident. Huddled around a small table in the lounge car, they worked to pick apart the details of their failed mission.

"It wasn't a total failure," Felix defended, no matter how he felt at the moment at the loss of Nathaniel. He sipped at his drink, spending a few moments trying to gather and convince himself of his own words. "We had good reasons to believe that a portal once existed there."

"It could have been closed prior, or damaged when construction crews were shoring up the remnant of the cathedral," Rosario explained. "If it had been disturbed or undercut too extensively, it would have deactivated. Or the extensive bombing, which destroyed the rest of the cathedral, could have caused irreparable damage, as you noted earlier, Felix."

Their leader nodded, turning his mind from grief back to logistics. There would be time to mourn later. Or darkness will overrun the earth and we're all screwed, he thought, laughing mirthlessly into his whiskey, rocks glass, hiding a grim smile.

Why the portal wasn't found or if it even existed at the site was irrelevant now, they all agreed. Switching gears, Felix noted the obvious.

"Darkness wanted the crown because it's the key. Without it, we're no threat to them."

"How did he know we had it?" Neal asked.

"That physically close to it, Leonard would have been able to feel it," Rosario said. "Just like how the portals can sense when a key is in its proximity. The demons can sense it, but for different reasons, strong polar opposites."

"Then why did he act like he didn't know we had it?"

"It's the type of messed up, mind games they like to play," Felix warned, feeling nauseous again at the loss of his young friend, who had overcome so much during his short lifetime.

"Can the crown help us?" Neal offered, still feeling his way through this entire endeavor.

"No, we need to be practically on top of it. We can't use it like a compass, getting even a general direction, I'm afraid. It's more like wi-fi," Rosario replied, trying to put it in terms that the gifted mortal would understand.

"We need to talk to a soothsayer. Convince them to put us on a valid path," Felix concluded, eyes down, but head shifted towards the coalition's subject matter expert.

"Oh, no. No, no, no, no," Rosario said with a violent and lasting shake of his head. "We can't go there."

"I'm out of ideas, Rosario," he said apologetically. "And you don't need to go. I will."

That didn't make his friend feel any better. The thought of even entering the same town was giving the librarian the willies.

"She'll know we're coming," he warned.

Felix nodded. Truth in that statement.

"Might even know we're in route," he continued.

Felix nodded again. "If she's paying attention."

"She's always paying attention," Rosario said. "And if this was your plan all along, Felix, then why are we going to Warsaw?"

Oriel and Neal looked up suddenly, surprised by the statement.

"We're going to Warsaw?" She asked.

Felix smirked again, taking another sip.

"We aren't going to Warsaw, are we?" Rosario asked, resignation in his voice.

"No, we're not. Sorry for the subterfuge, my friend. But, like I said, I will go see her without you."

Rosario shifted in his seat, clearly uncomfortable, but even he was surprised by his reply. "You know, I can't let you do that."

"It's probably wise that I don't go alone," Felix laughed, words tinged with stress, "but I will if I need to."

"I know you would," Rosario admitted, signaling the server for another round of drinks as though it might be his last, eyes nervously searching the countryside for any signs of danger. "Still can't believe I didn't notice our destination when we got on."

Switching gears, Oriel changed the subject back to something that had been gnawing at her. "Were those with Leonard demons also?"

"No, they were like Nathaniel," Felix said sadly, swallowing back tears at the loss. "Evil penetrates any number of ways, into the human soul, and the downward spiral allows it to fester, then rot. Darkness moves into the cavity and takes root. Before the person even knows it's happened, they become reliant on the evil growing inside. They aren't demons, but they're humans beholden to their new masters, the Dark Lords. Leonard, like most of the demonic tribe, can tap into that lack of hope and use the lost souls for their own bidding, as we regrettably witnessed today."

To keep them on task and get Felix's mind off any regrets, Rosario nudged Felix and motioned for him to get up. "If we're going to do this thing, we need to go have a chat with Nikolai."

They left to pay a visit to Nikolai's room, leaving Oriel to guard the crown. Directing her question at the lone participant still at the table, she posed it to Neal, who watched her expectantly, never knowing what was coming from the young woman seated opposite him.

"When we left the abbey and had lunch in Marazion, you handled the crown."

It was true. He nodded.

"Were you doing your thing, and we just couldn't see it?"

That's where this was going, he determined, smiling.

"I can hide it pretty well now or keep it from happening like at lunch," he confided, "but you're right, it wasn't always that way. With powerful objects, full of emotional baggage, it used to roll over me like a heavy wave that I couldn't hold back. I had to be careful with what I touched or it looked like I was freaking out or having a seizure. But then a few years ago, with rare exception, I could finally control when and where I opened myself up to the visions. Grateful for the control, frankly. It's nice not to be constantly overwhelmed. People get pushy when they know about my *gift*." He emphasized the word for Oriel's benefit, accepting that it was no longer a curse. "Know what I mean?"

"I do," she said, memories threatening to wash over her as well. It was a slippery slope when people learned you could do things for them which others could not. "So, you can control it now," confirming his assessment.

"Yes, unless I'm drunk or emotionally compromised," he said, surprising himself by the admission.

With eyes twinkling, Oriel gave him a mischievous look. "Let's test that," she said, leading him out of the lounge car by the hand.

Ch46 – Southern Germany

They returned to her room, the train car swaying ever so slightly. Stepping inside, they faced one another, eyes meeting and awkward smiles shared between them. Oriel removed the crown from her bag and set it squarely upon Neal's head before closing the distance and placing a tender and lengthy kiss on his lips.

He was clearly surprised, Oriel thought, watching him closely, as she eased back a step, but noticed that the man was smiling in a way that conveyed he wholeheartedly approved.

Relieved, she raised an eyebrow and asked in a husky voice, "You wanna do it?"

"Here? Now?" he said, nervous laughter escaping his lips, eyes searching the hallway beyond Oriel.

She nodded in agreement. "Yes."

"Oh yeah. Lock the door and pull the curtains," he said mischievously, taking a seat on the long bench, trying to get comfortable.

She performed the tasks, taking a seat next to him, hip to hip, placing a firm and steadying hand on his knee.

Neal shifted under her touch, clearing his throat, trying to focus his attention on what they were about to do.

"You're not drunk or emotionally compromised at the moment, are you?" Oriel whispered, lips only inches from his ear.

"A bit of both," he said, giggling like an infatuated schoolboy, his gaze meeting hers, faces flush.

The room darkened a bit, and a second view opened up around them. The ease at which it appeared and the vividness of the illusion caught him off guard, time racing by uncontrolled.

"Easy there, Neal," she teased, tapping his leg.

"Sorry, got carried away," he laughed.

The illusion stopped and started forward again in time, to when they first sat down moments earlier. Then, with more control, Neal reversed it in real time. Oriel wasn't sure why until Neal paused and then, in slow motion, stopped at the point just before she kissed him, spinning the room so they could watch it from a better angle.

Forward it went, in extreme slow motion, the passionate seconds drawn out for nearly a minute.

"That was weird," he said, apologizing, then thought better of it. "Not weird that it happened, just watching it at one-tenth speed, I mean. It was great," he stammered, feeling flush.

She smiled, thinking it was amazing. "I know what you mean," she said tenderly, trying to put him at ease.

Focusing, time raced steadily backwards.

In the mirage, Oriel has the crown, battle for the crown ensues in reverse, and then Lily could be seen withdrawing the crown from Oriel's backpack before putting it back into the bowling bag Felix had purchased in Cornwall.

She wasn't sure that Neal had caught the minor detail, the phantom video rewinding without pause, but she had certainly noticed it. While transferring the crown between bags, Lily had gone to great lengths to not touch the gleaming metal with her bare hands. Oriel wasn't sure what it meant, but would consult with Felix about it later.

The trip continued in reverse, back in the castle, down in the tombs. There were a few more moments where the mysterious child made an appearance and then decades earlier, when an occasional visitor paid a visit or staff cleaned up a bit. The tomb lay undisturbed until the day when Captain Abad Alvarez had been laid to rest and the crown placed with him.

"Keep going," Oriel encouraged, watching the time reversal slowing down. Not because death made her uncomfortable, but that a great mystery lay beyond Abad's mortal history.

They watched a portion of the captain's life, in between him moving the artifact from one secure location to another until it arrived back at the portal site, the battle of 1204. Abad, in full armor and wearing the crown, smile upon his face, slaps Felix on the shoulder and then walks backwards into the portal itself, removes the crown and lays it on the stones. A moment earlier, in real time, there is a bright flash and then a young boy, proud look on his face, is standing there with the crown on his head, hands on his hips, chin up.

That was exactly how Oriel remembered it; the last time she had seen the youth. She wanted Neal to stop here, to freeze time and the narrative, and go back no further, but answers lay beyond this point. In for a penny, in for a pound, she thought to herself.

"Slowly," she urged Neal, giving him permission and direction to continue.

Time unwound further. The boy, alive and well in the last moments of his life, strolled regally in reverse from the portal and started back down the hill. All kinds of hell was breaking loose around the young man, battle between good and evil, humanity and its shadow, unleashing terror on the world. Bodies defying gravity as they rose from the ground, shadows dissolving. The boy seemingly unconcerned as he continued down the hillside and into a small ring of bloodied soldiers dressed in various types of armor.

In the vision, the boy was turning towards a warrior about his own size. Even before he saw the now familiar, blazing sword in the fighter's hand, he recognized Oriel's contorted face, smudged with dirt and blood, lips snarled and filled with words of rage, though he couldn't tell what she was saying.

Secretly, his heart had known it was possible, even when his brain vehemently denied the possibility. Neal could feel his pulse quicken, body tighten, seeing her in his vision, the moment now frozen in time.

Oriel saw herself in that scene, still able to picture the death and destruction, smell the scent of smoke and blood, and taste the imminent defeat. Fortunately, Neal had blown past that point. People thought they looked bad in vacation photos, but her appearance at this moment was chilling even after centuries had passed. Her eyes turned from the vision to Neal's profile, Oriel watching for any reaction. One of her deepest secrets was just laid bare before a man she hardly knew. He was as frozen as the mirage, no signs of a reaction at first. Then he stirred, turning to look at her. Though it wasn't necessary, she nodded in confirmation of his unasked question.

"So, those Vindolanda tablets we saw in the Dublin repository," he began, looking into her eyes with a lifetime of gentleness, "really *were* your birth certificate?" Neal asked, trying unsuccessfully to keep a straight face.

Oriel broke out in laughter, her face flush, unable to contain herself. "Even before my time, smart guy."

Regaining some level of composure, they returned their attention back to the battle, both growing still, but for different reasons. Neal was learning about a tragic conflict that was rarely mentioned in historical accounts, while Oriel was reliving a chapter in her long life that she would rather have forgotten.

"Is that the turd?" He asked, remembering a story that Oriel had mentioned of the crown, portal, and the Chosen One, though she had conveniently neglected to mention that she had been there herself to witness it first-hand.

"Yes, that's him," she replied. Even after all this time, she still had an urge to smack the kid upside the head, but then felt bad about it. Not that he didn't deserve it and that she wouldn't do if he were here, but that in that magical moment, within the portal itself, the 'Chosen One' had been completely and totally annihilated, his body instantly burned to ash, only swirling vapor left to witness that he had ever actually existed. And the wind carried even that remnant away.

Neal unspooled time even further back. Worn by rulers, stored in boxes, secreted away in hidden caches. It continued in and out of hiding, beyond even Oriel, recognizing its varied times and locations. Eventually though, as if the film was reaching its opening credits, a large, stone room appeared, crown on the table, a ring of people inspecting the golden artifact resting upon a piece of faded cloth. Smiles, congratulations, and then a gentleman, tall with a broad build and powerful arms, placed it back into the cloth sack and backed out of the room. Across the way, he disappeared into a low-set, stone building, set off away from the others. Pulled inside by the crown's history, Neal and Oriel watched as the manufacturing process reversed via some kind of lost-wax mold technique. The artisan picked up an empty ladle and, as if by magic, the liquid gold poured up and out of the mold, defying gravity. Before the very last drop of gold had emerged from the forming crown, however, time came to a crawl, threatening to stop all together.

"When the crown ceases to be a crown, I can't rewind the scene any further," Neal said, "Even though the raw material of the object remains."

As Neal predicted, the first drop of gold to enter the mold appeared at its opening, dancing and shimmering as it sat there, unable to be drawn back up by Neal's gift, into the ladle where it had originated.

Their eyes watched, transfixed by the sparking bit of molten, yellow metal as it sparkled in frozen time.

"Can you rotate the scene?" Oriel asked, the question nearly caught in her throat.

Although noting her distress, he did as she asked and gave the room a gentle, mental nudge, the dark workshop, lit solely by the glowing furnace fire began to rotate, pivoting on the mold set upon the blacksmith's anvil in the center of the room.

Then the vision stopped, Neal finally seeing what had caught Oriel's attention.

"Is that Lily?" He asked in disbelief, seeing a proud look on the child's beaming face.

"And is that her father, Jacob?" Oriel whispered, leaping to her feet and breaking their connection. "We need to keep this to ourselves for now," she warned Neal, pleading with her eyes.

Neal nodded in agreement, needing no encouragement.

Ch47 – Prague, Czech Republic

"You, OK?" Felix asked Oriel, noticing that both she and Neal looked flush as the last two of the group climbed off the train.

"Who me?" She stammered. "Or Neal?"

"Either of you, I guess," Felix asked, gaze focusing on her, his eyes narrowing.

"Fine," she said, a bit more strongly that was necessary. "What wouldn't I, or he, not be?"

The exact situation that Oriel had hoped to avoid unwound perfectly, everyone in their small group scrutinizing the pair, including Lily, who seemed interested in what might have piqued Felix's interest.

"No reason," Felix said, motioning towards the exit. "Let's go."

It took a few minutes to find a vehicle large enough for all of them, but they were all feeling gun-shy about splitting up, even for the short ride to their destination.

"Do you want this?" Oriel asked Felix, motioning towards her bag.

"Oh no, it's safer with you. Where I'm going, they'll be sure to sniff it out. We can't risk losing it now that we're nearly at our journey's end."

"You mean where *we're* going," Rosario challenged, making sure that Felix knew the score. As much as he wanted nothing to do with the person they were going to see, he just couldn't send his friend in there alone while he waited safely outside.

Felix nodded, appreciating the gesture.

"Rosario and I will go inside. It should only take a few minutes to figure out if this is a dead-end. Otherwise, it might take a while to get what we came for. Everyone else, just monitor things and be ready to go on a moment's notice. Good?"

Everyone nodded as the SUV stopped at the curb.

"You'll wait for us?" Felix asked, slipping the driver a hundred Euro note. The man behind the wheel nodded and put the large vehicle in park.

"Keep running," the driver said in way of confirmation.

The man at the wheel was trying to act natural, but Felix could tell that there was tension in the air, an anxiousness which appeared after his fare told the driver where the group wanted to go.

The doors opened, and everyone stepped out. Felix and Rosario stared forward at the unassuming storefront while the others drifted away in various directions.

"Coffee?" Oriel asked Neal. She turned to Nikolai and Lily, but they had already moved on.

Neal nodded, the pair finding hot drinks in a small café just across a small grassy area, where they sat down inside by the front window with a view. They watched as Felix and Rosario milled about at the curb, frozen in place.

"Any idea what they're in for?" He asked her. Were these types of magical things going on around him every day and he just never noticed?

272

"I honestly don't know," she replied.

He wasn't sure it was a good thing that even Oriel hadn't a clue, but he seemed to feel better knowing that they were both in the same boat.

"Cheers."

"Too late to turn back?" Felix asked as they continued to hold their position.

Rosario laughed. "Yes, this was your idea, after all."

"Don't remind me."

"Not feeling it now?"

"No, it seems like a terrible idea."

"Desperate times," Rosario remarked, pushing Felix forward with a gentle hand.

He took the nudge and felt his legs carry him to the door, opening it for his friend. Rosario, though noting the strategy, held his ground.

"After you, I insist."

Resigned to his fate, Felix shuffled forward like a condemned prisoner.

Inside, seated behind a glass counter, burning cigarette in hand, sat an old woman, who eyed the pair with amusement, though the scowl on her face seemed to indicate otherwise. Stopped in his tracks, Rosario nudged Felix forward until he could let the door shut fully behind them. When Felix didn't move, Rosario looked around his friend's thin frame to see the source of the man's resistance.

"Remember us?" Rosario asked, hoping the woman wouldn't.

It didn't seem possible, but the old woman's scowl seemed to deepen, defying physics. She didn't answer, just continued to watch the two men who approached her counter with apprehension, remaining at a wary distance, shoulder to shoulder.

"Like what you've done with the place," Rosario continued, filling the silence that Felix seemed unable or unwilling to do.

The woman made a noise that could have been an agreement, he thought. Or it could have been phlegm, he wondered, pondering the woman's health.

"Lot of nerve coming here," she said finally, but in a way that seemed, to the two men at least, like she admired their tenacity.

"We're sorry?" Felix sputtered.

"But that," Rosario said, pointing at his taller partner, "was not an admission of guilt, you understand. It was all a great misunderstanding, Gypsy."

"I had to buy my yacht back at auction after the police impounded it," she said, in a clear accusatory fashion.

"How were we supposed to know the man we brought on board with us was with the authorities?" Rosario countered.

"He was your brother, I recall," she reminded him.

"We aren't really that close," he explained.

Looking to get things back on track, Felix took over. "I know things could have gone better, but you never told us about all the exotic animals you had on board, including that pack of wild lemurs running around the boat deck."

"Conspiracy," Rosario corrected, much to Felix's consternation.

"I don't think it was a conspiracy, Rosario. She simply neglected to inform us that they were an endangered species."

"A group of lemurs isn't a pack; it's called a conspiracy."

"I see. Thank you for the clarification," Felix said, regrouping. "We're not saying it was your fault Gypsy, and we're not admitting it was our fault. We're just here on a different matter, and we like to think that we've moved on from that entire sordid affair," he said, standing up taller, chin higher, his impromptu speech sounding better out loud than it had in his head on the trip over.

Gypsy, though, looked unconvinced.

"You have to admit, though, we almost got away. That yacht of yours is pretty fast. Not as fast as that NATO frigate, but even so, he nearly had to shoot us out of the water to stop us," Rosario added, hoping to sweeten their approach.

"You said you could make my yacht invisible."

"We never said that, Gypsy," Rosario said, shaking his head.

"Not you, him," she clarified, eyes swinging towards Felix.

"You didn't say that, did you?" Rosario asked, surprised.

"I nearly pulled it off," Felix replied, looking deflated. "Pride, some bravado, and a lot of alcohol might have been involved."

"What's the deal with Felix?"

Oriel pondered the question for a moment, trying to figure out where to even begin.

"Ever hear of the Picts?"

He shook his head.

"I would have been impressed if you had no offense."

"None taken, I think."

"They were a mysterious group from Scotland," Oriel began, "where Felix grew up."

"You were careful not to say that he was born there," Neal noted with a smile, testing the temperature of his coffee; still scalding.

She smiled back. "Touché"

"I catch on, eventually."

"But you are correct. Born *of* the magic, he was found in the village in the year 536 A.D. They took in him during a tumultuous time, global weather having gone off the rails, most likely because of a major volcanic eruption. Back then, the world ran on magic, science not even on the near horizon. Some wondered if his arrival was a bad sign, an omen of destruction. Others argued that his arrival signaled that a brighter future, pun intended, was coming. The leader of the tribe took in the infant Felix and raised him as his own. When things did, in fact, turn around and life returned to normal, the decision to keep the boy was celebrated. Felix took on an air of mystery after that and was a novelty of sorts growing up."

"That is crazy," Neal said, stunned by the story as much as by his age. "A year ago, before meeting Lily, I would have had you locked up if you had told me that tale."

"And now?" Oriel asked, eyebrows raised in expectation. Neal laughed, eyeing her. "Jury is still out."

"Keep up all this buttery talk, gentlemen, but what is it you want?"

Felix and Rosario exchanged looks, both clearly happy with how well things were going. They had not been optimistic.

"We need an active portal," Felix said, cutting straight to the point. Beating around the bush with Gypsy had never been a fruitful strategy.

"A portal, eh? You must have a key and a Chosen One," she said, summing up the equation.

"We might have a line on a potential key," he continued, "And a search is already underway on locating a suitable volunteer, but without a portal, none of it is worth anything to us."

"And you thought to come here and see me first?"

"The path of least resistance," Rosario said, taking over. "And we haven't seen our old friend in so long. Yes, we thought we would stop by to see you."

Gypsy could not completely suppress a smile, eyeing them both with suspicion. "Good thing I like you two. Come with me."

She led them into the back room, pushing through a pair of saloon-style doors that swung on stiff, unoiled hinges. They were in a rush, but followed obediently, patiently, as the old woman shuffled her way to the back of the store, continuing down a well-worn staircase into the darkness below.

Continuing more on feel and familiarity, she led the pair downward, light from above no longer reaching where they were headed.

"Long staircase," Felix noted, more to assuage his anxiety of the darkness than an observation.

"Almost there," Gypsy encouraged, the faintest hint of light glowing at the edges of their vision.

Another five minutes of descent went by before Felix and Rosario could convince themselves that they could indeed see a landing coming into view. Gypsy turned left when she reached the bottom, rounding the end of the banister. After their time in the darkness, only a ring of lit candles ahead was needed to illuminate their path. They followed her in that direction, over a roughly hewn floor carved directly into the stone upon which the building sat, high above them.

To the two guests, the area looked as though it had originally been a natural cavern, stone workers just smoothing out an occasional, inconvenient outcropping.

"Is that running water I hear?" Felix asked, the two men looking around curiously for the source of the sound, though none could be seen.

Gypsy didn't answer, stepping into the ring of candles, where a desk, some chairs, and a couple filing cabinets filled out the comfortable space. She pulled a cord on a desk lamp, and it sprang to life, her eyes watching them both as they gaped in awe at the sight stretching overhead.

Emerging from the darkness on one side of the cavern above them, only to disappear again after passing directly overhead, a river ran across the ceiling above. Similarities to the outer chamber of the garden could not be ignored.

"Unbelievable," the two men agreed in unison.

"Via Galactica," Rosario said, calling out the Roman moniker for the Milky Way, thoughts of the astronomical night sky feature coming to mind.

As they stood mesmerized by the undulating motion, light from the desk light reflected in its glossy surface, Gypsy picked through a cabinet before unfolding a large sheet on the table in front of them.

Pulling themselves regrettably away from the miraculous view, they turned their attention to the item, noticing the lightly drawn lines which, to the casual observer, could have easily been overlooked on its yellowed surface.

"Is this a drawing by da Vinci?" Rosario asked incredulously.

Felix edged closer, wondering what would have tipped his friend off, only then noticing that the script written in the corners was in reverse, in the famous inventor's style.

She nodded, clearly enjoying the impact that her show and tell was having on the two men.

Felix followed the lines of the drawing, studying the shape, its identity tickling at a memory in his brain. "Is it an island?"

"Yes, Tyrrhenian Sea. I do not know which one."

"Is that a watermark or part of the island?" Rosario asked, pointing to a peculiar blob on what he assumed was the eastern part of the island.

Felix edge closer, eyes searching. "Part of the drawing. There are a series of lines here that converge on that area. Starting point for our search."

"I can't tell you if it's open or not," she warned, "but I would start there."

"Thank you, Gypsy. Can we keep this search to ourselves, please?"

She waved a hand dismissively, as though she wouldn't consider an alternative.

"No one will hear it from me," she replied, carefully storing the document away.

"Thank you, again, Gypsy. We really appreciate it," Felix said, tempting fate by hugging the woman. Rosario stepped up to do the same. "But we need to go."

"You go. You climb faster than me."

They did, beginning the long and arduous climb back to the surface and their friends, while Gypsy switched off the desk lamp and shuffled deeper into the dark chamber, finding her way by memory alone. Stepping into an ancient-looking, but well-maintained mechanical lift, it took her silently back up to her shop, a playful smile on her lips.

"I think we've got an issue," Oriel said, tossing her cup in the trash as she made for the door. She spotted a few folks who were making a coordinated effort to not look like they were coordinating their effort, and who were closing in on the storefront and their ride from multiple directions. Nikolai and Lily were in sight, still milling about, but didn't seem to have taken notice of the approaching threat.

"I don't see Leonard," Neal observed, as they slid out of the shop and worked their way along the row of businesses, trying to get behind the new arrivals. "I count four?"

Neither did she, sneaking a casual look around. "I count five," she said, throwing her chin towards a figure directly on top of the shop, above the door where Felix and Rosario had entered thirty minutes earlier.

"Let's go down the side street, cross and start moving back in this direction," Oriel offered, preparing to draw her blade.

Felix and Rosario, buoyed by not only surviving their encounter, but getting the answer they needed, were nearing the front door of Gypsy's shop when they heard the gunshot ring out and the sounds of squealing tires. They edged the door open in time to see their ride racing away, the melee already in progress on the sidewalk.

Oriel had already taken down one attacker, body and gun lying separately on the sidewalk, while Neal was grappling with a second. Several more threats were closing in on Nikolai and Lily, who were surrounded on the grassy area across the street.

"Look out above you!" Oriel warned, smacking Neal's opponent upside the head with the pommel of her sword, lights going out in the attacker's head. They might be fueled by darkness and motivated by evil, she mused, but their physical forms were still painfully fragile.

Felix and Rosario were looking up as they stepped outside, narrowly avoiding the woman who had just leaped from the roof, trying to land on and injure the escaping pair.

Oriel pointed towards the far side of the square and yelled, "Run!" she said when she saw reinforcements appearing behind them.

Not needing any more encouragement than the woman lying broken on the pavement, the two men sprinted after Neal and Oriel, who had broken into a run to assist Nikolai and Lily. The odd pair were holding their own as the help arrived. Together, the coalition members sprinted for a narrow street, hoping to escape the trap, but they encountered more opponents coming at them from that direction. Forced to split up, their group fled in various directions, each left to fend for themselves.

Leonard watched as his easily corruptible puppets began their pursuit into the streets of Prague like a pack of wild dogs. That small group had to be stopped. They were trying to sow a different kind of chaos that would tip the balance and have unintended consequences. When everyone involved in the chase, either foxes or hounds, had disappeared from view, he turned his attention to the sad shop in front of him, and pushed his way inside.

The old woman was seated behind the counter, amused eyes watching him.

"What did you tell them?" he asked, cutting out the distasteful small talk.

Gypsy shrugged, lighting up a new cigarette with the old one she hadn't finished yet, and blew a large cloud of smoke towards the immaculately dressed demon. "The truth," she said.

"What truth? Your truth?"

"I told them exactly what you didn't want me to tell them," she said, laughing. "That truth."

He moved closer, ignoring the smoke, and edged right up to the front glass countertop, staring down at her.

"Don't suppose I can convince you tell reveal that truth to me?"

Gypsy made a face, as though such a thought was physically distasteful. "No, I don't think I will."

She wasn't the least bit intimidated by him, and it took everything he had to keep from losing his patience and slamming the tiny woman through the glass. Then again, image fresh in his mind, he opted for the carnage, reaching forward for Gypsy, who didn't seem surprised by the fast and aggressive attack. In fact, the speed of his adversary surprised Leonard, an old-style, straight razor appearing out of nowhere, her deft hand opening it with practiced ease and wielding it with deadly precision.

He grabbed her arm at the last moment and pulled her violently towards him, his own blade pushing past her sternum and between two ribs, burying itself to the hilt, straight through the heart.

Their eyes stared into the others. Even now, the woman only showing her defiance.

"You were always my biggest disappointment," she cackled, seeing the look of disapproval on his face.

"I'm sorry, mother," he whispered.

Both laughed, knowing that he didn't really mean it.

Ch48 – Northern Italy

Felix and Rosario approached the train, eyes searching in vain for any signs of the other four team members.

"We don't have the key," Rosario reminded him.

"I know, but they could already be on board."

The pair chose a dark corner table in the lounge and settled in, watching the doors located at both ends of the train car anxiously.

Nikolai arrived alone.

Lily arrived alone.

"Are they with you?" Felix asked each of them.

Both shook their heads and sat down as the train pulled away; the team relieved to moving again, but also disturbed that both Oriel and Neal were still unaccounted for.

"Any luck with your inquiry?" Lily asked, ready again to talk business.

"We got a line on a portal location, but without the key, it won't be of much use," Felix admitted.

Back and forth, the doors opened from each end of the car, unfamiliar faces coming and going.

Eventually, Oriel and Neal emerged, bag in hand, both looking tired but otherwise unscathed. She nodded to Felix and shifted the bag on her shoulder, indicating that the crown was still in their possession.

The coalition celebrated the small victory.

"Let's go back to our room and hang out there, where we'll be less visible," he offered.

They grabbed their next round and retired temporarily to the small suite that Felix had acquired for this trip.

"Any better odds with this portal?" Oriel asked, as they got settled.

"I think so," Felix offered. "Considering the source and the portal's obscurity. We've found no hint in other records of this location."

"I feel better about our chances, given that they attacked us again," Rosario said, laughing into his glass of wine.

The others joined in, toasting to their success. Adversity, Oriel knew, had that effect on those in battle. While the train continued south, the team laid out in various levels of detail what had transpired with each as they fled on foot from the storefront in Prague.

An hour later, when the train had reached a long stretch of track with no additional stops, the group decided it was relatively safe to venture to the dining car for a celebratory meal. Oriel had gone to her room to drop off her messenger bag, but was not letting her backpack, still containing the crown, out of her sight until they saw this entire thing through to the end.

On her way back past Felix's room, assuming that everyone had already moved on to dinner, she paused for a moment, surprised to see Rosario sitting inside alone. He wasn't looking out the window at the evening scenes racing by or doing anything other than staring at the wall opposite him. She thought about continuing on to the dining car, hoping to not be alone with the man who seemed intent on talking about a portion of her past that she would rather leave behind. But she had lingered too long and had caught his eye and he smiled, waving her inside. Something about the small piqued her interest, so she slid the door open as he motioned for her to sit across from him.

"Please," he insisted, noting her hesitancy. After she got comfortable, he continued, as though he had been waiting for just this very opportunity, rehearsing a prepared speech. "Are you really her, the Angel of Auschwitz?" he asked her again, point blank, but the tone, while still reverent, seemed different this time.

Oriel had thought that she had rebuffed his previous inquiry strongly enough that he wouldn't revisit it again, but she had been wrong. Taking a casual glance at the man, no one would picture him as someone who suffered confrontation well, but he wore a calm resolve at the moment that belied something more deeply hidden. She was hoping to nip his interest in the bud; pushing this entire dark chapter of her life back into a box where she could lock it away and forget it again, but it didn't seem like it was going to happen this evening.

"You are!" He started, scrutinizing her carefully, and answering his own question.

Oriel wasn't sure how Nikolai had found out, or why he had felt a need to make it public, but she figured that denying it any longer would simply delay the inevitable. Address it now and he'll move on, she thought to herself, watching him.

With an almost imperceptible nod, she confirmed his suspicion, but his reaction wasn't what she had been expecting. She could see tears filling his eyes, a genuine smile born out of love, wet trails streaming down his tanned and weathered face.

Rosario bounced in his seat, unable to contain himself. He tried several times to speak, but each time ended in failure, words fighting to race out of the man. Gaining some sense of composure, he looked at Oriel and just blurted out what had remained bottled up for so long.

"You saved my sister from the atrocities," he began, pulling back his sleeve to reveal a faded, but still significant tattoo, permanently etched onto his inner forearm. Although she couldn't make out the digits, she knew of their relevance and history. She realized now that his interest in her personal history was not strictly professional.

Rosario nodded when Oriel looked up, him seeing the recognition in her eyes.

"Imagine my horror at being there, finally knowing what was going on at the camp. It was worse, though, when we had overheard the talk amongst the guards, who mentioned that the rest of 'them' would arrive that evening on the trains. I knew my sister would be one of the last to arrive. It would be better that she died along the way than to endure the barbarity of that wicked place," he stammered through clenched teeth, memories storming back.

Oriel was mesmerized, feeling tears welling up in her own eyes, recollections of that time threatening to swallow them both up.

"I prayed to God then that He would take her up with Him and keep her safe and away from the camp and all the evil that went on there. Inhumane things that I thought impossible for one human being to do to another," he continued, shivering despite the relative warmth of the room. "She had been on that last train, I learned, years later, and that God had answered my prayers. But, instead of being taken up to heaven, as I had hoped, God chose a different way to save her. He sent down an angel to exact retribution upon the soldiers and their sympathizers, and free my sister, and all the others, from their captivity," he said, body shaking.

Rosario was struggling now, fidgeting at the fury that raged inside his tiny frame. "I was powerless then to do anything about it; to save even my sister from the horrors, but you, Oriel," he said, meeting her gaze, "You were the answer to my prayer. Then and now," he said, remembering what had happened to him in the garden.

Tears were flowing and a great dam of resistance finally broke in them both, long-held feelings rushing out, unabated.

"My Anna told me the train had come to an unexpected stop, still miles from the camp. She could hear a commotion amongst the soldiers outside the box cars. There was just enough room for her to see outside between the boards, shadows growing long. 'Her Angel', she called you, floated down from heaven, blazing sword in hand, and cut down everyone in sight without a single shot being fired. You looked over and noticed my sister watching, nodding to my Anna. She knew then that everything was going to be alright. The frightened people inside with her didn't know what was happening outside the train, but she did," Rosario said, the words spilling out faster and faster. "When Anna pushed her way to the door to open it, she had to fight off several people trying to keep her inside, not wanting trouble. But she slid it open, most fearing the worst. Despite the bodies, it was only good news, hope," he said. "Anna jumped down, while the others, more cautious and not knowing what was happening, eventually followed suit. While they looked at the scene, trying to make sense of what had occurred, my sister was looking franticly for her savior, the angel who had set them all free. I never thought I would ever get the chance to meet her hero; my hero," he said, standing and embracing Oriel when she rose to meet him halfway.

The man was sobbing now, wrapped in her safe embrace. In that moment, Oriel swore to herself that nothing was going to happen to this man if she had anything to say about it.

"They captured many of them, but not my Anna. She made it to the west and behind allied lines to safety. God bless you, Oriel, and He who sent you," he whispered into her shoulder.

Neal appeared at the window a moment later, his eyes catching hers, a look of confusion and concern on his face. He pointed to himself and then towards the dining car. She answered with a confirming nod, and he slipped away.

As though sensing an awkwardness, Rosario reluctantly let go, each trying to pull themselves together and make themselves presentable. "That is why, to this day, I cannot and will not wear stripes," he said, laughing through the tears.

They smiled, and it felt like a great release, no matter how dark the humor.

Continuing, he said, "I am not as convinced in the prophecy, despite Felix's assurance, that evil can ever be totally eradicated given our corrupted DNA and the state of this world, but if there's even a slim possibility, then we must try," he said, clearing his throat and blowing his nose.

She nodded in agreement, herself too choked up to speak.

"Live for the future, but never forget the past," Rosario said, knowing how badly Oriel wanted to lock away her history. It was a destructive act, he knew, based on his own personal experiences. "I faced down this evil once, remembering the dark stain it left behind, and I am here now to finish it," Rosario declared, weight lifting from his shoulders as he stepped towards the door.

They had entered this battle as allies, but were leaving this room as something far more.

Ch49 – Naples, Italy

"Don't get me wrong, Norway and its people had an inescapable charm," Rosario began, "but this is certainly more my style," he said, face pointed upwards into the warm, Italian sunshine. They were on deck of the ferry along with almost every other passenger, it seemed, their swift ride pulling out into the Bay of Naples.

"How far is our destination?" Neal asked.

"Twenty miles," Felix replied, motioning almost straight ahead.

At the rate the ferry was picking up speed, Neal estimated only thirty minutes of travel time until they reached the island they had learned about in Prague.

"How are we going to find it?" Nikolai asked. "I know of this island, and it's several square miles in size."

"Our friend Gypsy helped us narrow down the search," Rosario offered, face still pointed skyward, eyes closed.

"Are all the portals associated with religious sites?" Neal asked.

Felix shook his head. "No, not in the traditional sense. The portal system predates the religious sites we've been visiting. Many cathedrals and churches were built on specific locations because of the previous reverence by the locals. They were co-opted by those wishing to install a new faith, or were selected purely for a great location, which happened to coincide with a portal. The Mexican pyramid at Cholula is one such example. It's one of the largest pyramids built by native Americans and today, a western-style, sixteenth century church sits atop it."

Felix and Rosario relayed everything they knew about their destination, the island growing in size ahead of them.

"She told us that the portal itself isn't on the main island of Ischia, but will be found on that narrow spit of land there, taller than it is wide," Felix said, pointing. "If it's here, and I'm praying that it is, we will find it there, on the Castello Aragonese d'Ischia."

"That certainly narrows it down," Neal replied, taking in the craggy tower of stone.

The coalition members disembarked, bags and backpacks in hand, and found their way across the causeway and out to the outcropping of rock.

"We've gotten rooms in a small boutique hotel, which should allow us a decent look around before we have to widen our search, should the portal not be immediately at hand."

Before Felix could continue, a man in a sharply dressed white uniform approached, waved a hand, and flashed a bright smile at the group.

"Welcome to our small piece of heaven," he said in a boisterous tone.

They each tried to match his enthusiasm, but failed, even with the amazing view and tranquility that the place seemed to embody.

"Checking in?" He asked.

They nodded.

"Come, place your bags on my cart here and we'll make sure they get to your rooms."

The team set a few onboard, but Oriel kept her backpack close. Another hotel staff member appeared from nowhere and wheeled the cart away.

The man led the group up to the hotel and, upon reaching the front desk, stepped confidently around it and checked them in.

"You seem to wear several hats," Felix noted, much to the man's amusement.

"Yes sir, many, many hats. We are a very intimate establishment and all of us have several roles to fill."

He explained all the amenities, where to find everything, including a small pool, and the hours of the restaurant on the premises, before passing each of them their keys. "Please don't hesitate to call the front desk here, or stop me in the hallway, if there is anything you need, alright?"

They nodded, as the man with the luggage cart led them deeper into the hotel and to their respective rooms, carrying any bags inside for them.

Efficient, Oriel thought, closing the door of her room and checking out her accommodations. Certainly not the largest, but they were top-notch, even with a small window that she could open. Such were her requirements, noting the considerable, though not life-threatening, distance of her escape route.

She spent the twenty minutes allocated to her for freshening up and then returned to the lobby, where the rest of the team was waiting.

"Oriel has the crown. Neal, stay with her. Rosario and Nikolai will check out the neighboring spaces outside the hotel, while Lily and I try to get the lay of the land. We're not exactly going to see a 'this way to the portal' sign on the wall, but we might find some older places that look promising."

"Doesn't it have to be below us?" Oriel asked.

"Lowest levels are the most likely. With any of the portals, they can't be on upper floors nor can they be undercut by other rooms or passages," Felix reminded.

"Though there is a lot of virgin rock to our east, where it rises next to the hotel, so the portal could be in a cavern or other space off to our side," Rosario added, pointing in that direction.

The team split up and reconnoitered the areas of responsibility.

The amicable assistant manager, smile still plastered on his face, gave them a wave when he saw the peculiar group pass by the front desk. He loved his life, and he appeared to love his job, hoping one day soon, the retiring owner of this place might be agreeable to selling the hotel to him for a reasonable price.

With thoughts of ownership still swimming in his head, he continued to read through all the glowing reviews that the hotel had recently garnered, until the screen went black, everything on the front desk going dark and silent.

He would have to do something about the power though, if he wanted to make this place his own and to elevate it into a world-class establishment.

The man peeked under the counter but found that even the power-strip was dead. He flipped the switches a few times, though he knew the problem lay elsewhere. He stepped into the back room and found that the lights here, even the emergency ones meant to run on batteries, had failed. Making a mental note to get maintenance to swap them out for fresh ones, the man moved forward into the darkness, until he reached the back wall where he knew the electrical panel lay. Pulling his phone from his pocket, he held it up and examined the circuits, finding the local breaker flipped into its off position. He tossed it back into the 'on' position, expecting the lights to reappear, but nothing happened. He threw it off and on a few more times while his eyes searched for the main breaker.

Hearing a shuffle behind him, he assumed that the maintenance man on duty had seen the issue and had followed him into the back-spaces to investigate.

"Il problema non è qui," he called out over his shoulder, but he didn't hear the employee head back in the direction they had come. The man obviously wanted to have a look for himself to confirm that the issue wasn't with the panel.

He turned to let the man have a look for himself, but saw no one there. The open door at the far end of the hallway should have been visible, but a horror-filled vision of blackness blocked out the light. Before the cheerful man even had a chance to scream, the darkness rushed forward and swallowed him.

"See anything?" Neal asked.

Oriel was on her knees, peering through the keyhole into the space beyond. Light from a set of windows illuminated the room beyond, offering her a decent view of the space.

"Looks like a banquet hall."

"That's promising, I guess," he said.

"Why guess?" Oriel offered, a pair of tiny lock picks magically appearing in her hand. She had barely gotten them inside the mechanism when it clicked into place and she turned the handle, pushing the door open.

"Well, aren't you good at that?"

"Been getting a lot of practice lately," she said with a smile, storing the picks away just as quickly.

They wandered in, examining the space. No one was present, so Neal shut the door behind them, hoping their intrusion would go unnoticed.

Oriel had been right. A large bank of shaded windows ran along the right, outside wall, light streaming through the light-colored curtains. She edged open her backpack and pulled it closer to her face as she walked along the inner wall of the sizeable room, examining the crown with each tentative step. Her hopes of finding a sign were dropping rapidly with each meter covered.

"Anything?"

"Nothing yet."

As she neared the far end of the room, she thought she detected a slight glimmer in the polished, golden surface. She stopped moving, wondering if her eyes were deceiving her. Ducking her face even deeper into the bag, she confirmed she was seeing signs of life from the magical artifact.

"I stand corrected," she said, continuing further down the room until she reached the corner, the walls literally carved from the stone itself. What had only been a shimmer had grown brighter, her hands holding out the bag for Neal to confirm.

"I'd say we found something," he said, excited gaze matching hers. "Think there's an opening in this wall like the one we found in the seed vault?"

Rosario and Nikolai entered the hotel lobby twenty minutes later to find Felix and Lily already there, seated comfortably, off to one side. The pair looked up expectantly as they approached.

"Either you have great news or bad news," Felix offered with a grin, suspecting it was the latter by their disposition.

"Reminds me of Santorini," Nikolai said. "Many ups and downs and walls in-between."

"And other than a network of narrow footpaths, or the main route down to the causeway, there really aren't many public places we can search."

"We had the same luck," Felix answered for him and Lily. "Most of the public spaces are just your typical hallways and stairwells. They keep the other rooms and routes down into the bowels of this place locked up tight."

"Shall we go find our other two explorers?" Felix offered, the four wandering off in the direction where Oriel and Neal were headed.

Neal and Oriel exited the banquet room, not having found the opening they sought. Stepping out, they nearly ran into their four companions.

"The portal is close by, but there doesn't appear to be an opening through there," Oriel said, pointing over her shoulder to where the reaction had been strongest.

"Did you check in this direction?" Felix said excitedly, nodding further down the hallway.

The team rounded the corner and pushed through a set of double doors after Oriel had worked her magic again with her lock picks.

"Chapel," Felix confirmed, taking in the view.

"Reception area right next door. Handy," Oriel added, as the team fanned out, examining every corner of the room for any clues. She walked the perimeter, noting the strength of the shimmer.

"This doesn't make any sense," she said. "Nowhere else to go, but the signal is strongest here near the middle of the room." Looking down on the ancient tile, she found nothing remarkable, save for a small dimple in only one tile. Kneeling, she fingered the worn impression, easily overlooked by anyone who wasn't specifically looking for it.

"Nikolai, can you do that thing of yours? Like with the branch back in your village?"

Felix stepped forward, eyes searching, seeing nothing more than a chip.

"It's one of the symbols," she clarified.

"Are you sure?" he asked.

"We'll find out in a moment,"

Nikolai fingered the tile. Oriel could see the man struggle, nothing happening at first. They were a long distance from Gamsutl, she knew, remembering what Felix had revealed about the source of his power.

He lowered himself further, placing his entire palm on the ground, eyes closed, focused, lips silently moving. A few seconds later, the chip began to glow, more refined than the overall impression itself. Then, the entire tile receded downwards into the floor, the unexpected drop tossing Nikolai forward.

When it stopped, six inches below the floor of the room, the adjacent tile repeated the process, continuing twice as far as the first. Lily and Rosario danced to the side as it continued in sequence, one after another.

After a dozen steps had receded, the top of a tunnel became visible.

"I think we've found our entrance," Felix said, starting down the steps, Oriel dropping in right behind him.

The short tunnel continued straight, emerging into what looked to be a natural cavern. A series of stepping stones, set into a shallow pool of water, allowed the group to cross. There they came face to face with a dressed wall of stone, a pair of simple wooden doors set into its face. Felix pulled the doors open and made to enter, but the ubiquitous magical field held him at bay.

"After you," he said, stepping aside.

Oriel stepped forward into the space, no resistance, the crown glowing through the material of her nylon backpack. She continued, pulling the crown out and holding it in front of her.

"Oriel…." Felix warned, "let me in."

She continued forward, waving the artifact this way and that, until she had crossed to the far side of the room, the floor shimmering in a shade of light that matched the crown, the mix of colors in sync.

"Oriel," Felix repeated calmly. "Please."

She stopped, staring at the beautiful sight before her, the spectrum radiating outwards. She lowered the crown, returning it to the bag and then turning.

"Enter," she whispered.

"Why aren't you out front at the desk?" the owner asked his employee, who was still in the back room, facing the power panel.

The man didn't answer. He didn't even acknowledge the question.

"Why aren't you answering me?" his boss demanded, edging closer.

The man still didn't move or even shift, as though he hadn't heard the question.

The lights flickered and then they went out again, only a hint of light reaching the end of the hallway where the two men stood.

The assistant manager turned slowly, teeth of his wide smile glowing in the meager light.

"You work for me now," he growled, mouth not moving, the words emanating from the man's head, not his vocal cords.

Darkness engulfed them both.

The team assembled in the restaurant, shown to one of the tables on the small patio, a view of the setting sun. Because they didn't know what would happen tomorrow, they held a celebration of sorts tonight.

"Isn't it bad luck to celebrate before we're done with this thing?" Neal asked.

"We're not celebrating yet, the completion of our mission, Neal. Tonight, we're only celebrating what we've already accomplished."

Neal laughed, nodding. "Nice loophole, but I'll take it," he said, but his words faltered, eyes coming to rest on the doorway leading back into the hotel.

"Hey," Oriel said, standing at the edge of the patio, suddenly self-conscious, four pairs of eyes gaping at her. She continued towards the table, her heels clicking on the hard tiles. Neal rose as she approached, pulling out his chair and motioning for her to take his seat.

"You look amazing," he whispered, as she brushed past.

"Thank you," she said, with a nod, sitting down. Oriel had felt silly for packing the dress and impractical heels, but she was glad now that she had done it.

Neal took the seat next to her and the table returned to its prior state. Five of the team were now present. Lily, the last to arrive, showed up in the wake of their server, who took their order and retreated.

"A toast," Felix offered, holding up his drink.

The team clinked their glasses, and joined in, small talk filling the air until they had finished their meals and had stuffed away dessert.

"What happens now?" Rosario asked, bringing the business at hand back to the front and center as they watched the last of the sun drop below the edge of the horizon.

Felix flicked his gaze to Nikolai, hoping the last piece of the puzzle was already in route.

"A Chosen One has been located, and will arrive tomorrow morning."

"Let's hope you choose more wisely than I did," Felix bemoaned, Oriel rubbing his arm in consolation. "Sleep in, if you can, after all this coffee we've consumed, and we'll continue our session tomorrow in my room, starting at 9 a.m. We'll await our special guest, prep he or she for what they can expect, and then we'll move as a group through the chapel and into the portal room, where we will wish them good luck, and send them on their way."

Although Felix's words and body language were showing nothing by confidence, Oriel could see a hint of doubt in his eyes. Enough worry of a repeat of their colossal failure, that he hadn't allowed himself to fully commit his heart to the plan. He would follow through with the mission, she knew, but until the Chosen One had successfully gone through the portal and reached the other end, he wouldn't believe it possible. Success had proven far more elusive than any of them could have imagined.

"Who or what will they find on the other side?" Neal asked, curious.

"We're not entirely sure," Felix said, looking at his research partner.

"The prophecy is a little light on specifics in that area," Rosario said, looking equally uneasy.

With the sun down, meal complete, business concluded, and adrenaline of the day drained away, each team member said goodnight and returned to their rooms. The final three became just a pair, when Neal gave up and regrettably bid Felix and Oriel his own goodnight, then stepped back inside.

Oriel watched until he disappeared inside before turning her attention back to Felix. He was watching her with twinkling eyes and a smirk on his cleanly shaven face.

"Stop it," she said through a smile, reaching for her drink.

"I didn't say anything," he replied.

"You did, just not verbally."

"He likes you."

"I know he does," Oriel said, leaving out that the feelings were mutual. "Something to think about after we make the world safe for such things."

Felix didn't know what to say to that, glad though, that the conversation had finally come around to what had been preoccupying him the entire evening. On the surface, he had been engaged in the light-hearted conversation, but seeds of doubt had been growing inside him with each passing hour. "I hope it works out."

"With me or with the fate of the world?"

He smiled, looking up from the drink in his hand to her. "Just you. This other thing," he lied, with a wave of his hand at their surroundings, "Doesn't really matter to me."

That elicited hearty, but tired, laughter from them both.

"The magic might be mostly gone from this world, but I'm thankful that some of the greatest magicians are still around."

"Thank you for that," he said, eyes still on her as he tipped his glass towards her and they toasted.

"Then what's wrong?"

She was always very perceptive; he remembered. No use dodging the bullet now, especially with her. "I just don't know if fulfilling our quest benefited the world, or if it was just for my pride."

"That's just nerves talking, Felix. Why can't it be both?"

"If it works, then it serves both purposes. If it doesn't...."

"It's going to work," she said, patting his arm again. "The Chosen One will arrive. We'll go to the portal, activate it, send them through with instructions, and an ancient enemy will be defeated, just as the prophecy predicts."

Felix nodded, hoping she was right. "But until recently, the enemy that we've sought to vanquish for centuries had all but disappeared, undone by their own Machiavellian plots. I know that they never truly left, only changed their tactics to work their influence more in the background, but will our success really change anything?" he asked. "I failed the last time, selecting someone who was clearly not chosen, but we still ended up with an enemy who acted like they had lost."

"We didn't fail. We put genuine fear into the Sael Lords, who came very close to losing their influence on humanity forever. They ran and hid, no longer free to work in the open.

But they've gotten greedy, time dulling even their memory. This time, we're going to see it through and we're going to make this work, even if we don't know what it will mean."

"I was trying to think of what I would say tomorrow morning for our team pep talk, but I should let you do it," he said, eyes cast down, hand swirling the remnants of his drink.

"I'll do it if you want me to, but you know I hate public speaking."

"That's alright, I'll take care of it. Can't say that I won't borrow heavily from what you just said."

"Take what you want. Use it all. It's close to what you were thinking anyway, I'm sure." Oriel concluded.

"True dat."

"And when this is all over tomorrow, you can focus on what comes next."

He nodded. "Am I that transparent?"

"No, Felix, it's just a logical conclusion. I've just been thinking about it myself," Oriel said, getting to her feet.

Felix finished his drink and followed, stepping inside and heading for the stairs.

"Good night," they called out to the assistant manager, who said nothing, watching the pair silently through murderous eyes.

Ch50 – Ischia, Italy

"Big day," Neal commented, stepping out into the hallway, as Oriel emerged from her own room opposite his.

"Going to be exciting," she replied, and it was true, no matter the outcome.

They didn't find anyone they recognized at breakfast, and ate quickly, as the appointed time crept up on them. They returned upstairs and were preparing to knock on Felix's door when it was swung open by Rosario, who was monitoring the hallway for any foot traffic.

Oriel noticed the intense stare from the librarian, a tiredness in his movements.

"Everything OK?" she asked, stepping past.

"Just staying on our guard. We're getting close now."

"Chosen One?"

"Twenty minutes out," Nikolai answered from his perch near the window, eyes remaining pointed outside for any signs of trouble.

Whether it was Felix's idea to post guards, or Rosario and Nikolai had taken it upon themselves to fill the function out of duty or boredom, she didn't know. It certainly couldn't hurt if everyone stayed on their toes.

Lily was sitting in the only other chair, reading, while Felix paced the room, a bundle of nervous energy.

"Good morning," she said to the room, and got a mix of responses. "Get any sleep?" She asked Felix directly.

He responded by staring at her through bloodshot eyes. "Not much," he admitted truthfully, gladly taking the offered black coffee from her.

"Are we ready?"

"If there was anything else we could do to prepare, I'm not sure what it would be. Just in a holding pattern, waiting."

From behind the counter, where they had remained throughout the night, the two possessed hotel employees watched as a pair of unfamiliar faces stepped just inside the hotel entrance and paused for a moment to get their bearings. Seconds later, they walked through the small lobby and climbed the stairs.

"Them?" the owner grunted, more air than vocal cords.

"Yes," the assistant manager hissed. Shard was eager to attack, but wary.

"Attack?"

"Destroy."

"Now?"

"More," Shard growled, wanting reinforcements; desiring to overwhelm.

"Bring."

"Come," Shard commanded.

With nothing more than a powerful urge for mayhem and destruction exuded by Shard's blackened being, the darkness roaming the small island of Ischia sensed the desire and were drawn towards the Sael Lord like evil moths to a hellish flame.

"Come," he repeated.

"We've got movement," Rosario declared, hearing footstep approaching. When he noticed the pair approach, he swung open the door and ushered the visitors quickly inside.

Nikolai abandoned his post and came forward, wrapping Elana in a fatherly embrace before reaching for Anton and doing the same.

Rosario, looking confused and seeing no one else coming up the stairs, looked towards Felix and shook his head at the unanswered question.

The rest of the team, save for Lily, greeted the two teens warmly, both of whom exuded youthful exuberance in return.

"What do we have here?" Felix asked Nikolai.

"The council identified Anton as the Chosen One," he replied, face and voice beaming with pride. "He is here to fulfill the prophecy and to end the evil reign of the Dark Lords."

Felix looked relieved that the other half of the key had safely arrived, but also looked nauseous at the potential implications. His eyes drifted to Oriel, who exchanged a knowing look. She smiled and nodded, encouraging her mentor to run with it and not look back.

"Nervous," Felix asked Anton.

The boy shook his head and shrugged indifferently, as though it were any other day.

"He knows what he's in for, right?" Felix asked Nikolai, who questioned his son in their native language. After considerable back and forth, Nikolai smiled and answered Felix.

"Anton has been fully briefed and is aware of what is to be expected of him."

Felix would have taken the time to question the young man on what preparations he had been through, but Rosario became animated, stress evident in his voice.

"We've got company," he said, turning to the room to ensure they had received his message. "Two employees, standing in the lobby, staring up in our direction, were just joined by one more, who is doing the same."

"Shit," Felix mumbled under his breath. Any thoughts of additional preparations went out the window.

"There are several more people coming across the causeway," Lily said, standing at the window where Nikolai had been positioned, "But I can't be sure that they're connected with any of this."

"It doesn't matter. We need to go now, before they get between us and the portal entrance. Rosario, are they all still in the lobby?"

He nodded.

"Okay, let's go. Oriel, can you ensure we have a clear path?" He asked, taking the backpack from her.

She nodded, drawing her sword from its hiding place that Neal had yet to discover.

"Nikolai, you'll follow her with your two children?"

The man nodded, staging the three of them behind Oriel at the door.

"Lily next, with Neal, while Rosario and I defend against any rear attack. If the way is clear, do not stop for us." Felix knew that with Oriel in the lead, the path to the objective would remain open. The only worry was for the enemy overtaking them from behind and already flashbacks to the battle of Auvergne were tugging at Felix's confidence. Before he had a chance to reconsider, he took one last moment to confirm that everyone was on board with the plan.

Everyone nodded in agreement, and Rosario took one last look.

"Four in the lobby now,"

"Four or four hundred, it doesn't matter, as long as they aren't between us and the portal," Felix acknowledged, trying to sound calm. "If you will do the honors, Rosario," he said. "No longer any reason for subterfuge."

Rosario threw open the door and Oriel exited first, staring down and blowing a kiss at her familiar foe, wondering if Shard would lead the charge against them today. She turned the other way and lead the rest of her team deeper into the upper reaches of the hotel, senses, and sword at the ready.

The rest of the coalition streamed out behind her, following closely at her heels.

"Pursue."

"Attack."

"Kill."

"Destroy," the mortal vessels voiced in unison.

The darkness urged their physical forms into action, demanding muscles to obey. Lumbering awkwardly up the stairs in rage, the darkness pressed forward, seeking revenge.

Oriel was making great time, even as she was cautiously awaiting an attack from all quarters. They passed the banquet room, doors shut and secure, and hustled down the hallway and around the next corner, reaching the chapel doors without resistance. Instead of the intricate lock picks, she opted to kick in the doors to save time and surprise any of the enemy who might lie in wait.

No one was present.

Charging forward, she could see that the entire room was empty of people. So far, so good, she thought, hustling to the center of the chapel, sword at the ready, as Nikolai kneeled down and worked his magic. The steps disappeared into the floor, as they had the previous day, albeit at a pace that Oriel would swear was half as fast as it had been during their prior visit. Both teens smiled at the neat device, no real concern showing on their faces.

Even before all the treads had come fully to a stop, Anton and Elana were eager to descend, but Oriel stayed the pair, wanting to go first.

"Let me," she said, charging downwards, sword leading the way into the darkened tunnel below. She paused for only a moment, quickly sweeping the chamber, seeking any enemy. Unlikely, given the proximity to the portal, but she wasn't taking any chances. Oriel found nothing amiss, concerned by the lack of a visible enemy. She would rather have them lined up and waiting for her than the eerie silence that filled the cavern.

"Come down," she said, leading the teens to the edge of the water and then across the stepping stones, without incident.

Nikolai came across, followed by Neal and Lily.

"Keep moving," they heard Felix yell, but didn't see him.

Oriel charged forward again, to the final set of doors, and after throwing them open, was both surprised and relieved that the portal chamber was empty, devoid of any obvious enemy.

"Here," Oriel said, holding out her sword to Neal. He was ready to take on the enemy with only his fists but felt better, despite the awkwardness of the weapon, to have the magical blade in his hands.

"Just don't cut yourself with it," she said, laughing despite the seriousness of the situation.

He nodded, eyes watching the stairs across the way which led down from the chapel above.

Felix charged down the steps, not slowing down as he sprinted across the stepping stones. Rosario appeared a moment later.

"Go," Nikolai said, directing Anton to follow Oriel into the portal chamber, while he and Elana remained behind with Neal.

Neal did the same, indicating that Lily should also go inside, and she did so.

Felix raced by, closing and securing the doors behind him, the flimsy latches providing only token resistance should anyone want inside, but success could come down to mere seconds.

The four soldiers of light stood shoulder-to-shoulder, facing their opponents, four soldiers of darkness emerging into the chamber, eyes searching.

Feeling a bit of chivalrous guilt, Neal wondered if they should also send Elana inside for her safety, but when he looked in her direction, the young woman wore a determined look on her face which reminded him of Oriel. She was also wielding two nasty looking weapons, blackened slivers of metal that looked more like long daggers than swords. In her hand, the blades appeared far more natural than what he was feeling, the unfamiliar grip of Oriel's sword in his own hand. He felt better, he determined, that she would fight alongside himself, Rosario, and her father, when the four possessed humans shuffled into view.

"You guys aren't looking so hot," Neal opened, drawing their attention to him.

Rosario laughed, the combination of Neal's observation and his response seeming to irritate their leader, who stepped closest, examining the water, and stepping stones for any signs of magic or deception. He seemed to find neither, creeping right up to the very edge and eyeing the four defenders who dared stand between him and his objective. His mouth moved in an unnatural way, as though he wanted to speak, but nothing came out at first. With an escape of air, intelligible sounds spilled out all at once.

"Give us the key," it hissed, eyes searching each of them for any signs of the magical artifact. He sniffed at the air as though the crown gave off a scent that it could detect. "Know it's here. Give it to us."

"Sorry," Neal said to their leader, recognizing the body it inhabited as the jovial assistant manager whom they had met upon their arrival. The transformation turned Neal's stomach.

"Give it to us," it repeated, eyeing Neal, who it assumed was speaking for the group.

Not too bright, he remembered Oriel saying. "What do we get in return?" He asked, trying to buy the rest of their team as much time as possible.

Shard examined Neal more closely now, not expecting his enemy to bargain.

"What do you want?" Shard hissed, eyes searching for signs of subterfuge.

Every second, Neal had been told, could be critical. He suspected that drawing out this conversation was far more valuable to their mission that what he would hope to accomplish with a sword, even one as powerful as Oriel's blade.

Neal rambled off a half-dozen wants, having no inclination at ever giving the beast what it wanted. "And the Detroit Lions to win the Super Bowl," he added, for good measure.

The last item seemed to throw Shard for a bit, the monster catching on to Neal's tactics as the seconds ticked by, the other dark shapes growing closer and impatient.

"Die," Shard hissed, no longer interested in negotiating.

"A bridge too far with that last one, I guess," Neal said, raising the sword in preparation for battle.

Shard spotted Oriel's blade in Neal's hands, and seemed to hesitate, as though remembering all the pain that the sword and the woman had inflicted on it over the centuries. Then it seemed to put the pieces together. The woman was behind the row of defenders, just out of sight. While her weapon was here, held by someone new. That meant his target was defenseless and cornered in the room beyond. Nowhere to run.

Its black eyes watched the ripple of energy slither along the blade's edge, memories of past encounters with the sword and its owner clouding its memory. A dark stare shifted again to the doors behind the defenders, sensing something of interest just beyond the wooden barrier.

The temptation of blood lust and gorging became overwhelming. The logic it had just employed was pushed easily aside. As though reaching a decision, and acting as one collective mind, the four attackers reared backwards, faces pointed towards the ceiling, let out a loud, deep scream, and shed their human forms, flesh crumbling in heaps to the stone floor.

"I really didn't need to see that," Neal mumbled under his breath.

The four team members waiting at the portal's edge turned as one and stared at the doors when the ear-piercing, morale demoralizing roar reached them. Shaking it off, they tried to collect themselves and focus on the task at hand.

"Okay, Anton, ready to do this?" Felix asked, stepping towards the portal.

"I'm ready, sir."

Felix smiled at the young man's manners. So different from the last Chosen One, he thought, praying that the outcome this time would be different. "The crown, please, Oriel."

She passed it to him, the key already glowing from its proximity to the portal, and he set it squarely upon the young man's head.

"I can do this," Anton said, misinterpreting Felix's hesitation.

He smiled. "I know you can," Felix said, ushering the boy forward, Oriel watching, his eyes meeting hers.

Two of the bodies, which Neal didn't recognize, landed as though they had merely fainted, mostly intact. The two hotel employees, however, weren't so lucky. Flesh, corrupted by the darkness, slumped to the ground, limbs twisting in unnatural angles as though their bones had been liquified. The assist manager fell forwards and landed face down in the shallow water, unmoving.

The four defenders, seeing the unholy demonstration, were motivated to not allow such a thing to happen to them.

Merging into one wall of rippling, mottled darkness, with only a single, twisted face featuring one working, dark eye, the mass moved across the stones towards the coalition.

"Here we go," Neal whispered, raising the sword and rushing to the water's edge, hoping to repel the darkness as it attempted to regain its footing on his side. Neal nearly went down though, surprised by how nimble the black mass moved, no legs needing stepping stones to get across the shallow pool. At the last moment, he shifted his weight and swung the sword as though he were splitting wood with an axe. From his last encounter with this enemy, he had been expecting little resistance when his weapon encountered the smoky creature, and had altered his slash accordingly. The magical blade, however, seemed to encounter the beast as though it was made of solid flesh, and quickly stalled its forward progress. The relatively light impact of the weapon did little to deter the monster, as Shard's consolidated form surged forward, propelling Neal backwards through the air.

As though anticipating the physics of the encounter, Elana stepped sideways to provide Neal with a clean landing spot. To his credit, she thought, he had hung onto the sword, shaken off the impact, and had gotten up quickly.

While the other three engaged the darkness, Neal found a gap and waded back into the melee. He slashed with far more gusto this time, the monster roaring in displeasure at the intense attack, only egging on Neal to whip the blade into the darkness as though he were beating a rug.

"C'mon!" Neal yelled, remembering how Oriel's taunting had unhinged the evil Lord. It worked, darkness rippling as it tried to split and attack, regroup, and throw its mass at the defenders, looking for a weak spot. Over and over again, Shard concentrated its attack on one member, then shifted to the next, when each successfully held the line against its attack.

Then there was a bright flash, light leaking around the wooden doors, temporarily illuminating the cavernous space.

The beast stopped, backing up a step, one-eyed stare focusing on the doors beyond. When Neal turned, he saw what had seized the monster's attention. Oriel, crown in hand, looked defeated. Beyond, he could see Felix sitting on the floor, back against the wall, head held in his hands. Lily stood near the portal itself, eyes staring down at the floor, motionless.

"Anton?" Nikolai asked, eyes searching frantically for his son.

Oriel shook her head. "I'm sorry," she whispered, voice catching in her throat, unable to look up at the father.

"Oh God," Neal replied, looking sick, as Oriel leaned into his arms for support.

Taking in the sight, and knowing that the threat had been eliminated with the closing of the portal, the darkness solidified, its broken glass like voices crowing in victory.

"Check out time is noon, scum, don't be late."

What sounded like a chorus of laughter echoed in the hard space from the black mass as it evaporated from view.

"Anton." Nikolai repeated, this time no longer a question. He dropped his weapon and stumbled forward into the next room, a moaning upon his lips as he kneeled upon the portal, eyes cast downwards, hands searching for any remnants of his son.

312

Moments later, however, his moaning stopped, Nikolai's body growing still, silence ensuing. When his face swung upwards, he saw the group standing shoulder to shoulder in the room, including his son Anton, cradled protectively under Oriel's left arm. His eyes shifted from his son's look of confusion to Oriel, whose gaze stared back at him with cold, calculating menace. Nikolai's eyes shifted again, this time to the glimmering crown that she still held in her right hand. Knowing now what the young woman was going to do, and knowing that Oriel would not hesitate, Nikolai pushed himself up, planning to launch his body at the woman.

But Oriel, anticipating his move, held out the crown as though she were offering it to him. It was just out of his reach, but close enough for the two magical artifacts to detect their proximity. In that instant, the crown and portal flashed, magical energy surging between both objects from somewhere beyond.

If Nikolai thought he was quick enough to escape certain death, the speed at which the magic surged forth dashed his hopes. The darkness, which had wormed its way into every strand of the man's DNA, violently unwound, cells spinning as though they were gravitationally bound to the portal.

Knowing what was about to happen, Oriel turned Anton towards her, and Felix blocked Elana's view, to spare each child a memory they would not want to share.

There was no sound, other than a quiet crackling of energy associated with the bright flash, as the remaining flesh was burned away. On the stones, a smudge remained, the only evidence that Nikolai had ever existed.

Ch51 – Ischia, Italy

Oriel lowered her arm, the glowing crown and portal dimming. She handed the artifact to Felix and drew both children to her, holding the pair tightly as though they might also vanish. "It's going to be okay," she said to each of them, ensuring both that they would be alright. Oriel would see to it herself, if there were no other family to which they could turn. They seemed shocked at what happened, but were clearly made of stern stuff, neither losing it, which was remarkable.

Neal was watching the entire scene, trying to make sense of what was happening. He had a desire to ask a lot of questions, but knew that now was not the right time for that.

Oriel released the teens and turned back to the business at hand, ready to discuss their plan, when she froze, eyes on Felix.

"It has to be done, Oriel," he said, lowering the crown upon his own head, ready to tempt fate and test the portal himself. "If we had sent Anton in there with this crown on his head, he would have been killed. I can't have that on my conscious too."

314

"Which was all part of Nikolai's plan, Felix, to close this portal and put an end to our mission."

"I need to do this."

"I agree it has to be done, but you can't do it," she said.

"I want to do this," he corrected.

"I know you do," Oriel said, stepping forward, reaching up slowly and removing the gleaming artifact from his head.

"We have to try."

"We will," she assured him, lowering the crown onto her own head. Watching his eyes, Oriel could see that although Felix would protest, he secretly knew that she was right. She smiled, encouraging him. "You've known it all along."

He nodded, tears streaming down his face, knowing that she was the Chosen One; always had been the Chosen One. But even now, he couldn't bring himself to say the words out loud.

Oriel stepped forward and hugged her mentor and friend, finally releasing him. Centuries of history they shared.

"It's you," Neal said from behind her, the words that Felix couldn't bring himself to utter. "You're the Chosen One."

"I'll be back," she promised, turning and wrapping her arms around his neck and planting a chaste kiss on his lips.

"I'll be waiting," Neal replied, regrettably releasing his grip.

She said goodbye to the kids, received an unexpected hug from Lily, and then turned to find Rosario watching her, a mix of emotions on the man's face. "Off to save the world again?"

Oriel laughed. "Someone has to try."

"If anyone can, I know it will be you," he admitted, stepping forward and taking her into a fatherly embrace. "God's speed."

"Thank you, Rosario."

She neared the portal, feeling the vibration on her head, as much as seeing the glow growing in intensity around her. Before her courage could falter, she stepped to the center of the magical space, turned, and smiled at each of them.

One second there, one second gone.

"Did it work?" Neal demanded; chest tight.

"It did," Rosario whispered. "No Oriel, and no crown."

Felix bent at the waist, hands on his knees, looking like he might be ill.

"Now what?" Lily asked.

Ch52 – The Twilight Garden

A familiar scene greeted Oriel when the blinding flash died away. This time, though, she found herself on the other side of the impenetrable barrier, alcove, dais, and tree in front of her. She turned to view the rest of the garden, the space apparently now open to her without restrictions, and noticed, despite the clock in her head telling her that it was late morning, dusk was hanging over the land.

"It's always twilight here, if that's what you were thinking," came a voice from an unseen source.

It was exactly what she had been thinking, though it wouldn't have been a hard guess to make.

From beyond the foliage at the edge of the clearing, Oriel could see a woman walking towards her. She relaxed a bit, sensing no threat from the approaching stranger, but remained wary out of habit.

"I mean you no harm," the woman said, stopping a safe distance away.

Also, what I was thinking, Oriel thought, wondering if the woman could read her mind.

"And no, I can't read your mind," she added, smiling.

"I think that's what you would say, if you could read my mind," Oriel replied, with a grin of her own to convey that she was not being entirely serious.

"Welcome to the Twilight Garden, Oriel."

"Not a mind reader?" She asked, skeptical.

"No, not a gift of mine," she said. "That was what your friends called you when you were here last." The woman motioned to the alcove, and Oriel's eyes followed, though she didn't immediately understand what she should have been seeing.

Oriel paused, questions faltering on her lips, head turning towards the tree, eyes searching. She didn't see anything, but her ears detected something. She knew what was about to happen, but couldn't explain where the thoughts were coming from.

The woman watched with her in silence, as though their time together didn't need to be rushed. A full minute passed before Oriel detected unmistakable movement near the far entrance. Seconds later, visitors drifted into view, their voices growing louder as they fanned out around the dais and we're examining the tree.

One arrival approached the barrier, eyes searching as though they knew that someone was here and was watching them.

"You could sense that we, observing," the woman noted with interest.

Oriel watched as 'Earlier Oriel' hovered near the edge of the barrier, as though knowing that what she sought was here on the other side, just out of reach.

Although she was mostly convinced that she hadn't died when stepping into the portal, watching her previous life from a few days ago felt like an out-of-body experience, a part of her life flashing before her eyes. It was both cool and unsettling.

She listened to her friends speak, the dialogue matching her memory. Then, like Neal's gift of time rewinding, the scene raced forwards a few minutes, then stopped, her eyes turning to her mysterious host.

"It's not me, but you," the woman revealed, gaze watching.

Turning her attention back to the dais, Oriel moved the scene forward, up to where Shard and his unholy cohorts descended into the space. Rosario stumbling backwards in slow motion. 'Earlier Oriel', sword in hand, already in motion, somehow aware of the imminent threat.

The two women watched the battle unfold; Oriel intrigued by seeing it from this angle, knowing how things would end. She wasn't focusing on her fight though, her mind tugging at an unanswered question, but watched as Neal, tentative at first, then with more confidence, engaged the enemy.

Neal, she remembered, a twinge of an emotion racing through her body that she couldn't readily identify, distracted her, and she missed the critical moment. Panicked that she has blown her only chance, the scene stopped, and spooled backwards, before continuing again in slow motion.

"This is handy," Oriel admitted, smiling.

This time, she was focused on the battle, eyes locked on Neal, as the circle of fighters closed ranks, discipline holding back the enemy's attack. Time slowed further, as Oriel commanded, each movement drawn out in fine detail.

Then it happened.

She watched as Nikolai turned sideways, sensing an opportunity, and struck Neal on the back of the head with his elbow. The man spun again on his heels to reengage the dark enemy, his attack continuing on Shard's minions. While looking convincing in the heat of battle, it was weak from this new vantage point. Nikolai had been pulling his punches, as the expression went.

319

With the blow to Neal and him temporarily out of the fight, the distraction proved costly as the advantage quickly shifted in the enemy's favor.

"You already knew," the woman commented.

"I did, but I feel better having confirmation," Oriel replied. "Nikolai was also the one who invited the Dark Lord and his minions inside here, wasn't he?" she asked, motioning towards the dais beyond the barrier.

The woman nodded. "Yes, we've shut them out again, but they know where this entrance is located, and I suspect they'll be watching it more closely in the future."

With the melee ended and Earlier Oriel and the coalition members departing, Oriel turned her attention back to her host.

"Eve," the woman answered.

"I'm making this far too easy," Oriel replied, wondering where this conversation was going. "That's not an apple tree, though," she said, referencing the woman's name and the biblical connection.

"You're right. It never was. But the Christian bible never said it was an apple that Adam and Eve ate."

"Really?" Oriel asked, memory searching.

Eve nodded in confirmation.

"So, you're not the Eve of Genesis?" Oriel asked, to set the record straight.

"No, I am not her."

"And the writing on the branches and trunk of the tree?"

"Like the garden, it pre-dates even my arrival here. It could be the original, God-breathed script, before humanity tried to build the Tower of Babel. Or maybe it isn't. We're not sure."

"Can you read it?"

Oriel watched Eve, as a sense of loss or the recall of a distant memory, drifted over the woman's delicate features, then vanished just as quickly. "Regrettably, no, though we've tried."

"There are others here?" she asked, looking around but seeing no one else.

"Quite a few, some of whom you'll meet in time. Come, let's sit."

The woman led Oriel to the bench beneath the tree, the glyphs on every branch glowing brightly as they approached and got comfortable.

"No one else expected?"

Eve shook her head. "No one is currently on their way," she said cryptically, ensuring her guest that all was well.

"We just watched my friends and me battling the forces of darkness right here. While it was happening, could I have come over to this side and helped them?"

"You could have, but then we don't know what the repercussions would have been."

"My witnessing myself didn't cause a rift in the space-time continuum or anything, did it?" Oriel asked, half-heartedly worried that there might still be a cascade of changes coming.

"Not at all," she said, seemingly unconcerned at both the reference and any issues it might have caused. "You're one of the few people to have ever stood on both sides of the dais."

The thought was both heavy and pleasing to Oriel, as she pondered the situation.

"Could I have stayed and talked to myself?"

"Yes, but that is frowned upon, given the potential alterations that it might have evoked in your actions that day and up until this point."

"Very tempting," Oriel had to admit.

"I know it is. Everyone would be."

"Fortunately, the moment has passed."

The woman smiled. "Here on the dais, time is relative. With a simple thought, you could rewind and replay the fight that just finished. You could start the loop over again when you and your friends first arrived, and have them find us both sitting here instead of finding an empty chamber."

"Is that what my friends were hoping to find here, you, not me?"

"I believe so. We've made ourselves known to some visitors in the past."

It was heady stuff, and Oriel shook her head, hoping she was strong enough to resist the temptation.

"Very few are sensitive enough to use the dais. You knew we were just on the other side of the barrier, invisible to those who stand on this side. In fact, you are one of those even more rare individuals who can travel here using the portals," Eve said, nodding to the crown she still wore.

Oriel lifted it off her head and set it in her lap. "I assumed it was the power of the key that did most of the work."

"It is, but very few can survive the journey."

Oriel wasn't sure if the woman knew of their past attempt to use the portal to send a Chosen One to this spot, as the prophecy predicted, but kept that failure to herself.

"But you can use them, can't you?"

The woman studied her curiously. "Yes, they were designed for us to travel between your realm and ours."

"But many of the portals are closed now."

The woman shrugged indifferently. "We created them for a different purpose and a different time."

"No reason to keep them open and operating?" Oriel inquired, curious.

Instead of answering, the woman turned to her left, towards the barrier, and stared expectantly, no one visible in the clearing beyond.

A moment passed before a tall man came through the magical barrier and stepped down onto the dais, walking towards them.

Eve rose and joined the man, standing together, facing her.

"Jacob?" Oriel asked, the man's face recognizable from the vision that she and Neal had shared on the train.

The pair seemed mildly confused by their guest knowing the man's identity. Oriel felt some satisfaction that she had finally brought something fresh to the conversation.

That means Lily is also from here, Oriel surmised, head swimming at the implications.

What in the world was happening? She wondered.

EPILOGUE 1

While the idyllic island setting of Ischia would have appealed to many tourists, what had just transpired there for the remaining coalition members had spoiled any enjoyment that the place might have provided. Looking to distance themselves from the rocky outcrop and the experiences they shared, the team left by ferry as soon as possible. Lily, for reasons known only to her, had said her goodbyes, and had left for the airport as soon as their feet were back on solid ground.

The three who remained, Felix, Rosario, and Neal, had selected a seaside hotel on the neighboring island of Capri, just off the harbor road of Via Cristoforo Colombo. Tourists were everywhere, heading in all directions, as the three men sat under a sunshade on the street-side patio, sipping on limoncello and eating panino caprese, the scenery and salt air adding to the experience.

Neal was enjoying the downtime, but thoughts of Oriel not being here to share in the reward seemed to diminish the pleasure of it all. "Any idea where she is at the moment?"

Neither Felix nor Rosario needed to ask of whom he was speaking, Oriel having been on their collective minds, after all. They set down their food, not out of a loss of appetite, but one of contemplation.

"The prophecy talks about how the Chosen One will go forth, and what they might achieve, but it tells us very little about where it will happen."

Rosario shook his head, not having much to add. "There are many sources that reference the prophecy and they're very consistent. Whether that means they were all derived from a single source, or were arrived at by different means, I can't say."

"But if we're able to accomplish everything that the prophecy states is possible, then we sent the best person for the task. Oriel was the one who had sniffed out Nikolai's deception to jeopardize our plans and close the portal, even if it meant sacrificing his own son," Felix said, raising his glass and invited the others to do the same. "To Oriel, and her success."

They toasted, all in agreement with the choice and the sentiment.

While it seemed like the best strategic move, long term for humanity, Neal couldn't help but feel sorry for himself, as selfish as it sounded in his own head.

"She'll be back," Felix concluded, confident in his remarks.

"What should we do in the meantime?" Neal asked.

"Have you ever been to Paris, Neal? We need to help Rosario out by returning something that doesn't belong to him," Felix said, eyeing the librarian with a mischievous smile.

Rosario swallowed hard. "Not going to be easy," he mumbled into his wineglass.

"Nothing ever is with you, my friend," Felix stated with a deep laugh.

EPILOGUE 2

Leonard sat alone at a small table outside his favorite café in Amsterdam, enjoying a perfectly pleasant morning. He was ruminating on what the meddling success of the human coalition, as they so eloquently liked to call themselves, might mean for his kind, as he enjoyed his strong, Café Americano blend and fresh pastry, still warm from the oven. The demon was disappointed at the loss of one of his most prized sources of information, still confused about how the gifted man had failed in his mission to stop the portal's use, and where he had disappeared to following its successful activation. The man's children had returned unscathed to their mountainous retreat, but so far, his contacts could not locate Nikolai himself. He smiled mischievously, picturing how he would go about wrenching answers from the man once his demons caught onto his scent. He couldn't hideout in another time, indefinitely, he knew, the magic of the mountain only powering the man's gift for so long.

He popped the last bite of pastry goodness into his mouth, even demons enjoying a guilty pleasure now and then, but its enjoyment faltered as the acrid odor of cigarette smoke washed over him, ruining the experience. Leonard sneered as he turned to the table behind him, the inconsiderate patrons sitting upwind, only to find to his mild, though not completely unexpected, surprise, an old woman seated alone, gnarled fingers wound around the burning tube of tobacco.

His mother blew him a kiss before blowing out an even larger cloud of smoke in his direction.

He said nothing, rising from his chair and strolling onwards along the canal, her taunting laughter echoing after him.

EPILOGUE 3

Lily walked into the large salon, which fronted the first floor of the Georgetown townhouse that acted as her base of operations. The affluent neighborhood allowed her easy access to the key players in not only the US government, but influential people who lived and worked in the area for a hundred different nation states. Although it would appear to anyone searching the premises that she might live on the home's upper floors, she rarely stayed at this location, choosing a more secret, and well secured location, known only to her.

"The boy scout not with you?" a man seated on the couch asked, referring to Neal.

"He's on vacation," Lily said, taking her customary seat, eyeing each of her three guests.

"Did you find what you were looking for?" The only other woman in the room asked, sharing the dark leather loveseat with the first man, though there was no affection shared between the two.

Lily reached into her bag and withdrew an object, bronze, about a foot long. She passed it to the woman, who examined it, not understanding its significance. It moved next to the man seated with her, who looked bored, and passed the bronze object onto the last man, who sat in a single matching chair, that completed the U-shaped arrangement around the dark, unlit fireplace. With one arm in a sling, he turned it in his free hand before giving up on the mystery. If Lily wanted them to know about the item, she would tell them all in good time.

He stepped forward, returning it to Lily, who set the artifact gently on the side table next to her, careful with the item she had invested so much time and energy in acquiring.

"And the woman?" The woman to her right inquired, more interest showing. "Did you find her and was she everything you thought she would be?"

Lily smiled, precociously. "Her too, and she's the real deal."

"Will she be joining us?"

"Oh, yes," Lily replied, confident in her assessment.

www.ingramcontent.com/pod-product-compliance
Lightning Source LLC
Chambersburg PA
CBHW072128250626
47159CB00007B/2607